Would he reenlist?

"What if you get bored staying in one place?" Heather asked.

"It's not the places that attract me," Rick said. "It's the people. In the army, I had my men. We were a team… almost like a family." He paused, studying her closely. "Maybe I'm looking for something else to fulfill me."

Like a family of his own?

"There might be more benefits to staying in one place than I realized." Rick slid his hand over hers and squeezed.

The way he was looking at her made Heather blush. And when he leaned forward, cupped her cheek and grinned at her, the warmth spread down to her toes.

His lips brushing softly across hers made her head go light.

Yet…this was another man who might put himself back in the line of fire.

Dear Reader,

Lynn Patrick is a pseudonym for longtime writing partners Linda Sweeney and Patricia Rosemoor.

Patricia is a master gardener, trained by the University of Illinois Extension service. She volunteers, holding workshops for enthusiastic local gardeners, mentoring a high school eco-club and working garden walks to hand out information and answer gardening questions. Her experience inspired the idea of having a heroine whose goal was to be a landscape architect who wanted to design and install beautiful gardens using mostly native plants.

As she did for scenes in *Home to Sparrow Lake,* Linda got the lowdown on her niece's twin daughters to add authenticity to scenes with Heather's twins.

We hope you enjoy *A Forever Home.*

HARLEQUIN HEARTWARMING

Lynn Patrick

A Forever Home

Recycling programs
for this product may
not exist in your area.

ISBN-13: 978-0-373-36640-8

A FOREVER HOME

Printed in U.S.A.

www.Harlequin.com

LYNN PATRICK

Lynn Patrick is the pseudonym for two best friends who started writing together a few decades ago. Linda is a professor with a reading specialty, and Patricia writes as Patricia Rosemoor. Together they enjoy creating worlds that are lightened by the unexpected, fun and sometimes wonderful vagaries of real life.

Books by Lynn Patrick

HARLEQUIN HEARTWARMING

SHALL WE DANCE
THE MARRIAGE ASSIGNMENT
HOME TO SPARROW LAKE

HARLEQUIN SUPERROMANCE

343–GOOD VIBRATIONS

SILHOUETTE ROMANCE (as Jeanne Rose)

913–BELIEVING IN ANGELS
1027–LOVE ON THE RUN

SILHOUETTE SHADOWS (as Jeanne Rose)

26–THE PRINCE OF AIR AND DARKNESS
55–HEART OF DREAMS
64–GOOD NIGHT, MY LOVE

HARLEQUIN INTRIGUE (Patricia Pinianski writing as Patricia Rosemoor)

707–VIP PROTECTOR
745–BOYS IN BLUE
785–VELVET ROPES
791–ON THE LIST
858–GHOST HORSE
881–RED CARPET CHRISTMAS
924–SLATER HOUSE
958–TRIGGERED RESPONSE
1031–WOLF MOON*
1047–IN NAME ONLY?*
1101–CHRISTMAS DELIVERY
1128–RESCUING THE VIRGIN*
1149–STEALING THUNDER*
1200–SAVING GRACE*
1261–BRAZEN*
1292–DEAL BREAKER*
1345–PUREBRED*

*The McKenna Legacy

To our very understanding and gracious editor,
Laura Barth.

PROLOGUE

An unusual noise woke Cora Stanton at two-fifteen a.m.

At least she thought it was a noise.

Squinting at her illuminated bedside clock, she groggily rose to her elbows, listening intently. There was plenty to hear with the wind whipping around the creaking eaves of the old mansion and the crash of waves as Lake Michigan hit the shore some yards away. The shadow of branches clawed at the wall nearest the bed.

But it wasn't branches scraping or the wind or the waves she'd heard…

It had been a thud.

Cora jumped as she heard the sound again. She sat up, trying to locate where the noise had come from. Definitely inside the house. But where?

No one was sleeping on this side of the house but her. Her flesh crawled at the thought of a stranger creeping around the passage outside or messing about in another room.

Not wanting to turn on a light and alert the

intruder, she crept out of bed and went to the door. She turned the lock, then grasped the knob to crack the door slightly for a view of the hallway outside. Nothing. No one. It seemed empty and quiet in the faint glow of a night-light.

She stood there for several minutes, waiting, listening…until her feet got cold.

No more thuds. No thumps.

Closing the door, she locked it again and made her way back toward the bed and her slippers lying beside it. Could her imagination have been playing tricks on her? Easy enough to conjure up noises on a windy night in a big, old house.

As she slid into the slippers and grabbed her robe from a nearby chair, she had second thoughts. Surely she'd lived here long enough to distinguish familiar sounds from strange ones. She'd definitely heard something. Could it have come from the attic? Squirrels had gotten in once and maybe they'd found their way back again. She'd have to call the extermina-tors tomorrow.

There was nothing she could do now except go back to sleep. But the adrenaline flowing through her veins had wakened her com-pletely. She'd go downstairs and fix herself some warm cocoa.

Pausing in front of the windows overlooking the trees and the beach and lake beyond them, she glimpsed a sudden movement. Was it a person? She froze, then pulled back the curtain. In the dim light of a waning moon, something dark and human-shaped darted out of the shadows. It stopped, swung around…

"Ah!" breathed Cora.

Then just as quickly, the figure disappeared, blending into darkness again.

Now it was her pulse that thudded in her ears.

CHAPTER ONE

LATE. TODAY OF all days. Heather couldn't believe her bad luck.

Her first day on the job site and both the twins decided this was the morning to drive her crazy. That was normally Taylor's job, but to make the situation worse, Addison joined her twin in doing everything possible to put Heather behind, starting with their refusal to get out of bed when she called them. They'd ended up running around the house like little banshees instead of getting ready, then threw buttered toast at each other at breakfast so they both had to change clothes. Which meant her neighbor, who'd agreed to watch them for an hour before escorting them to school with her own son, had left without them.

Now she had to drive the girls to school herself, and Heather couldn't believe it when she found Taylor sitting in the middle of the living room floor and playing her favorite DVD of her father before he'd gone back for the second tour of duty that had gotten him killed.

"You're Daddy's little girl," Scott told Taylor, kissing her on the cheek. *"You'll always be Daddy's girl."*

"Forever and ever?"

"Forever and ever. Cross my heart."

And even though her twin hadn't been there when this was recorded, the then-three-year-old Taylor had asked, *"Addison, too?"*

"Of course, Addison, too."

Heather blinked away the threat of tears and turned off the television. Moments like this brought back the heartache. Even though Scott had died three years before in Iraq, he was still alive in all their hearts.

She cleared her throat. "Taylor, come on. Addison is already outside. We have to go now."

Once through the kitchen, they headed for the SUV. Heather noted Addison was focused on a dog hanging back on the property but watching the little girl hopefully. He looked like some kind of a border collie mix.

"Mommy, look at the dog!" Taylor said excitedly.

"We don't have time for that. C'mon, Addison. Both of you, get in."

Maybe if she didn't look at the dog, she wouldn't feel guilty just leaving him there. Loose. Probably scared and hungry.

She was already late for her new job.

She checked to make sure both girls were strapped into their booster seats, then got into the driver's seat, and with a last look at the pooch, she took off for the school. He would find his way home, or his owner would find him. She had enough to worry about without adding a possible lost dog to the list.

Five minutes later she was getting the girls out of the vehicle. No kids on the playground. School had already started, so the twins were late, too.

"I don't want you to go to Kenosha, Mommy," Addison said, sniffling as they walked toward the entrance.

"What if you don't come back?" Taylor added. "Like Daddy." Her eyes shone with unshed tears.

Heather stopped, slipped an arm around each little girl and hugged them tight. "Of course I'm coming back. I'll be going to all different places with my new job, but they're not far away. I told you that you'll see me later. *In* Kenosha. Uncle Brian is going to drive you to your new day camp this afternoon, and after work, I'll pick you up. We can sing songs in the car all the way home."

Taylor blinked and swiped at her eyes with

the back of her hand. "I learned a new song in kiddygarden—"

"Me, too!" Addison interrupted.

"And I can't wait to hear you both sing it." Heather kissed one little blond head, then the other. "But right now, let's get you to your classroom."

She walked them inside the building and apologized to their teacher for being late, then practically ran back to her SUV.

Thankfully she'd found a day camp close to her job site. For now, Brian or their sister, Kristen, would pick up the twins and deliver them to afternoon care for her. Once school was out, the twins could be at the camp all day.

Finally heading for Kenosha, she called Tyrone Smith, one of the two people on her team.

"Me, again," she said. "I'm on my way. I should be there in fifteen minutes."

"No rush." As usual, Tyrone's tone was smooth and easy. "We trippin'."

"Tripping? I hope that's another way of saying you and Amber are working hard."

"And havin' a good time."

Hearing hip-hop music in the background, Heather had to force herself to keep her own voice even. "You're clearing the land along the beachfront the way I asked you to, right?"

"Exactly."

"Okay." Not that she was actually sure it was okay. She didn't know either member of her team well enough yet to judge. "Keep clearing."

The area was becoming overgrown with Lyme grass, an invasive non-native beach grass that posed a threat to several rare native plants. Heather wanted to replace whatever they removed with native varieties.

"Just remember to only remove the grass that has bluish leaves," she added. "They should stand out clearly from any native dune grass still present."

"I got it the first time," Tyrone said.

Heather flinched. She might be the boss of the team, but she didn't want to come off as "bossy." "I'll be there as fast as I can."

The short drive from Sparrow Lake seemed interminable.

Take deep, slow breaths, and enjoy the ride, she reminded herself. *Let go of what you can't fix.*

She'd existed in a pressure cooker for the past couple of years. An army widow at twenty-one, she'd managed her aunt's quilting store to make a living while raising the twins and earning a degree in landscape horticulture. In order to cope she'd had to learn how to counter stress with relaxation techniques.

Sometimes they even worked.

Now her sister, Kristen, had decided to change careers and was back in Sparrow Lake and running Sew Fine while Heather was embarking on her new career. The final project for her advanced landscape design class had been a design challenge sponsored by a nonprofit called Environmental Partners, Inc., otherwise known as EPI. She'd won the challenge and the opportunity for a paid internship that could turn into a full-time job.

This internship was a dream come true for Heather. She'd started gardening when she was a kid and her mother had no time to do anything but work to support their family. By high school, Heather had been drawing plans for friends' yards and figuring what kinds of plants should go where. She'd known then she wanted to get a job working in landscaping. But her plans to go to college had been cut short by her early pregnancy and Scott's determination to enlist. For years she'd had to be content with the gardening magazines she'd collected, the knowledge she'd gathered from them and a dream that one day it would all come together.

Now she actually would be able to put that knowledge to work and in a way that would help improve the earth by creating a sustainable landscape.

When she arrived in Kenosha at last, Heather drove through the historic district along the Lake Michigan shoreline. The houses on Third Street were old and huge and lovely, as was much of the current professional landscaping. Flanagan Manor was the biggest and showiest of the bunch.

She couldn't contain her excitement as she turned onto a drive that led into the huge lakeside estate surrounded by black wrought-iron fencing. She would get to work here for a good part of the summer, redefining the grounds of the mansion built in Victorian times and once owned and expanded by the wealthy Chicago bootlegger, Red Flanagan, who'd been famous for trading bullets with his chief competitor, Al Capone. The mansion had gone through several more owners since the 1930s, after the federal government claimed the property as payment for Flanagan's tax evasion.

One wing of the huge old home had been turned into a bed-and-breakfast by the current owner, Benjamin Phillips. The Phillips family lived in Chicago and used Flanagan Manor as their "summer cottage." Apparently, the bed-and-breakfast paid for the estate's upkeep. Heather had met the owner, of course, but the family wasn't currently in residence.

The main building itself was a showpiece, a gorgeous historic greystone with a portico lakeside and a porte cochère at the side entry, so passengers could alight from their vehicles heedless of inclement weather. Close to the mansion at the top of a gentle incline sat a stone terrace with some plants in large containers and a faux Italian fountain that didn't work anymore. An old two-story coach house that mimicked the mansion sat directly behind it. The huge expanse of grass fronting the lake tumbled down to a few modest dunes and a small beach. The rest of the shore on both sides of the mansion was lined with boulders, and to the south, a weathered boathouse was attached to a decrepit dock that jutted out into the lake. Once the site where illegal Canadian booze had been unloaded, the dock and boathouse no longer seemed to be in use.

Heather had no idea what the Phillips family intended to do with them in the future.

Her focus was on the surrounding nature.

Heather had been chosen to design and supervise renovation of the grounds, which would include reintroducing native plants to support not only stormwater containment, to keep the runoff from the lake, but also a balanced ecosystem. Many insects needed a specific plant for food. And those insects were food for small animals and birds. The landscaping would be both practical and beautiful, and she was thrilled that her work would be enjoyed for decades to come by myriad guests and visitors and the owner and his family.

Parking in back of the mansion alongside other service vehicles, she grabbed her portfolio with the design plans she was still working on, then left the SUV. The long, narrow lot along the north side of the building was reserved for guests, but today there were only a few cars. It had probably been full for Memorial Day weekend, but kids weren't out of school yet, and the tourist season hadn't geared up. The perfect time to get started.

Looking for her team, she headed across the south lawn, passing the century-old, glass-paneled conservatory on the southeast end of the mansion. Having had a quick tour of the inside, she knew that it wasn't being used to its full potential. No plant aficionado in the family. Mr. Phillips had suggested he might want her to renovate it. No promises, but the prospect excited Heather.

To her relief, Tyrone and Amber were busy at work on the gently rolling dunes near the shoreline, loading the invasive plants they'd removed into a wheelbarrow. About to call out to them, she stopped when she realized they would never hear her over the combined racket made by hip-hop music coming from a boom box on the beach and the roar of a nearby lawnmower.

Wait a minute! Why was anyone other than her team doing anything with the lawn? Mr. Phillips had told her to set the boundaries for EPI, so any groundskeeper should have checked with her first.

Glancing back, Heather noted a *giant* lawn-mower was eating up the south lawn at an amazing speed. The man riding the machine was pretty amazing, too. From the length of his leg, she'd guess he must be at least six feet tall. He had a sculpted body—she could appreciate the muscles all too obvious beneath the thin, white T-shirt—and undoubtedly sculpted features beneath a shock of dark-brown hair streaked with gray. Or so she assumed from his jawline. The rest of his face was pretty well-hidden behind mirrored sunglasses.

She'd never seen him before…but then she hadn't been introduced to anyone who worked on the estate other than Cora, the housekeeper, who was in charge of the mansion.

Though she thought about approaching him to find out exactly who he was, Heather decided that could wait. She felt less in charge wearing an old cap to protect her face from the sun, a practical gray sweatshirt and a pair of jeans loose enough to work in. Not that Mr. Sunglasses intimidated her or anything.

Her pulse threading a little unevenly, she moved away from man and machine and headed for her team. Tyrone Smith and Amber Miller had both been working for EPI for more than a year, but because neither had gotten any kind of formal education, they did the hard labor, not the design or planning. That was up to her. So, the week before, after she'd met them, they'd all made a trip out to the estate—Tyrone and Amber to deliver the heavy equipment they would need and Heather to go over the plans for the site. She'd made further changes in her designs since and figured she would be refining until the job was complete.

As Heather approached Tyrone, he looked up. Tall and skinny, he wore his hair in cornrows, and the ends of the braids brushed a too-big T-shirt honoring a dead musician.

"Hey, Amber, the boss is here!" he yelled. "Better turn down that music!"

Her light blond hair pulled up into a ponytail, her eyes a soft gray, Amber was probably only eighteen or nineteen, a couple of years younger than Tyrone. Dressed in a T-shirt and shorts and her feet encased in work boots a lot safer than her partner's tennis shoes, she bent over to shut off the boom box. As the music stopped, the young woman who looked too small to be so strong stopped, too, her hands on her hips like she was waiting for orders.

Heather might be used to giving orders at the store, but this was different. She had no history here. No real experience. Behind her, the mower noise grew louder, and she glanced back to see Mr. Sunglasses riding over grass he'd already cut. That wasn't good. And how low had he set that mower? Grass should be cut no shorter than two inches. At least not if you wanted it to live.

Was this something else she needed to take care of?

Okay, she had to admit it. The thought of giving *him* orders intimidated her just a little. Okay, maybe a lot.

Forcing a smile, she turned back to her workers. "Looks like you got a lot done."

"Well, we've been working since eight," Amber said.

Heather's face grew warm, but she chose not to make excuses. "When you've finished with the beach area, we should start removing sod for the rain gardens."

She'd planned on two freeform rain gardens on the mansion's lake-facing side, leaving room for a wide, stone pathway down to the beach between them.

"Retaining wall or no?" Tyrone asked.

Something she'd been undecided on the week before.

Heather nodded. "The slope is gentle enough, so we can install twelve or fifteen inches." If the slope were steeper, a big storm could wash away a taller retaining wall, but a small one should do well. "That way, we can create flat areas with a shallow bowl for the new plantings."

"How much of the lawn are we going to remove?" Amber asked.

Considering the estate grounds were nearly an acre, equivalent to the size of a football field, and knowing her budget, Heather said, "Not as much as I would like, but it'll be a great start. We have four areas of concentration. In addition to this beach area and the rain gardens, we'll plant a prairie with native grasses mixed with flowering plants as a backdrop over there." She indicated the south end of the grounds. "And then an expanded garden starting from the terrace, with another seating area at the other end, then here, around the buildings. All that will require more lawn removal. The rest of the lawn will remain, at least for this year."

"There's not going to be much left if The Terminator keeps going," Amber said, looking beyond her.

"The Terminator?" Heather turned to see the man mowing the same section for a third time.

"He's killing that grass," Tyrone said. "Are you sure the owners want any left?"

Heather sighed. "I'm sure." She'd actually had to scale back her plan a bit due to their budget. New plantings weren't inexpensive, especially for an estate of this size, so she better save that grass.

"I saw him roll right over some bushes, too," Amber said. "He just hot dogs that thing around like he's driving a sports car."

Heather sighed. "Okay. I guess I have to go talk to the guy. He doesn't work for EPI, right?"

Tyrone shook his head. "Nope."

Great. "Go on back to work while I take care of this."

The Terminator. He did kind of look like the movie character, wearing those mirrored sunglasses.

Not wanting to confront a stranger her first hour on the job, Heather nevertheless trekked back up the incline. The landscape was now her responsibility, and she couldn't sit by and see the lawn destroyed, not when there would be so much of it left when they were done planting.

Moving in behind him, she cleared her throat, then called, "Excuse me!"

The Terminator kept going—apparently he hadn't heard her—and he was moving so fast, she nearly had to run to keep up with the riding mower.

She raised her voice. "Excuse me! Sir!" When he didn't answer, she jogged faster and grabbed his arm. "Hey!"

He suddenly stopped and she ended up just about running smack into him. Stopping the machine instantly, he jumped off. The next thing Heather knew, she was on the ground, his hand on her throat, pinning her in place and knocking off her cap. It all happened so quickly, she had no way to defend herself. Frightened and angry, she lay beneath him, shaking inside, staring wide-eyed into his half-hidden face.

"What are you doing?" she croaked. Her heart was thumping double time. "Let go! Please! I wasn't attacking you, okay?"

As if suddenly realizing he'd overreacted, he shook himself, stood and said, "Sorry, I didn't mean to do that." He held out a hand to her. "You just startled me."

Reluctantly, she took his hand and let him pull her to her feet. The breath seemed to whoosh out of her, and she could feel her pulse where his fingers wrapped around hers. "Sorry," he said again. "Really."

As if burned, she pulled her hand free. "I—I, uh, just wanted to talk to you."

He reached over to shut off the lawnmower. "About?"

"Well, that." Her heartbeat steadying, she nodded at the fancy mower.

"You want to do the mowing?"

His lips curved slightly. Was that a smile? Hard to tell in a face that seemed to be made of granite. And one that was mostly hidden behind mirrored sunglasses. She wondered if he wore them for effect—if he wanted to seem mysterious or dangerous for some reason.

Not caring to make matters worse, she said, "Uh, no, I don't want to do the mowing. I just want to know why *you're* doing it."

"I'm the handyman. Rick Slater. Mr. Phillips just hired me a few days ago."

He didn't look like a handyman. Heather frowned at him. "And he told you to mow the lawn?"

"Phillips didn't give me orders to do anything specific. He just expects me to take care of the place in general. You have something against me cutting the grass?"

Did she? Heather wondered. This wasn't something she'd talked about with Mr. Phillips or EPI, so she merely said, "I'm in charge of renovating the landscaping. Heather Clarke."

His lips curved again. "*You're* in charge? Then you must be that community college girl who's doing an internship here."

He seemed amused by the idea of her being in charge of anything. How young did he think she was, anyway? She was a very mature twenty-four. Not that she felt inclined to tell him so.

"I'm the *woman* who is doing the internship, yes." Trying not to be irritated with him— she was fighting a losing battle—Heather said, "Mr. Phillips told me I could decide what we're doing with all the plants and the lawn. Do *you* have experience with landscaping?"

"What kind of experience is necessary to ride a lawnmower around? Feel free to give me advice. I'm new at this."

Then why had he been hired?

"First, you need to adjust the lawnmower so it doesn't cut lower than two inches, or you'll destroy the grass," Heather told him. "Then only go over it once. And if you're just riding from one place to another, raise the blades entirely." She flicked her gaze around the area until she saw the bush Amber had told her about. "Apparently you've also sent a few shrubs to the big garden in the sky...so don't mow the bushes, okay?"

He held up his hands, palms out. "Okay. You're the boss. Your company does want the lawn mowed, right?"

From his expression, she was certain he was silently amused at her expense.

"Sure, mow any of the lawn that's open— once." Heat sizzled up her neck and her spine went stiff. "I need to get back to my team. We have a lot of work to get done today."

With that, she whipped around, leaning over to pick up her fallen cap. She placed it firmly back on her head, tucking stray strands around the edge. All the while, she felt his gaze bore into her as she walked away. It took willpower not to glance back and look at him one last time. Tension coiled in her until the lawnmower started up again. She relaxed a bit, then realized her team had stopped work to watch the encounter. They were both grinning. Well, great. No respect from The Terminator...she could take that. But the people she would count on to follow her directions were another matter. If she didn't have their respect, it was going to be a *long* summer.

She tried to play it cool as she joined them. Hoping they couldn't sense her pulse racing or her stomach churning, she shrugged nonchalantly. "He's the new handyman, but it seems he doesn't know what he's doing."

"He looks pretty competent to me," Tyrone said. "Like he's been in the military. Or maybe he's a spy. The way he flattened you on that ground in two seconds was amazing. Whoohoo!"

"Well, she *did* ambush him," said Amber, grinning. "He didn't even see her coming."

Both Amber and Tyrone laughed as Heather clenched her jaw. "I was only trying to catch up with him."

"Well, you caught him all right." Noting his boss's somber expression, Tyrone raised his brows at his coworker.

But Amber wasn't paying attention. "A spy, hmm? Yeah, I dig that. A real hot one."

Rick Slater might be hot, but Heather didn't feel in the least like smiling. "A spy for what?" She couldn't help but be sarcastic. "Protecting the country from invasive plants?"

Although *spy* was going a little too far, Heather could believe Rick had been military at some time. Probably an officer. He held himself with an authority that had bothered her. Considering her husband, Scott, had been killed in Iraq, she had no desire to get to know any man who was former, current or future military.

She only hoped the little show The Terminator had given Tyrone and Amber by making her look silly hadn't damaged her relationship with her team.

CHAPTER TWO

RICK KEPT GLANCING over to see what Heather Clarke and her team were doing as he finished mowing the lawn area around the mansion. He'd enjoyed annoying her just a little. She was plenty bossy for someone so young. *Young.* Yeah, she was, no matter the tempting curves she'd hidden under that baggy sweatshirt, curves he'd felt beneath him when he'd had her on the ground. No sense in thinking about that or about her at all.

No sense in thinking about anyone, not when he was here to do a job.

He had to redirect his mind back to his mission.

Mowing the lawn was simply part of his cover, though he had carefully adjusted the mower higher as Heather had suggested. He didn't want to be a grass destroyer. He snorted at the idea and remembered how Heather had glared at him when she'd made the accusation. Hmm, her narrow, makeup-free face had pulled into the cutest expression, and her blue eyes had gone all steely, when she'd been irritated with him...

There his mind went again, off in the wrong direction.

Raising the blades, he rode the lawnmower to the far side of the mansion, stopped and turned it off. Then he dismounted and walked along the flower garden that bordered the building. The task gave him the opportunity to covertly inspect the area where he'd found a man's footprints early that morning. Though he hadn't seen any signs of a break in, he was certain someone was sneaking around the grounds. If only he could figure out why. Whoever had left those tracks beneath the windows probably was up to no good, as Ben Phillips feared.

Strange things had been going on at the Flanagan estate for the past several weeks—a broken window, random diggings, tampered locks. Phillips had grown concerned, as he should have been, considering the family had quite a collection of century-old stained glass in the house, in addition to pricey antiques and a butler's pantry filled with silver service. Also, there was the safety of the staff and the bed-and-breakfast guests to consider. With the tourist season about to heat up, Phillips had hired Rick to secure the estate and investigate the source of the trouble. And to stop it from going any farther, of course. Because Phillips had fired the last handyman/groundskeeper, he needed someone to do small repairs around the place—hence Rick's cover.

But Rick had now been all around the mansion and the other buildings on the property, and he hadn't seen anything more to clue him in as to what was going on. Figuring he needed to change tactics, he left the mower outside the coach house. Built to house carriages drawn by horses and walled with the same kind of fancy paneling as the house, it was now a combination garage for his employer and storage area for equipment. There was even a small shop area to make repairs. And upstairs, the second floor apartment that had been inhabited first by a carriage driver, then a chauffeur, was now Rick's temporary digs. He'd only brought along some clothes and a bunch of books—the mysteries and thrillers that kept him company at night. The challenge of figuring out who did what and why had entertained him since he'd read the Hardy Boys as a kid. Undoubtedly the reason he'd been drawn to this particular job.

Rick was used to temporary digs. He'd never had a real home, not even when he was a kid. His dad had been military, and Rick, his brother, Joe, and their mom had moved from base to base all over the world with him. Their parents were retired now and living in Florida. And Joe had settled in to a job at the Pentagon.

Sometimes Rick wished he'd been smart enough to get out before the horrible attack that had turned his dreams into nightmares. When terrorists had attacked his team on a special mission in Afghanistan, two of his men had lost their lives. He and Keith Murphy had barely survived. He'd relegated to memory every detail of the event and the deaths of the men he'd called friends.

Afterward, he'd never felt the same about being a lifer. When his tour was over, he'd left the army. Still, Rick wasn't settled, inside or out.

Guilt over his men's deaths lingered, always just below the surface.

He hadn't yet found any reason to want to remain in civilian life.

And he didn't know if he would ever call any place home.

The only reason he'd come to Wisconsin had been to reconnect with Megan Anders, an old girlfriend, the daughter of a commissioned officer. He'd dated her off and on for a couple of years, and the last he'd heard, she'd settled in Milwaukee. Unfortunately, he'd had no clue she'd gotten married since he'd last seen her.

Still, he liked the area, and having nowhere else to go, had stuck around, taking a job with Lake Shore Security, the company that had placed him in his current undercover job.

Getting to know the other employees on the estate was essential. It was day two and he'd barely met any of the help, so Rick decided to go inside the mansion and get cozy with them. He hadn't had a chance to talk to any of the three full-time staff alone. Maybe he could get something out of one of them that would put him on the right track. The only person on the property who knew his real mission was the housekeeper, Cora, who'd been with the Phillips family for decades. He assumed that she was loyal and would keep his identity to herself, or the owner wouldn't have told her who he was.

He entered through the huge kitchen, which still had an old-fashioned feel despite the new appliances. The large cabinets looked original to him, though they'd been painted white and sported new hardware. Gray-threaded white marble counters gave the cook several large preparation surfaces. Right now, however, she was busy at the stove, stirring something in a big pan. The smell made his mouth water.

He sized up the woman. Probably in her early forties, Kelly Bennett wore a white chef's coat over gray trousers and had tied her red hair back from her face.

"Smells great," he said.

She glanced at him. "Oh, Rick, good morning. I'm making carnitas, a southwestern pulled pork. You can try it later, at dinner."

"I'll be looking forward to that."

Actually, he was looking forward to any meals he could catch here. He wasn't a very good cook himself. And eating in a mess hall had never been much of a treat. So he was grateful for Phillips's invitation to catch lunch and dinner with the other full-time employees on weekdays. On Saturday and Sunday, the cook only made brunch and only when there were guests.

"It's pretty quiet here at this end of town," he said. "Not much action."

"Well, no, not now. There will be shortly. We have two guests arriving tomorrow. More on the weekend. We won't be full seven days a week until mid-June, when school lets out. After that, all eight guest rooms are booked solid for most of the summer."

Rick waited a beat, then said, "I thought I heard something last night." If someone had been out in the garden as the fresh footprints indicated, the person must have made some kind of noise. Unfortunately, Rick hadn't heard anything because he'd been too far away, sound asleep in the coach house.

"Heard something?" Kelly repeated. "Like what?"

"I don't know. But it woke me." A small fabrication.

"Maybe you had a bad dream."

"I would have remembered. Well, usually I do." He waited another beat. "So you didn't hear anything?"

Phillips had told him that the cook, housekeeper and concierge all lived in the mansion.

"No. And I'm a light sleeper." She went back to stirring her carnitas. "Nothing last night."

"Another night, then?"

Keeping her back to him, she shrugged. "Old houses have strange noises sometimes. Is there something else you need?"

Rick wanted to ask her more, but he got the idea she wasn't about to elaborate. At least not yet.

"Actually, I came in to see Cora."

"She said she wanted to do some reorganizing in the library."

"Thanks. See you when it's chow time."

He left the kitchen via a hallway that took him to the rotunda. The large, round multistory room in the middle of the building separated the two wings. An original mural of the heavens covered the domed ceiling and extended to the upper walls, where a balcony ran full circle, allowing guests to admire artwork on the walls or look down to view the activity on the first floor. The lower walls were enhanced with a rich wood wainscoting, and a carpeted stairway with hand-carved railings led to the second floor.

The rotunda did double duty as the check-in area for guests and as the concierge office. Behind the antique mahogany desk hung a large portrait of a thin, wiry man with wild red hair that stuck straight up. The man stood next to an elaborate seven-branched silver candelabra complete with glowing flames.

Red Flanagan himself, Rick assumed. Odd that Phillips would showcase a portrait of a mobster. Then again, that a mobster once owned the estate might be part of its appeal to visitors and the reason they called it Flanagan Manor rather than Phillips Manor.

At the moment, the cavernous room was empty, so he sailed right through. Phillips had given him a set of plans of the mansion, so Rick knew that the kitchen, dining room, drawing room and music room sat below two floors of guest rooms with baths, and the library, main entrance and conservatory sat below the owner's private quarters. The Phillips family had a drawing room and huge master suite on the second floor and four more bedrooms with individual baths on the third.

Entering the library, he saw Cora Stanton on a rolling ladder, straightening some books on a high shelf. Sections of every wall were lined with shelving from floor to ceiling, all filled with books. He cleared his throat to get her attention. She glanced back and saw him.

"Ah, Rick, there you are. I wanted to talk to you."

"Good. Then we're on the same wavelength." When she arched her eyebrows in question, he said, "That's why I'm here."

She immediately descended the ladder.

As Flanagan Manor's housekeeper, Cora was, in effect, in charge of the estate. All employees answered to her. An attractive older woman of around seventy, she wore dark trousers and a lace-trimmed white blouse. Her silver hair was cut in a short, modern style, and designer glasses hung from the chain around her neck.

"Benjamin told me why he hired you, of course, and I must say I'm relieved. I admit that I've been a bit spooked by some of the things happening in or around the house lately, and I hope you'll get to the bottom of whatever is going on. I'm at my wit's end worrying."

"Phillips gave me the short explanation, but I need to know more from someone who is actually living on the property full-time."

"Let's sit, shall we?"

She indicated the upholstered sofa and leather chairs before the massive ceramic-faced fireplace with an equally massive wood surround and mantel, where a small fire had taken the chill of the spring morning from the room.

They took the two chairs, so they were facing each other.

Concern furrowed Cora's brow. "I've run this estate for more than thirty years, and I've never had to worry until recently. I don't feel safe anymore, what with the noises and sightings and attempted break-ins." She shivered.

"What kind of noises?"

"Thumping in the walls. Supposedly there were secret passageways and tunnels at one time and I'm wondering if somehow something or someone got into one of them."

Rick started. Secret passageways. *Underground.* That was something Phillips hadn't told him about. A shudder ran through him, but he covered quickly.

"I have blueprints of the house, but I didn't see any note of hidden access," he said.

"Well, no, there wouldn't be, not on the original plans. When Red Flanagan bought the estate, he had the passageways and tunnels and perhaps a secret room or two built into or under the house to support his illegal business. Then the Feds took over. It's said they walled off the entrances to the house itself before they sold the property. You know, to discourage any more illegal activity. That was nearly eighty years and two additional owners ago."

"Where were the entrances to these supposed tunnels?"

She shrugged. "I have no idea. I never even had reason to think about them until the past few weeks."

Rick remained silent for a moment. Secret tunnels…secret stash? Was that what the intruder was looking for? Something the person thought Red left behind and the Feds hadn't found? Made sense.

"So start from the beginning," he said. "When did you first suspect someone was up to no good?"

"About five weeks ago. I woke in the middle of the night because I thought I had heard a noise. I looked out at the lake through my bedroom window and movement nearby caught my eye. A dark, shadowy figure. Someone was on the property, but the gates were locked. The person either climbed the fence or came via the lake itself."

"You're sure it wasn't an employee or guest?"

"It was April and the middle of the week. We have very few guests at that time, and none that night. Day employees—maids, mostly—don't have keys. So the only ones legally on the property were the cook and concierge, and both Kelly and Gina said they were sound asleep."

She went on to tell him about other incidents, a few Phillips had already related. It was sounding more and more like the intruder was searching for something specific.

"Has there been any kind of property damage?"

"Not with the first few incidents, which is why I wasn't too alarmed. But then a couple of weeks ago, I heard breaking glass." She sighed. "Fortunately I am a light sleeper. Or just an old woman—they say people my age tend to wake up more easily in the night."

"You're not old," he reassured her.

She shrugged.

He went on, "So you investigated?"

"Not then. I was alone. So not until morning."

"Well, you're not alone anymore." Rick

handed her his card. "My cell number is there. Program it in to yours. Should you hear or see anything suspicious at any time, call me immediately."

She took the card and slipped it into a pocket. "I will sleep better knowing that you are around and that I can call on you."

"Good." Rick got to his feet. "If you think of anything else—anything at all that might help—let me know."

Leaving the library, Rick figured this was going to be a piece of cake compared with some of his experiences in a special operations intelligence team. He was going to have to install several security cameras not only around the mansion but also in several other places. The coach house for one. The old boathouse, too, just in case an intruder decided to come in by the lake. Tracking back the way he'd come through the rotunda, he saw that Gina Luca, dressed in a black pencil skirt and a bright red blouse, was standing next to her desk.

"Rick, it's so good to see you again. How are you getting along so far?"

"I'm doing fine with a little guidance," he said, thinking of his encounter with the college girl.

Gina's lips curved in an inviting smile. "I'd be happy to help you with whatever you need."

With jet black hair that trailed her shoulders, dark brown eyes and a body that would make most men take a second look, Gina was a little too high end for Rick's taste. He preferred his women earthy and a little feisty.

Now he was thinking of Heather on the grass pinned under him, his hand to her throat, ordering him to get off…

He really hadn't meant to go on the attack like that. His training had kicked in at the most inappropriate time.

He nodded at Gina. "I'll let you know when I need something."

Like information that would help him break the case.

FOR NEARLY AN hour Heather helped Tyrone and Amber clear the persistent, invading grass from the beach area.

"Wait till my younger sisters and brothers hear where I get to work," Tyrone said, looking out to the lake, blue-green today, waves swelling and rushing in to shore with a lick of foam.

"How many siblings do you have?" Amber asked as she dumped another plant into the wheelbarrow.

"Three of each."

Heather started. "Seven kids?" She had her hands full with two. "Your poor mother."

"Me and my seventeen-year-old sister, Chantel, help her take care of the younger ones."

"You?" Amber said, sounding disbelieving.

"Hey, I like kids, especially after they get past that crazy stage."

"When is that?" Whenever it was, Heather wasn't looking forward to it.

"Actually, there's two crazy stages," Tyrone said with authority. "Everyone knows about the terrible twos. But it's the psycho sixes that get to me. That's when they become jugheads, think they know everything and get into trouble. Darnell decided to investigate a boarded-up house for ghosts and ended up with a broken arm. And LaVonda tangled with a hornets' nest. Man, was she ever a mess. I'm glad we're on our last six-year-old. That would be Vaughn."

Heather could hear the affection in Tyrone's voice when he talked about his younger siblings and thought it was both sweet and unexpected.

"So what about you?" he asked Amber.

"Two older brothers. Big lugs. Always trying to take care of me whether I want them to or not."

"That's what big brothers are supposed to

do," Tyrone said, then turned his attention to Heather. "Your turn, boss."

"Younger brother, older sister. And I have twin six-year-old girls."

"Twins!" Tyrone puffed himself up and swaggered a little. "You need advice on how to handle them little girls, you can come to me."

Heather laughed. "I'll keep that in mind next time they make me want to scream."

They all laughed together, a good sound. Heather decided that, despite the shaky start, they would make a compatible team.

Noting they were almost finished with this section, she stepped back. "I'm going to get the sod cutter from the coach house so we can start clearing our rain garden areas next."

Tyrone saluted her. "By the time you get the equipment, we'll be ready to go."

"If you see The Terminator," Amber added, "say hi for us."

The Terminator. Right. Not having heard the lawnmower for quite some time now, Heather found herself looking to see what he was up to. And then she remembered being pinned under that big, muscular body. Heat crept up the back of her neck. *Rick Slater,* she told herself. His name was Rick Slater. Thinking of him as The Terminator was bound to get her in trouble.

She headed for the coach house, a miniature

version of the mansion. Same gray stone, same windows, same small details. Her team had put most of their equipment in a storage room with plenty of shelving. But the sod cutter was bulky and weighed more than three hundred pounds, so they'd left it near the lawnmower and other large equipment. Of course, The Termin…*Rick*…had removed the mower earlier.

So when she turned on the light and approached the sod cutter, she noticed it was sitting at an odd angle. The first thing she thought was that Rick must have whacked it getting the lawnmower out of the coach house. She tried straightening it so she could turn it on and back it out but had no success. It was definitely wonky. A closer look showed her the rear pivot wheel was out of alignment.

How had the sod cutter been damaged?

Heather tried not to panic, but the breath caught in her throat as she realized the implications. She was in charge of this contract, which meant she was in charge of the equipment. Any damage was her responsibility.

If the sod cutter was inoperable…how bad was it? Her hand shook as she pressed it to her chest. *Oh, please, I hope I don't have to replace it.*

"Hey, what's going on? Is something wrong?"

She whipped around to find Rick coming

into the coach house. She could see that he'd left the lawnmower directly outside. He was still wearing his sunglasses, so she couldn't read his expression.

"Yes, unfortunately there is. The sod cutter wasn't like this when we delivered it last Friday."

"Like what?"

"Broken."

"And you haven't used it yet?"

"No. It's the pivot…" She indicated the damaged wheel. "You didn't bang into it or anything when you moved the lawnmower, did you?"

"Hey, I didn't touch it, honest." He crouched down to inspect the damage. "It looks like it can be fixed."

"I sure hope so. A new sod cutter would cost thousands of dollars. I don't know how I would pay for it. I don't even know how I can pay for the repair."

She was still managing website orders for Sew Fine, mostly at home, but she might have to arrange more hours at the store to make extra money.

Rick straightened. "Hey, it's going to be all right. Calm down."

"I-I'm sorry." Now that he was closer, she could see the part of his face not hidden by the sunglasses. He appeared concerned. "I'm a little strapped for cash lately, and I'm a single mother, so I have to worry about how I'm going to feed my kids." Though she didn't want to rely on anyone else, her family would come through for her if she ran into a financial problem. She took a deep, calming breath. It would all work out somehow.

"You have kids?" He sounded a little surprised. "Plural?"

She nodded. "Two. Twin girls. Addison and Taylor. They were six last month."

"Six-year-olds?" Now he sounded amazed. "How old are you?"

Remembering he'd called her *that community college girl,* she asked, "How old did you think I was?"

"I don't know. Nineteen. Maybe twenty."

She smiled despite herself. "Thanks, but I'll be twenty-five in a few months."

"You could have fooled me. You *did* fool me." He reached out and gently touched her shoulder. "I can see why you're worried with kids and all. But relax already. Your company must have insurance on its equipment."

"I—I guess." Appreciative of his sympathy, she said, "I hate even telling them something's gone wrong on the first day. I was hoping this would turn into a full-time job after we finished this project."

"Maybe you won't have to tell them anything," Rick said. "I probably can fix the wheel."

Thinking of the way he'd wrestled with the lawnmower, she asked, "Seriously?"

"Just because I don't know my way around a lawn doesn't mean I don't have other talents. I used to take cars apart and put them back together for fun. Yes, seriously, leave this to me. I'll take care of it."

Starting to like Rick more than she thought she would, Heather let out a relieved sigh. "If you can do that, I'll…well, you deserve some kind of reward. I'll owe you."

His mouth curved slightly in a ghost of a smile. "I'll keep that in mind."

She blinked at him and swallowed hard. "Um, when do you think you might be able to get around to fixing it?"

"I have a couple of things to take care of first that won't take long. If I don't need to order a new part, I should have it to you early this afternoon."

"Thank you!" She could hardly believe he was being so great to her after her negative thoughts about him. "I guess I'd better tell my crew our plans have changed. We need to build a composter anyway, so we can recycle the sod we remove. We'll start on that."

Luckily, she'd had her workers bring the materials to create a couple of large composter holding units—wood and galvanized chicken wire. Not pretty, the composters would be built at the far end of the property and hidden by native grasses that would reach six feet high by midsummer.

Shifting into a positive mode, she started to leave but turned back when Rick called her.

"Hey, Heather. If anything else unexpected happens—not just to your equipment but anything else that bothers you around here—make sure you let me know. I'm going to take care of everything."

She suddenly felt warm inside.

"Will do," she agreed, wondering why his assurances made her feel so good. Maybe it was because she hadn't had the protection of a caring male in a very long time.

But as she headed back toward the beach area, she wondered what Rick meant by "anything else" that bothered her.

It almost sounded as if he expected something to go wrong.

A GUT FEELING convinced Rick that the sod cutter had been damaged by their mystery intruder. When he'd stooped down to get a closer look at the pivot wheel, he'd noticed a smear of dirt on the machine that looked like a footprint. Someone had stood on it, and perhaps the weight had bent the wheel.

The question was...*why would someone stand on it?*

After his discussion with Cora, he was pretty convinced the person was looking for entries to the secret tunnels. Maybe he'd had to climb over the equipment to search.

Who knew?

Rick had to admit the coach house was a perfect place for a secret entrance. Not much traffic in here, so low probability of any witnesses. He started inspecting walls for some indication of a hidden door, but the paneling made it hard to see any irregularities. And the lack of good light everywhere but in the storage area frustrated him.

And as he searched, he thought about Heather Clarke. At almost twenty-five, she was still eleven years younger than he. But why was he even thinking about the difference in their ages? He might like her, but he wasn't looking for someone to date. He was looking to do his job—to stop whoever was up to no good around the estate.

Still, he was distracted. He couldn't shake

Heather's distraught expression from his memory. As a single mom, she obviously had some money concerns.

Stooping down to take a better look at the sod cutter's pivot wheel, he remembered how Heather's tension had eased when he'd told her he could probably fix the equipment himself. And when he did, he hoped to see a big smile on her pretty face.

All the reward he would need.

CHAPTER THREE

HEATHER PUT A tuna casserole into the oven. She was grateful that Rick had come through for her and that she and her crew had been able to make short work of cutting out the two areas for rain gardens. Now she wondered what she could do to properly thank the man. Not that she had time to think about The Terminator at the moment. The nickname made her smile, made her *want* to think more about the resourceful man.

But right now, she had to concentrate on getting Addison and Taylor fed. Which meant making a salad to go with the casserole. A salad they would complain and fuss about before she got them to eat it. She fetched lettuce and a tomato, then carrots from the fridge and took them all to the sink, where she rinsed everything off. Addison loved carrots and Taylor could be bribed to eat them with a little French dressing on the side. She glanced around. The kitchen could use a makeover, but thankfully, it was spacious enough to be eat-in. The house was a neat bungalow with a living room, kitchen, two bedrooms and a single bath. All she'd been able to afford using her late husband's life insurance.

A screech from outside made her wonder what was going on now. Apparently a morning of school followed by an afternoon of day camp wasn't enough to wear out the twins. She grabbed a bowl and a cutting board and began chopping. The girls were playing in the backyard, and from the sound of their squeals and heated words, they had energy to spare.

Putting together the salad, Heather couldn't even remember what that kind of energy felt like. Although she loved her time with the girls, they took everything out of her. She simply couldn't keep up with them no matter how hard she tried. At one point when she was managing her Aunt Margaret's store, she'd considered giving up on school. But then her sister, Kristen, had returned to Sparrow Lake and taken over Sew Fine. Having lost her fancy marketing job in Chicago, Kristen hadn't known what she wanted to do at first but, luckily, her family and a new romance with the town's police chief meant she was in Sparrow Lake to stay, and Heather was thankful for that.

She smiled wanly, thinking about how

gladly she'd stepped down from the store manager job and taken the easier one of overseeing online sales. Much of which she could do at home after the twins were in bed. The only problem now was money. They were living on an even tighter budget than before.

A budget that would have been ruined if she'd had to pay to repair the sod cutter.

Rick crept into her thoughts despite her determination. There was just something about him...

And he certainly had come to her rescue this morning. Nothing she did could possibly convey her gratitude because she was hoping this internship would be the turning point in her life. If EPI hired her full time, she could give up working for Sew Fine for a fulfilling job with enough pay and benefits that she could finally relax. Then she would have more time to concentrate on the girls.

Which sounded like heaven after the past four years of pushing, pushing, pushing. Whoever had thought it was possible to "do it all," especially if you were a single mom, was deluded. Yeah, you could do it all if you didn't mind feeling like a zombie half the time. Her own mother had remarried and moved to California about the same time Scott had died, so Heather had been on her own.

"Hey, look what we got!"

Hearing Taylor's chirpy voice, Heather smiled and turned to see. But though her daughters were both beaming at her, her own smile quickly evaporated. Standing between them was a scruffy dog with orange-brown and white fur and a pointed nose. The same dog who'd been watching them get into the SUV that morning.

"Whose dog is that?" Heather had hoped it belonged to a neighbor and had simply been wandering around.

"He's ours!" Addison said. "We found him!"

Heather shook her head. "Oh, no, he's not ours."

"Yes, he is, and he's starving." Taylor went to the refrigerator and pulled out a package of turkey slices. "He needs to eat."

Heather was about to say no when she took a better look at the dog. He did seem a little thin and he was staring at that package of lunch meat with the most hopeful expression on his sad little face. "Okay, one slice of turkey."

But when the dog practically swallowed the slice whole, Taylor pulled out another and gave that one to him, too, saying, "His name is Kirby."

"Sweetheart, don't give him a name because we're not going to keep him."

"Why not?" Addison asked. "He's real nice."

Watching the dog devour a third slice of meat, Heather said, "I'm sure he is. But—"

"C'mon, Mom," Taylor wheedled.

"I don't have time to take care of a dog."

Or the money. Being a responsible owner meant paying for shots and vet bills in addition to food, and the family budget was at the straining point now. Not that she wanted to burden her six-year-olds with her financial worries.

"I'll take care of him by myself!" Taylor insisted.

"No," Addison protested, "I'll help."

Heather knew Taylor couldn't take care of the dog herself, not even with Addison's help. The twins didn't have that kind of focus yet. When something interested them, it was only for a short while. And then they moved on to the next thing.

"You can take care of him for tonight. But tomorrow, I'm driving him to the local shelter. They'll either find his real owner...or they'll find him a good home."

"Mo-o-om!" the twins cried in unison.

"That's enough." Noticing the lunch meat package was empty, Heather said, "Well, it seems the dog has had his dinner." She pulled a bowl out of the cabinet and filled it with water.

"Now it's time for you to get ready for yours. Go wash your hands so you can set the table."

She put down the bowl of water out of the line of traffic. The dog immediately stuck his muzzle in and started drinking as he gazed up at her with shiny brown eyes. He was such a cutie. She couldn't help herself. She patted his side. Whistling through his nose, the dog immediately whipped his head around and licked her hand. She melted inside just a little.

"Don't worry, boy. I'll make sure you get a home."

As long as it wasn't hers.

An hour later, the kitchen was clean and Heather was on the computer, which she had set up in the bay window area of the living room. Someday it would be nice to have a bigger place, one with a real office space. She was going through Sew Fine's newest online orders and figuring out what supplies she would need to order to replenish stock.

Directly after dinner, the twins had absconded with the dog to their room. Heather could hear them now, talking to him and giggling. She smiled sadly. They were having a good time, and she hoped their little hearts wouldn't be broken when they had to give up the dog in the morning.

Hearing a vehicle stop in front of the house, she left the computer to see who it was. To her surprise, her sister was coming up the walk. Wearing a lavender dress and four-inch heels to match and her blond hair gathered in a sleek ponytail, Kristen was carrying a dress bag. Apparently, she was delivering Heather's bridesmaid's dress. Kristen and Alex's wedding date was approaching all too rapidly.

Heather opened the door. "Hey, Kristen, what a great surprise." They hugged, and she took the dress bag from her sister. "You didn't have to deliver the dress, though. I could have picked it up myself."

"But then I wouldn't have been able to see my favorite nieces," Kristen said as the twins came running out of their bedroom, the dog on their heels.

"Aunt Kristen!" they yelled together, each twin launching herself onto Kristen, who laughed and gave them big hugs.

The dog stopped short and started barking. Kristen started. "Whoa, what's this?"

"Our new dog," Addison said.

Before Heather could object, Taylor added, "His name is Kirby."

Over the twins' heads, Kristen locked gazes with her. Heather squinched up her face and shook her head *No*. In return, Kristen rolled her eyes.

"Girls, give your aunt some breathing room. It's time to take your baths." When Taylor's face lit up, Heather clarified, "I mean the two of you, not the dog. You're not to let him in the tub. Understood?"

Taylor's face fell. "Okay."

"While the tub is filling, get your pajamas ready and brush your hair and teeth. And don't get in until I tell you it's okay."

She let them wash themselves now but not without supervision.

The girls flew to the bathroom, the dog trotting behind.

"You actually think they're *not* going to let their four-legged friend get in with them?" Kristen asked, laughing. "I remember that time I babysat and gave them a bath. When my back was turned, they brought every doll and toy horse into the tub, even though I told them not to."

Hearing the water running, Heather laughed. "I'd like to say they're more mature than they were a year ago, but that's wishful thinking. Maybe I'd better get the dog and keep him with us in case they get any ideas."

She went into the bedroom, where the girls

were tossing their pajamas back and forth over the dog's head so that he kept jumping, trying to get the clothes whipping through the air.

"Enough. I'm going to take the dog into the other room with Aunt Kristen." She looked straight at the dog and tapped her leg. "C'mon. C'mon, boy." He sat down. She patted her leg again. "Let's go." She whistled. "C'mon, boy." He yawned.

"His name is Kirby," Taylor sing-songed, and the dog got to his feet and trotted over to her. "See?"

Naming him was a mistake, but what else could she do? "C'mon…Kirby."

The dog now came to her. Heather patted him on the head. "Let's go see Aunt Kristen."

By the time she got to the living room, Kirby trotting ahead of her and looking back to make sure she was coming, Kristen had already opened the garment bag to reveal the bridesmaid's dress made of sheer apricot-colored material.

"Oh, it's gorgeous."

"You need to try it on," Kristen said, handing it to her. "I want to make sure it's perfect."

"I'm not the bride. You're the one who has to look perfect." And Kristen *would* look perfect, Heather thought, having seen the elegant cream-colored wedding dress at Kristen's last fitting.

"But you're my matron of honor and my sister. We have to look perfect together."

"Okay, I'll try on the dress."

Heather and Kristen started for the bedroom with Kirby next to Heather, bumping against her legs as they passed the bathroom. The bathtub water was running and the girls were in their room, giggling.

"Teeth!" she reminded them before closing her bedroom door. She was already removing her sweatshirt. "I haven't had a dress that fancy in...well, never."

Kristen laughed. "Then it's about time."

Amazingly, the dress fit Heather perfectly, though the fancy style felt a bit foreign to her.

"It looks great on you," Kristen said.

Heather checked herself out in the full-length mirror on the back of a door. Kirby parked himself next to her, and she thought the color of his fur was almost the same color as the dress.

"It is nice," she had to admit, "even if it isn't me."

"How did I ever get a sister so uninterested in clothes?"

"How did I ever get one so interested in labels?" Heather came back.

Luckily, Kristen had insisted on buying the garment for Heather. Or rather, Kristen and Alex. Between the two of them, they could afford it. Not that Heather still didn't feel a little guilty. She promised herself she'd make it up to both of them someday.

Kristen asked, "You don't hate the dress, do you?"

"No. It's very pretty." Heather smoothed the fabric of the skirt with her hands. "I just don't look like me wearing it. I'm more comfortable in jeans and a T-shirt or sweater. And I'm going to have to do something with my hair. The color is so mousy against the bright apricot."

"Your hair is shiny and thick," Kristen said, "but I do wonder how a shade lighter would look on you."

"I actually thought about putting in some blond highlights."

Kristen grinned. "Now that's the spirit! You haven't exactly been enthusiastic about this wedding—"

"No! You know I like Alex." And she was thrilled to see her older sister so happy. "I've just been too busy to enjoy things as much as I would like."

Heather took off the dress and carefully hung it up. She listened for the girls. The water was still running, but she didn't hear their voices. She opened the door. "What are you two up to?" she called.

"Brushing teeth," one of the twins answered, sounding as if the toothbrush were in her mouth.

"Okay, I'll be there in a couple of minutes." Closing the door again, she said, "You and Alex make the perfect couple, and I'm so happy for you." She pulled her old clothes back on. "I just don't want the relatives who'll come in for the wedding pitying me or something."

"Pitying you? Why would they?"

"You know, because I'm a widow and all."

Heather opened the nightstand drawer where she still kept a small photo of her late husband. She ran a fingertip around his face. Her memories of Scott were getting a little hazy, so every night before she went to bed, she looked at the photo and called up a nice memory of the two of them together.

Heather went on. "I know they're going to ask me about Scott—how he died, how I'm doing without him, how my poor girls are doing growing up without a father."

And what could she say? She still missed him. The girls missed him, Taylor especially. She'd watched that DVD so many times that Heather was beginning to worry it wasn't healthy for her daughter. Still she couldn't take the little girl's Daddy away from her.

"Wow," Kristen mused, "you've imagined a whole scenario with the relatives."

"Do you have a better one for me?"

"Yeah, bring a date. With you on another man's arm, they won't be able to ask you about Scott."

"Except that I'm not dating anyone."

And hadn't ever dated any other man in her whole life other than Scott. Part of her didn't want to. His death had left her so broken-hearted that she couldn't ever see herself taking another chance on love.

"So start dating," Kristen insisted. "Aunt Margaret invited John to be her date."

"I'm glad they connected. It's nice to know it's never too late for love."

Aunt Margaret was nearing seventy and John was five years older. They'd only met the summer before, but they made a perfect couple. Heather had to admit she envied that. She just didn't know if she was ready for another relationship.

"It's not too late for you, either," Kristen was saying. "You could start slow. If you're uncomfortable calling it a date, ask a male friend to accompany you."

"I can't think of anyone to ask."

The only single man of an appropriate age she'd met lately was The Terminator, and he certainly wasn't her type. She was glad when the girls yelled, "Mo-o-om!" and knocked the image of him right out of her head.

"Bath time," she told Kristen.

"And time for me to leave."

Heather opened the bedroom door and saw the twins wedged in the bathroom doorway.

"C'mon, Mommy," Addison said. "Bath time!"

Taylor echoed her twin. "Bath time!"

"Give me just a minute to see your aunt to the front door."

Kristen was already halfway there, the dog shadowing her. She stopped and gave Heather a quick hug. "Just remember what I said about asking someone to accompany you to the wedding."

"I doubt I'll be able to forget."

An image of Rick Slater was in her mind again, tempting Heather as Kristen left, and she closed and locked the front door behind her sister.

She hesitated just a moment to think about Rick…to wonder what he might look like without those sunglasses…

What sounded like a tidal wave accompanied by little girl squeals brought her around.

"What's going on?" she yelled before realizing the dog had disappeared.

It seemed everyone was getting a bath tonight.

WAKING IN THE middle of the night had become an unwelcome habit for Cora. And it didn't take an unusual sound to rouse her from sleep. It was simply the expectation of some sort of noise occurring. Tonight she didn't remember anything unusual. She awakened, lay there for a while, then rose to fix some chamomile tea in the little electric teapot she'd set up in her bathroom. The teapot made things easier in that she didn't have to leave her suite. A small nightlight made the bedside lamp unnecessary.

Sitting in the comfortable chair beside the bank of windows, she sipped her tea and watched flashes of lightning illuminate the sky over the lake, followed by a rumble of thunder. A storm was brewing. Perhaps it had simply been thunder that had invaded her dreams.

She hated having to be on guard all the time.

At least a private investigator was now in residence.

Not that he could be everywhere at once.

A cool breeze that smelled of fresh rain

lifted the curtains. Thinking that perhaps she ought to lower the windows, Cora put down her cup, rose and leaned on the sill.

Storms over the lake had always fascinated her, so she didn't immediately adjust the windows. Instead, she looked out from her attic-level quarters, which gave her a perfect view of the show. For a moment she was mesmerized by the electric light dancing in the sky.

Until another movement closer by captured her attention.

She dropped her gaze to search for the source.

Lightning flashed again and she could see the second-floor balcony and the small wiry man with red hair standing on end who perched there, back stiff, body wired with tension.

With a start, she thought she recognized him. *Red Flanagan?*

Could it be? He certainly reminded her of the man in the portrait hung in the rotunda.

Shocked, Cora gripped the windowsill and held her breath.

The sky went dark and she blinked several times, then took another look that made her stomach whirl.

The balcony stood empty.

Lightning flashed again, confirming that no one was there now…if anyone had ever been there at all. She'd thought the intruder was a flesh-and-blood man. But now she wondered. Surely no one these days could look exactly like an eighty-year-old portrait.

Trembling from the inside out, she closed the windows, and with shaking hands, locked them.

Not that locked windows could stop a ghost...

CHAPTER FOUR

STANDING ON THE balcony off the second-floor family drawing room with the housekeeper, Rick kept his voice low. "This should be a perfect place for one of my cameras." He didn't want to alert any other employees on the property as to what he was doing. It was possible someone working here knew the intruder and was sharing information, whether on purpose or not.

It was early morning—too early for Heather and her EPI workers to be on site. Truth be told, he was looking forward to Heather's arrival, but he wanted to make certain that, before she and her workers swarmed the property, he had time to install at least a couple of the security cameras he'd picked up from his company in Milwaukee the night before.

"So this camera will show you if anyone...or anything...is on the property at night?" Cora asked.

"Well, not just this camera," Rick said, wondering what she meant by *or anything*. "I brought enough of them to cover the area in each direction around the building, plus the coach house and the boathouse."

The housekeeper nodded. She seemed tense and nervous, and she looked as if she hadn't slept well.

He tried to reassure her. "Don't worry, I'll catch whoever has been messing around on the estate grounds. These wireless cameras are the best. They have spectacular night vision as far as three hundred feet. And they're set on motion detectors that will start the camera and make digital recordings on a computer that can signal me on my phone."

He would have to hook up each camera to a 110 AC source, a consideration in choosing locations. He also needed places that would provide camouflage for the cameras. If the intruder became aware of them, he could simply cover up the lenses. If he didn't destroy the equipment. So Rick had to hide each camera very carefully. He would position this first one between the balcony's balusters, near a planter with greenery that hung in long strands through the opening. A perfect nest for the lens.

"So the cameras would be able to see anything out of place?" Cora asked.

"As long as it's moving."

"Does it have to be…"

"What?" he asked.

Cora cleared her throat. "Um, alive?"

What exactly was she getting at? Rick wondered. "Well, uh, if someone threw something into the area covered by—"

"Not an object. That's not what I meant."

"Then…what?"

"I saw something last night." Cora wrapped her arms around her middle as if trying to protect herself. "At least I think I did."

Rick was getting a weird feeling about this. "Go on."

"It was a figure. Male. It *looked* like a small wiry man with red hair standing on end—"

"Looked like? What is it you're trying to say, Cora?"

"I thought I saw Red Flanagan."

Silence. Part of Rick wanted to laugh at her imagination. But he didn't want to insult Cora. She'd been stressed about whatever was going on around the mansion at night for weeks now. Perhaps it had become too much for her.

"You don't believe me," she said, her words almost whispered.

"Red Flanagan has been dead for what? Half a century?"

"I know that! I just said it looked like him. Like the portrait in the rotunda."

"Hey, easy. I'm on your side. I just don't know what to think."

"What if Flanagan Manor is haunted?" Cora asked.

Rick could see that she was serious. "I can't say that I believe in ghosts."

"I didn't think I did, either. But after all that's happened in the past several weeks…"

"If you did see Flanagan's ghost, why now? What made him come back? Before all these curious events, did something significant happen on the estate? Some big change?"

"I—I don't know. I'll have to think on it."

Rick didn't believe in ghosts and he started to say that he'd never heard of one leaving footprints or breaking equipment by standing on it. But he was distracted by the sound of an engine. Both he and Cora turned to see a silver sedan pull up to the mansion. The driver's door opened and a distinguished, silver-haired man exited.

"Oh, David—I mean Mr. Guildfren—is early."

The man advanced to the trunk of his car and pulled out two suitcases.

"A guest." Apparently one she knew by name.

"Yes, a regular. He's an antiques dealer who appreciates the history of this estate. He's been coming here for the past three years for a few weeks in the summer and again during the winter holidays."

Color flushed Cora's cheeks, and her avid expression suggested a certain fondness for the man.

"I can take it from here," Rick said. "If you have other things to do."

"Are you sure?"

"Positive."

"All right then. Call me if you need me."

Rather than waiting for his response, she whipped back into the drawing room, a changed woman from the tired, nervous one of a few minutes before. The spring to her step informed him of her affection for the guest. Rick wondered if the feeling was reciprocated, and if so, if they had ever done anything about it. Cora had said the man was a regular, visiting the bed-and-breakfast twice a year. She hadn't been able to hide her excitement at seeing him.

He needed to get to work. Luckily there was an outlet nearby, providing a source of electricity.

As he set the camera in place, he felt hollow. He'd never had a long-term relationship with any woman. Being military for nearly all his life, he'd never been in one place long enough. His on- and off-again romance with

Megan had been the closest he'd gotten. And being part of a special ops team had brought him to some pretty grim places. None were so grim as the last. Once he'd landed back here in the States, he hadn't known what to do with himself. The army had always been his home. Giving civilian life a chance had its own difficulties.

He'd been back for several months now, but no woman had even interested him.

Not until he'd met Heather Clarke.

TAYLOR COULDN'T BELIEVE Mommy could be so mean. First Daddy never came home like he promised. Now Mommy was going to give away Kirby.

"He's my dog!" she said with a sniffle as they approached the counter. Dogs were barking and cats were meowing, too. She looked around and tears filled her eyes. "You can't put poor Kirby in jail!"

"Sweetheart, he's not your dog," Mommy said. "And the Sparrow Lake Animal Shelter isn't a jail."

"Then why are all the animals locked up?" Tears slipped down Taylor's cheeks.

Addison took her hand and squeezed hard. "They're so sad!"

"Not so sad, honey." The white-haired lady

behind the counter smiled at them. "The animals don't all get along with each other, so we keep them separated for their protection. But they all get some time out of the cages every day. We have several volunteers who come to take care of them and play with them. The animals here are treated very well."

"Then I want to volunteer," Taylor said.

"Me, too," Addison added.

"I'm sorry, girls, but you're too young."

Her mom held up the rope she'd used for a leash. "We found this dog yesterday, and I was hoping you could take him and either find his owner or find a new home."

"I'm very sorry, but we're full at the moment. Actually, we're usually full. So many animals lost or thrown away." She sighed and shook her head. "But we can put him on a waiting list. You never know when one of our dogs will get his forever home. Here's a form to fill out." She slid a piece of paper over the counter. "We'll also add him to the list of newly lost animals in case anyone is looking for him."

Mommy started scribbling, and Taylor got down on her knees and hugged Kirby tight. "You don't have to come here yet," she whispered. "So you're still mine."

"What's a forever home?" Addison asked.

The white-haired lady smiled again. "That's

what we like to say when we place one of our dogs or cats with a new family. That they've found the home where they will live and be happy forever."

Taylor thought Kirby had already found his forever home. Now if only she could make Mommy change her mind…

She'd already lost Daddy. It wasn't fair if she had to lose Kirby, too.

HEATHER ARRIVED AT Flanagan Manor early after dropping off the girls at school. She got out of the SUV, brand-new leash in hand, and the dog rushed for freedom. It took all her strength to keep Kirby from wiggling past her.

The dog, she corrected herself. She didn't want to think of him by name, didn't want to get too fond of him, no matter how sweet and lovable he was.

"Hang on a minute," she muttered, meaning to clip a lead to the collar she'd bought him after she'd learned there was no room at the shelter.

Yet.

He was on a waiting list to get in, and in the meantime, Heather would try to find him a good home herself.

"Okay, come on out." She gave the leash a small tug.

The dog lunged out of the SUV and, in his excitement to stretch his legs, nearly jerked her arm out of her shoulder socket.

She slammed the door, yelling, "Hey, slow down!"

Having checked with Alex, she'd been assured no one had called the police station to put out an official alert for the little guy, which was a real shame. He so obviously loved people. He must be missing his owner. When she got some time, she and the twins would put up notices around town with a picture of the dog. Surely someone would recognize him.

Either that or offer to give him a new home.

She headed toward an area near the parking lot where the dog could relieve himself without ruining any landscaping. As she tried to figure out where she could tie him up while she worked, she heard footsteps behind her.

"Hey, who is this?" came the unmistakable voice that made her picture granite features accentuated by mirrored sunglasses.

Heather turned to see Rick coming from the general direction of the coach house. "This is a dog the girls found yesterday," she said. "I tried the animal shelter first thing this morning, but no luck. It's full, and I couldn't stand the thought of leaving him in the pound where he'd have a week or two to be claimed before they would euthanize him, so I'm going to find him a home."

"Here?"

"No." Hope suddenly blazed through her. "Unless…if I can't find his owner and you want him…"

Rick put up a hand to stop her. "Not what I meant."

She sighed. "It seems no one wants this poor guy." Except for the twins, especially Taylor.

Keeping the dog was out of the question. But it seemed finding any owner—old or new— was nothing more than a pipe dream.

"He's a nice-looking dog."

Rick crouched down to dog nose level and ruffled Kirby's ears. In return, the dog threw his head around and licked Rick's hand. Heather smiled at the instant bond. Rick was a nice guy, as he'd proved the day before by fixing the sod cutter for her. She thought about her sister's suggestion to have a friend escort her to the wedding. But Rick really wasn't her friend. She barely knew him.

"What are you calling him?" Rick asked.

Heather jerked back to the present situation. "Dog."

The mirrored sunglasses turned up toward her. "Seriously?"

"Okay, the girls named him Kirby, but I'm trying not to think of him that personally."

Giving the animal a last pat, Rick got to his feet. "Your bringing him with you to work is pretty personal."

"It's not like I had a choice. He was barricaded in the kitchen all night with a makeshift bed and food and water. And he still chewed one of the shoes I left by the back door. I can't leave him in the house by himself. Who knows what kind of mess he would make? What he might ruin."

"He seems pretty young to me. He needs a kennel. You know, a big cage."

"Except that he's not my dog."

Rick grinned at her as if saying, *Sure he's not.*

Flushing, Heather looked around. Anywhere so she didn't have to connect with his know-it-all smirk. "Now I just have to find a place to tie him up while I work."

"What about over there by the coach house?" He indicated the area he meant. "It's nice and quiet. I'm the only one who lives there," he said, "in the second-floor apartment."

"What, no wife or partner?" she asked before realizing it was none of her business.

"Nope. I live a solitary life."

She tried again. "Maybe you *could* use some company."

"Maybe, but since my future is up in the air…"

Heather sighed. Too bad. Finding someone to take the dog off her hands this soon would have been too easy, of course.

She looked over to the coach house with its nice open expanse and a big maple tree for shade. And there was bizarrely long grass to make a comfy bed. Apparently, Rick hadn't applied his mowing skills—or lack thereof—to that particular section of grass yet. Maybe it was because he couldn't ride the mower under such low-hanging branches.

"Looks like as good a place as any. Thanks. I need to get stuff from the car."

"Let me help you."

"You can hang on to the dog for me." She handed him the leash.

Taking it, he said, "Sure. Kirby and I are buddies already, aren't we, boy?"

"So you're a dog person?"

"I'm an animal person. When I was growing up, no matter where we lived, there were always stray animals that needed to be fed and taken care of. I took as many of them in as Mom would allow, which was quite a few, actually." He quickly added, "I'm just not in a position to take on an animal now since I don't know how long I'll be here."

Too bad. He sounded exactly like the person Kirby needed. Heather would never have guessed that Rick had such a soft spot for animals. She had to admit she liked that about him. Opening the back of the SUV, she pulled out water and food bowls, a bag of food and a chew toy, plus a few other toys he'd gotten excited over. She'd gone into one of those giant pet supply stores that allowed owners to bring in their dogs. She'd had to take him inside to get the right size collar. Then he'd instigated her into making some of the other purchases.

Eyeing everything she was carrying, Rick cleared his throat. "Right. Not your dog."

She gave him her best irritated expression. Buying this stuff had broken her budget, but she hadn't been able to help herself. "Someone had to feed him, and no one else volunteered." *Not yet.*

"He's going to eat the toys?"

"I was hoping keeping him busy would keep him quiet." She'd told herself not to buy anything except the bare necessities, but she'd felt so sorry for the dog that resisting had been useless. "The last thing I need on the job is a barking dog."

She started off toward the coach house, Rick

keeping pace with her, and Kirby—*the dog,* she reminded herself—racing ahead, leash taut, even though the little stinker didn't know where he was racing to.

Standing under the tree, Heather looked up to the branches, too high above her. "I need to be able to tie him to something that will keep him put."

"I'll find something," Rick said. "You could set out his water and food."

Heather flicked her eyebrows up. Suddenly, Rick had taken over. Still, grateful for the offered help, she did as he said while he took the dog into the coach house with him. She filled one bowl with kibble and took the other to the hose attached to the side of the house to get the dog some water.

In the meantime, Rick returned carrying a three-foot length of steel with holes in it. The dog danced around her, inspecting everything she touched. As she set down the bowl of water and the dog crowded her to get a drink, Rick used the hammer he'd brought to pound the steel more than a foot into the ground.

"What is that?"

"Just something I found in the shop. Looks like someone was building a storage unit and left the castoffs."

When he clipped the dog's leash to one of the holes, she said, "My, you're inventive."

"Just call me resourceful."

"Okay, thanks, Resourceful." She snorted but choked back further response.

The mirrored sunglasses aimed her way, and he rose to his full height. "What?"

She grinned up at him. "Actually, my workers already have a nickname for you."

"What?" he asked a little louder.

"They've been calling you The Terminator." Which, with his features set in a frown at the moment, he absolutely resembled. "It's the sunglasses." She wasn't going to bring up his skinning the grass or plowing down the bush. "Remember, in the movie, he always wore those mirrored sunglasses that made him look so dangerous."

"They think I look dangerous?"

At first *she* had, too, especially after he'd flattened her. But now that she knew him better, not so much.

"Tyrone is convinced you're a spy," she informed him.

Rick's turn to snort. "A commando, maybe, but not a spy."

"Android?" she teased.

"Thoroughly human, I promise." His lips quirked. "You believe me, don't you?"

"Maybe if I could see your eyes. The sunglasses do come off, right?" She'd never seen him without them.

In answer, Rick slipped off the shades.

His eyes were blue. A clear, sharp blue. And they were large and fringed with thick lashes, quite at odds with the granite features that suddenly took on a softer appearance. His eyebrows were thick, too, and they quirked upward as she scanned his whole face. Nice features. High cheekbones...determined jaw... tempting mouth. She shook away the last and told herself he was decent looking. That was it. Nothing out of the ordinary.

Still, he'd make a great-looking escort at Kristen and Alex's wedding...

"Well?" he asked.

Her pulse was thrumming. Could she do it? Ask him?

"It's just nice to know what you actually look like," she admitted.

"You approve?"

Not wanting him to get a swelled head, she avoided a direct answer. "I don't disapprove."

She was stalling, trying to make up her mind.

"So you're neutral," he said.

"Like Switzerland."

She loved that he was taking the conversation in stride, even seeming amused. She appreciated a man with a sense of humor.

He was grinning at her when he asked, "You've been to Switzerland?"

"No. You?"

"I've been to a lot of different countries all over the world," he admitted, "but that's still on my list of places to see. I love traveling and learning about different cultures."

In a lot *of different countries?* "But you're not a spy, right?"

"Nope."

"So why all the traveling?"

"My father was a lifer. Army. Different bases all over the world."

"Oh." Now on alert, she asked, "What about you?"

"Not a lifer. At least I wasn't planning to be. I just kind of got sucked in for so many years because it was what I knew." His expression changed, grew a little grim. "War isn't pretty, so when my last tour ended, I wanted to see if there was something else for me. So I decided to give civilian life a chance before I make up my mind whether or not to re-enlist."

As he spoke, her pulse crashed.

Army...thinking of re-enlisting...

Instantly reminding her of her late husband, Scott. He'd been killed along with several other men when their truck had rolled over a land mine.

His answer made her uncomfortable, and Heather was glad to see the EPI truck pull up. "Oh, look, Tyrone and Amber are here with some of our supplies."

As if tired of being ignored and wanting to be part of the conversation, Kirby barked and looked from her to Rick, who bent over and patted the dog.

Disappointment filled Heather. For a moment, she'd thought…but there was no way she was going to ask a man who might re-enlist in the army to escort her anywhere. Rick might be nice. And good-looking. But she'd lost one man to war. She'd been devastated, and so had her girls. What if Rick decided civilian life *wasn't* for him? He might want to re-enlist. What was she thinking? She wasn't ready for a long-term relationship anyway and didn't know if she ever would be. She couldn't take that kind of chance with her heart again. She'd just been thinking about Kristen is all, but Rick simply wasn't the right man for her, not even to escort her to a wedding.

Heather gave the chew toy to the dog, patted his head and gave Rick a tight smile. "Time to get to work."

Turning her back on them both, she raced to

the truck in the parking lot. Both of her workers were already in back. Tyrone was moving bags of compost to the rear edge of the truck and handing them off to Amber, who was dropping them down onto the dolly.

"Wow, look who's early," Tyrone said when Heather got closer. "So what is the spy up to this morning?"

"Tyro-o-one." Amber poked his leg. "Hi, Heather."

Heather laughed. "At the moment, he's up to taking care of the dog my kids found last night."

She couldn't help but look over to where Rick sat with the dog. They were both watching the workers with lazy interest.

Thinking about going to the wedding alone, Heather felt a twinge of disappointment.

Too bad about Rick.

He was just someone she couldn't let into her life. She needed to keep a professional distance.

To that end, thinking he could help haul stuff where it was needed, she yelled, "Hey, Mr. Sunglasses, since you're not doing anything, why not come over here and give us some muscle?"

Rick got to his feet almost immediately and

sauntered toward them. The dog sat at alert and watched.

"I still think he's on some secret mission." Tyrone kept his voice low. "We should see if we can crack him. A point for every detail we learn about him. Whoever gets the most points gets free pizza for lunch."

"I don't think that's such a good idea," Heather said.

"Why not?" Amber asked. "It's all in good fun." Then, "Hey, if you can take over here, I'll fetch the wheelbarrow."

Which would make things go even faster. "Great." Heather grabbed a bag from Tyrone and lowered it to the stack already on the dolly. "This is pretty full. I'd say just one more."

Tyrone handed her a bag, then jumped down from the back of the truck. "I'll take these over to the rain garden."

The idea was to move the supplies directly to the site where they would be used. Which meant bags of compost and potting soil would be piled up in several areas for the next couple of weeks. They would need the bags of mortar and the quarry gray blocks to build the rain garden retaining walls today. A lot more was coming—boards for raised beds and Wisconsin bluestone for another terrace with built-in seating and a fire pit. Heather was trying not

to order too much at once. The bed and breakfast was about to get busy, and she knew the
owner did not want his guests to be inconve-
nienced. That was why she'd decided to start
with the beach area, the walkway and rain gardens—they were all directly between the mansion and the lake.

Rick jumped up on the back of the truck as
Tyrone left with the full dolly. Leaving her
alone with the man.

Not exactly what she'd had in mind.

"Are you sure you can handle this?" Rick
asked, placing another bag at the edge of the
truck.

"Of course."

Not that Heather was certain at all. Nor did
she mean hauling weight. She was stronger
than she looked. But just thinking about Rick
had put her on edge, and working this closely
with him was probably a mistake.

Thankfully, Amber returned with the empty
wheelbarrow.

"You two fill that while I help Tyrone un-
load the dolly," Heather said, already running
off to catch up with him.

Over the next hour, they worked together
smoothly, and Heather kept getting snatches
of conversation between Rick and Tyrone or
Rick and Amber. Or rather…interrogations.

"So, what did you say your name was?" Amber asked.

"You can call me...The Terminator."

Heather bit her lip so she wouldn't laugh out loud.

It was on.

"Where is it you said you were from?" Tyrone asked Rick a little later.

"Here, there and everywhere. No particular place."

Zero for Tyrone.

"Are you married or do you have a significant other?" Amber asked.

"You're a little young for me," Rick returned.

The game went on as they unloaded and delivered the bags to the work sites. The last job was to get the blocks in place to start on the retaining walls. When the truck was empty, Rick excused himself, said he had something to take care of. On his way back to his apartment in the coach house, however, he stopped to visit with the dog. Kirby seemed thrilled by the attention.

Heather was a little thrilled, too. She couldn't keep from watching the man.

"I couldn't get a single thing out of him," Tyrone said, his voice rife with disgust.

"Me, neither." Amber cleared her throat. "I

wonder why he said to call him The Terminator."

Heather bit back a smile as she turned to face them. "His name is Rick Slater. He's single. He's army. And he's trying out civilian life to determine if he can make it or if he's better off re-enlisting."

Tyrone scowled. "Hunh. I guess we get to buy *your* pizza today."

CHAPTER FIVE

THE EPI TEAM worked straight through the day,
pausing briefly only for lunch. As promised,
Tyrone and Amber bought a couple of pizzas
to pay off their debt to Heather. Heather herself
sprang for soft drinks and some small salads
to offset the carbs. The group offered pizza to
Rick, but he grinned and said he was already
having lunch inside the mansion. It seemed
that he got free room and board in return for
his services, Heather noted. Maybe his salary
as a "handyman" wasn't all that high.

Later, as afternoon wore on, they were ready
for a break. Heather collapsed on a bench beneath a small but shady Hackberry tree and
sipped some iced tea from the cooler she'd
brought. Tyrone stretched out for a catnap near
a copse of bushes and Amber wandered off to
take a closer look at Lake Michigan. The day
was gorgeous with full golden sun that made
the water sparkle as blue-green as the Carib-
bean. Not that she'd ever been to the Carib-
bean, Heather thought wryly, but she'd seen

pictures of its turquoise seas and inviting white beaches.

Travel would have to wait for another day. Another year. Probably for another decade or two. At the moment, she had other kinds of beauty in her life, and the most important two soon came running toward her across the lawn, shrieking with excitement. She waved to the neighbor who had dropped them off so she wouldn't have to leave work early.

Then Heather steeled herself for impact and leaned forward to grab both twins in an expansive hug. She dropped kisses on their little heads.

"Mommy!" cried Addison.

"We had hot dogs for lunch!" announced Taylor.

"Ooh, I bet that made you happy!" said Heather. Although she considered hot dogs to be junk food, the camp had promised healthier versions with all-beef meat and whole grain buns. "We'll leave as soon as I finish things up here. What did you do today?"

"We made Native A-mer-i-can bracelets." Addison showed her mother her wrist. She was wearing a bracelet of woven threads bedecked with several colorful beads. She had a similar one on her other wrist and, Heather noted, what appeared to be numbers in messy black marker smeared across the palm of her hand.

"Here's mine," added Taylor, showing the bracelet she'd made.

"Very pretty," said Heather, equally admiring, then returned to the smeary numbers on Addison's skin. "What's this?"

"Addison has a boyfriend," chanted Taylor in a sing-song voice.

Addison giggled. "Chad wants me to call him. He wrote down his number." Then she pointed to the second bracelet she wore. "He gave me this, too."

Taylor continued to chant, "Boyfriend... boyfriend..."

"I didn't know you were such a little temptress." Heather had to laugh.

Addison frowned. "What's a temptress?"

"Oh, just someone who's popular," Heather fibbed. She ruffled both girls' hair. "Can you two find something to play with while I finish up?"

She had to change her clothing before they left because she was due at Sew Fine for a bridal shower this evening and she couldn't wear her landscaping clothes. She needed to pick up Aunt Margaret and drop off the twins to be watched by her brother, Brian. With all the wedding activities going on, the coming weeks would be very busy, and she could already feel things accelerating.

"Let's make a house under a tree!" cried Addison, taking off.

"We can play with Kirby!" shouted Taylor, following her sister.

Heather wanted to make sure they were safe. "Don't go down by the lake!" she called. "Stay out here where I can see you."

As she watched the twins run across the lawn, she saw that Tyrone had sat up and was watching them with a big grin. He looked wide awake and ready to get back to work. Now all they had to do was rustle up Amber so they could be ready to pack up and leave in another hour.

RICK HAD HEARD all the shrieking and came out to stand beneath the shady overhang at the mansion's back door. He wasn't used to children, hadn't had much experience with them, but he thought Heather's pair were certainly cute. Dressed in a bright green T-shirt and shorts, one little blond-haired girl was jumping up and down along a planting bed near the edge of the lawn, while the other, all in purple, seemed to be wrestling with the dog Heather had shown up with that morning. Obviously an animal who liked kids, the dog looked like

he was having a great time, yipping and lick-
ing his attacker in the face when she turned
him on his back.

Rick laughed, enjoying the entertainment,
though he figured such energy must drive any
adult crazy at times, including their mother.
Heather had said she was single. What happened to the girls' father? he wondered. Raising two kids alone was a huge responsibility.

Rick was approaching the girl with the dog
when he saw her start yanking on the leash
clipped to the post he'd planted in the ground.

"Need some help?" he asked.

She looked up at him suspiciously, her blue
eyes narrowing. "This is my dog, Kirby."

"You want to take Kirby for a walk?" He
figured the dog could use some exercise after
being tied up all day. "Maybe I can help you
get him to heel."

"I want to walk him by myself."

"Well, okay." Rick released the leash, which
the little girl immediately snatched out of his
hand. "Be careful, though. He weighs about as
much as you do." Which he'd estimate was at
least forty pounds.

"Kirby, Kirby!" cried the other twin, running up to see what was going on.

"Hi," Rick said. "And who might you be?"

He knew their names, but he didn't know who was who.

"I'm Addison." She gestured to her sister. "And this is Taylor."

"Glad to meet you both. I'm Rick."

"Can I try on your sunglasses?" Addison asked.

She had such a charming smile, Rick couldn't resist. He took them off, and while he squatted to slip them onto her small face, Taylor and the dog took off.

"Hey, be careful!" Rick yelled.

Taylor made no reply but at least she was heading across the lawn, half skipping, rather than going toward the lake.

"I like these," said Addison, posing with one hand on her hip. "Don't I look good?"

"Just like a movie star," Rick told her.

The frames were so big, they immediately slipped right down the child's nose. She pushed the glasses up to perch on her head. "Where'd Taylor go?"

Rick turned to see, and before he could take the sunglasses back, Addison sped off, shrieking, "Taylor! Kirby!"

"Wait…" Rick started to give chase, then decided against it. Hopefully, his glasses would survive and he'd get them back in a few minutes.

He looked around for the EPI staff. Heather and Tyrone were carrying boxes and tools to the edge of the veranda, where Amber loaded them in the wheelbarrow, probably to store them in the coach house. It was nearing the end of the work day. Rick waved when Heather glanced around, He wondered if he should offer to help, but she looked right past him, obviously more concerned with what her kids were doing. Rick gathered up the dog food and toys from the long grass, placing them in one spot so Heather could easily load them when she was ready to go.

Meanwhile, Addison had settled down beneath a tree and was piling up some of the loose rocks near its base and talking to herself. Rick couldn't see Taylor or the dog, but some excited yips told him they were nearby.

He gazed back at the mansion, thinking about the security cameras he'd installed. He wondered if he should test them out, make sure they were hooked up correctly to the computer. And did he have enough devices? Maybe he should put one up by the rear door, just in case someone tried to sneak around the back of the house. He'd been concentrating on the lake side where Cora had claimed to see things after dark.

"Kir-r-by!" came a high-pitched yell, followed by delighted giggling. "Go, go!"

Rick turned to see the dog running at top speed across the lawn, right past Tyrone, who stood staring. Behind the dog and his tautly stretched leash came Taylor. Her feet were moving so fast, they seemed to glide across the top of the grass. She grinned ecstatically while making a *w-h-e-e-e* sound.

But Rick was concerned. As he'd pointed out to her, the dog weighed as much as the little girl. What if she fell? "Hey, too fast!" he shouted.

Taylor paid no attention. He frowned as the pair came toward him. Instinctively, he took action, jumping forward to grab the leash while at the same time scooping the child up by her middle.

Both the child and the dog were surprised and just about knocked breathless. The dog snorted and choked a little, dancing in place.

"Sit," said Rick, and the dog actually followed orders.

But Taylor started flailing around. "Let go! Let go!"

"Hey!" said Rick, pummeled by small fists and feet. When she smacked him good in the face, he put her down. "Whoa!"

"Kirby's my dog!" yelled Taylor. "You're not my daddy! Leave us alone!"

"I'm not trying to hurt you," Rick told her. "You were going too fast."

"My dog!" Taylor screeched, trying to rip the leash out of his hand.

But Rick wouldn't give it to her. "I think both of you need some obedience training."

"Obedience training?" Suddenly Heather appeared, looking very concerned.

Tyrone joined the group, stopping next to Rick.

Taylor started to cry. "Mommy! He's mean! He took Kirby away!" She ran to her mother and wrapped her arms around Heather's legs.

Heather stroked her child's hair, frowning at Rick. "What's going on here?"

"He hurt me!" Taylor sobbed.

Rick wondered if Heather believed him capable of such a thing. He didn't like her scowl. "I just caught her as she and Kirby ran by," he explained. "Maybe knocked the air out of them a little, but they thought they were at the races. I was afraid she'd get hurt."

"Little girls can be just as tough as little boys," said Heather, sounding defensive. "Taylor's a tomboy."

"There's a lot of rocks and cement around here to fall on."

"She actually was running wild with the dog," Tyrone said in Rick's defense.

Heather appeared uncertain. Rick realized she might not know him well enough to trust him. And she was a mother, protective of her children. He couldn't fault her for that.

Taylor continued to sob. "Kirby's my dog."

Heather crouched to take the child in her arms. "Mr. Slater was just trying to help you with him," she told Taylor, though her glance at Rick remained doubtful. "Shh, shh. You're all right. Let's get ready to go home." She stood, then asked Rick, "What did you mean by obedience training?"

"I was just talking. Honestly, I didn't mean any harm," he told her.

"Obedience training is for dogs, not for human beings!"

"Of course—"

Heather interrupted before he could apologize. "We're leaving as soon as I can change clothes. The girls are tired. They've had a long day."

"Sure." Rick figured he needed to back off for now. Hopefully, Heather would be calmer by tomorrow.

She asked, "Tyrone, can you come here for a minute?"

"Coming, boss!" He jogged over to her and the twins.

"Girls, this is Tyrone. Tyrone, meet Addison and Taylor."

He gave them an intent look. "You two aren't twins, are you?"

"Yeah!" they both yelled.

"Could you keep a close eye on them for a few minutes?"

"Sure thing."

"And the dog?" she added.

Rick handed Tyrone the leash as Heather gathered up Kirby's supplies and walked over to her SUV.

"Hey, I got a game we can play," Tyrone told the girls.

"Yay!" Addison said, "What game?"

"C'mon, I'll show you."

Taylor looked torn between wanting to play and wanting to continue sulking. When she looked at Rick, her little features pulled into a stormy expression before she stalked off to follow the others.

Leaving Rick to wonder whether her dislike for him would rub off on her mother.

He hoped not.

He liked Heather Clarke. A lot. Maybe a little too much.

Even though Tyrone was in charge, Rick kept

an eye on the girls and dog. Tyrone seemed to be good with them, especially with Taylor, who settled down quickly. Rick couldn't help but feel inadequate, remembering how the little girl had gone hysterical on him.

He turned away, his mood altered, but before he could head for his digs, the phone in his pocket alerted him, the signal telling him someone had triggered one of the security cameras, which was virtually impossible since it was broad daylight.

Unless someone was in the boathouse.

BECAUSE THE BATHROOM available to EPI was small and only had a sink for washing up, Heather had decided to find another place to clean up and change into her clothes for Kristen's bridal shower. She knew the boathouse had a shower, but once she entered the place, she was a little dismayed. The interior of what was in reality a nearly century-old boat garage was dark and dingy, and if there was any place to hang up her dress, she couldn't tell. But once she'd trekked across the grounds—making sure to look nowhere in Rick's direction because she now felt so conflicted about him—then raced along the dock and entered the building, she was committed. If she didn't hurry, she would be late.

The old boathouse had been built over the water alongside the dock. The planks of the dock were in questionable shape, and one had even snapped when she'd stepped on it. Probably the reason a sign indicated this was for family only use. Mr. Phillips had said repairs were scheduled once the landscaping was finished.

Once inside, she looked around and noted three boat slips with lifts and an open area in back where ropes and cushions were still stored. The canvas-covered motor boats now hung a few feet over the water, and she could hear the waves below lap against the piers.

Spider webs decorated the interior, giving the place a haunted feel. Probably no one had used the building since last summer. If then. Making for the bathroom area in back where, after swimming or boating, family members could clean up before going to the main house, she almost walked into a web that stretched several feet across. Once inside the bathroom, she hung her dress on a hook in the wall.

The place gave her the creeps and the faster she got out of there the better.

Unzipping her jeans, Heather dropped them and managed to get her feet free. No way was she taking off her work boots in here. A little water wouldn't kill them. She took a fast shower, after which she turned her shirt inside out and used it to dry herself since she'd forgotten to bring a towel. Then she slipped into one of her favorite dresses, powder blue with a scoop neck and uneven hemline.

Looking down at her now wet boots that she'd have to wear until she got back to her SUV, Heather laughed.

Feminine.

Right.

Maybe she should fix her hair in an upsweep. She had a fancy clip in her purse.

Either the bathroom light switch wasn't working or the bulb was dead. She took her things back into the boathouse proper, where she was able to turn on a single bare bulb hanging from a wire in the ceiling. It would have to do.

From her purse, she took a hand mirror and set it on a wall ledge. Then she brushed her hair and pulled it up. She was having a hard time seeing what it looked like, so she held up the mirror and turned this way and that, making silly faces as if posing for a photo. Good enough, she guessed, trading the mirror for the hair clip so she could fasten her hair. Peering in the mirror again, she pulled little tendrils around her face. A swipe of lipstick and she gave her reflection an air kiss and was done.

Good thing because she suddenly got a weird feeling, like someone was watching her. She took a fast look around but saw no one and heard nothing.

The place itself was spooky enough to ignite her imagination.

She picked up the discarded clothing and gladly left the boathouse, making a quick escape along the dock. As she headed back across the grounds, she smiled when she saw Taylor sitting next to Tyrone and hugging the dog. Then Addison had to take a turn.

She couldn't help herself. She looked for Rick.

He was still out there, leaning against the tree. He slipped what must be his phone into his pocket and then looked her way. His instant smile seemed appreciative, the dress undoubtedly surprising him. When his gaze dropped down to her work boots, the smile morphed to a big grin.

Flushing, Heather yelled, "C'mon, girls! We're leaving now. Keep the dog on his leash." She'd already packed his bowls and toys in the back of the SUV. "Thanks for keeping an eye on them, Tyrone."

"No problem, boss. See you in the morning." He waved and jogged to the parking lot, where Amber waited for him in the truck.

Arriving at the SUV before the girls, Heather threw in her jeans and T-shirt and traded her work boots for some strappy sandals with modest heels. She wasn't into four inchers like her sister wore. Another glance out at the coach house and tree told her that Rick had left the area.

Leaving her with a flicker of disappointment.

She'd barely closed the hatch before the dog and kids surrounded her.

"I'll take the dog's leash," Heather said. "You two get into your seats."

The twins now insisted they be allowed to do it themselves. Of course, after getting the dog in the front passenger seat, Heather checked to make sure they were strapped in safely before sliding behind the wheel.

Addison was trying to set a familiar pair of mirrored sunglasses over her little face. They barely perched on her nose but she flung her head back and put one hand behind her head, trying to look glamorous.

"Ooh, I'm a movie star," she said.

Heather asked, "Where did you get those?"

"From Rick. He's real nice and let me try them on."

Taylor scowled at her sister. "You look like a big bug."

"Do not!" cried Addison, shoving Taylor.

Taylor shoved her back, nearly dislodging the glasses. "Do too! A creepy, stinky bug!"

"Hey, stop that right now!" Heather demanded, reaching a hand back to separate the twins. "You're going to break them."

Thinking she should get the glasses back to Rick, Heather was a little relieved that he was nowhere in sight. He didn't need them now anyway, and she would be sure to return them in the morning.

Addison placed the sunglasses back on the top of her head and Taylor scowled.

"All right," she said, "Make sure you leave those in here, Addison, so I can give them to Rick in the morning.

"'Kay. Can't Kirby sit back here?"

Heather eased the SUV out of the parking spot. "There's not enough room for the dog back there, sweetheart."

"I want Kirby!" Taylor whined.

Heather glanced back to see her daughter's stormy face.

The dog whistled through his nose and stared at her. She gave him a comforting pat and drove off.

"You don't want Kirby to be uncomfortable, do you?"

Taylor gave a dramatic little sob. "No-o-o."

Heather sighed and hoped that was the end of that. Taylor could be impossible when her will was thwarted. And the little girl was undoubtedly still upset from her go-to with Rick. Heather wondered what had really been going on, but Tyrone had stood up for Rick, so she had to believe he had been worried that Taylor would hurt herself. It was difficult not to side with her child, but it seemed that in this case, she shouldn't. Rick had done the right thing in keeping her safe.

She headed the vehicle toward the highway and thought maybe she needed to apologize to him in the morning when she returned the sunglasses.

Luckily, as she drove, Addison distracted her twin, Kirby sat staring out the passenger-side window and the ride back to Sparrow Lake proved to be uneventful.

Heather drove straight to Aunt Margaret's. Brian had agreed to watch the twins and the dog as long as it could be at their aunt's place with the new 44" LCD television he'd bought for her with his earnings from the store. Not that Aunt Margaret watched much TV. But now that Brian was in college, he had to catch every game so that he could discuss the results with his new friends.

"We're here, girls," she said, pulling up to

the lakeside house with the brilliant chartreuse front door.

"Yay!" Addison shouted. "There's Uncle Brian!"

The dog got to his feet and barked.

"And Aunt Margaret!" Taylor yelled.

Brian was halfway down the walkway, and Aunt Margaret was getting up from one of the comfy cushioned chairs she'd set on the front lawn. Always colorful, she was wearing white pants with a chartreuse tunic that matched her door but was at odds with her spiked red hair. The large rectangular box she picked up—her shower gift for Kristen—was equally colorful with artfully wrapped ribbons of different colors. Heather grinned and waved to her aunt and little brother before getting out of the vehicle. The dog tried lunging past her, but she caught him by the collar.

"Not so fast."

"Here, I'll take him," Brian said, grabbing the dog's leash. "Neat-looking dog."

"He's real nice, too," Addison said.

Taylor added, "And he's *mine*." She gave her mother a defiant look. "His name is Kirby."

Heather wasn't about to contradict her now. No time for an argument. "You two be good for Uncle Brian. Help him make dinner and clean up, okay?"

"'Kay," Addison said, running to get a big hug from Aunt Margaret.

Taylor was busy wresting the leash away from Brian.

"Don't worry, sis, I'll get it under control."

Heather knew he would. He'd changed a lot from the irresponsible boy he'd been the summer before when he'd moved back to Sparrow Lake from California to live with Aunt Margaret. The plan had been for him to go to the university, but community college was a better fit for now.

"I have confidence that the twins will find a way to either entertain you…or drive you crazy."

Brian winked and got Taylor and the dog in hand.

Heather hugged Aunt Margaret, took the present from her and put it in the back of the SUV next to her own.

"This should be fun," Aunt Margaret said once they were on their way.

"I hope so. I could use some fun."

"The twins aren't fun?"

"I mean away from the girls."

"I have something that will give everyone a little lift."

"Everyone? Aunt Margaret, you didn't hire a male stripper, did you?"

Her aunt whooped. "Now why didn't I think of that?"

Thank goodness! "Whew!"

"You're relieved? Not disappointed?"

"At least I know I won't be embarrassed." Heat flushed her neck just thinking about it.

There'd already been a larger shower with townspeople and a few relatives who lived outside Sparrow Lake, but tonight's gathering was simply to have a good time, with the women closest to Kristen—her aunt, her sister and the other bridesmaids. Heather had bought her sister a pretty red negligee and a certificate to have a glamour photo taken while wearing it. That was all the rage now and a memory that the groom was sure to appreciate in years to come. She couldn't wait to see what the others had chosen.

A few minutes later, they were inside Sew Fine, the last to arrive.

"There they are now!" said Shara Lessley, a beautiful young African-American woman, her hair in narrow braids with tiny sparkling beads woven into the ends.

"Come get some punch, ladies," Gloria Vega said. "No one makes tastier punch than me. Fruit juices and seltzer and sherbet."

"I can attest to how delicious it is," Kristen

confessed, grinning. "I cheated and tasted it already."

"As you should," Priscilla Ryan said. "Being this party is in your honor."

Shara and Gloria, both employees of the quilting store, and Priscilla, Kristen's best friend from high school, stood around the punch bowl with the bride to be. Kristen was beaming as she ladled punch into little cut glass cups that matched the bowl.

Heather thought her sister looked happier than she'd ever seen her. Thinking about her own shower, Heather blinked away the sting from her eyes. She wasn't going to ruin this night with sad memories of Scott. That she could compartmentalize so easily now surprised her. It meant that she had finally finished grieving for him. Not that she would ever forget him—how could she with two beautiful reminders of their love? But she had to admit that she finally felt ready for something new and wonderful to happen to her, too.

"Here you go, honey," Gloria said, holding out a cup of punch.

Heather took it from her. "That's a great blouse," she said, admiring the layers of cutouts and embroidery in the white cotton.

"Thanks." Gloria beamed at her. "My sister

brought it back from Mexico when she went to visit our grandmother."

Priscilla set down a tray next to the punch bowl. "Everyone try some of my cheeses. I brought three kinds, plus crackers and seasoned almonds."

"Yum," Kristen said. "I love cheese."

Priscilla had recently moved back to Sparrow Lake from Green Bay. Kristen had said it was because her old school friend was trying to start over after the relationship with her latest boyfriend went sour, and she'd vowed to find the right job to make herself happy at work. Conservative when it came to her clothes, Priscilla always wore colors that were a little dull against her bright red hair and clear green eyes. Today, her slacks and blouse were both beige.

Heather asked, "So what have you been doing with yourself since you got back to town?"

"I've been getting my new business going— an artisan cheese shop."

"So when you said 'my cheeses' you meant—"

"That they're ones I'm going to sell," Priscilla clarified.

"What fun." Heather grinned. "When does the shop open?"

"Actually, I'm opening it Friday with a tasting. Everyone is invited. Do you think you might come?"

"Hmm. A grown-up activity." Something Heather could look forward to. "I'm pretty sure I can use an extra big pizza to bribe Brian to babysit. If the twins don't give him too hard a time tonight."

"Great. And you can bring someone."

Uh-oh, there it was again. "I'm...uh...not exactly dating anyone right now."

Priscilla sighed. "Yeah, me, neither. Always the bridesmaid..."

Kristen had told Heather that Priscilla had been a bridesmaid several times in the past few years. Apparently Kristen was the last of her old friends giving up the single life.

"We can always hang out together," Heather offered.

"Wait!" Gloria said. "The two of you have dates for the wedding, right?"

"Uh, no," Heather said.

"Nope." Priscilla's cheeks flushed nearly as red as her hair. "I can't seem to meet a guy I can connect with long term. So if any of you know an eligible man, send him my way, would you?"

Eligible man? The only one Heather knew was Rick, who was definitely not meant for her, not when he was thinking of re-enlisting.

But that didn't mean he might not be right for someone else. Still, not wanting to get Priscilla's hopes up for nothing, she kept her thoughts to herself for the moment.

Everyone sampled the goodies and chattered.

In the midst of their talk about the wedding, Kristen changed the subject. "What happened to that cute dog the girls found yesterday? Kirby, was it?"

Heather sighed. "We still have him. He's on a waiting list at the shelter. I'm hoping to find his owner. Or if not, a new home for him."

"Won't the girls be disappointed?"

"Taylor especially," Heather admitted. "But I have a tight budget as it is. If only they'd found him a few months from now, when my work situation is settled."

"So you like the dog?" Kristen asked.

"Of course I like him. But I need to be practical, and—"

"We need to get down and dirty here," Shara broke in.

Gloria whooped and Heather grinned. Enough with the dog already. She'd been sad thinking about his fate. Time for a little fun with her sister. Gloria and Shara had set up a gift-giving area between the table of quilting kits and one holding bolts of velvet.

The first gift was from Priscilla.

"Crystal toasting glasses with a bottle of champagne for the wedding day," Kristen said. "How beautiful."

"I want you to have a special cheese to go with it," Priscilla told her, "but I'll have to bring it to the wedding. On ice, of course."

"And here's something for the bridal bed." Shara handed Kristen a pretty pale pink and silver bag with matching ribbons.

From it, Kristen lifted a big silver pillow cover, quilted with silk and laces and decorated with pale pink sequins that read *Just Married*.

"Oh, how lovely."

"And I have something less pretty and more fun," Gloria said.

Which proved to be massage oils and scented candles. Heather grinned as Kristen opened one of the bottles and inhaled.

"Mmm. That will certainly set a romantic mood."

"Now for something totally different," Heather said, handing over her gift.

Kristen opened the card first. Her eyebrows shot up. "A photograph?"

"Wearing what's inside."

Kristen opened the box and lifted the negligee.

"You bought *me* a present?" came a male

voice. Having just arrived, Police Chief Alex Novak stepped behind Kristen, kissed his fiancée's cheek and winked at Heather. Tall and good-looking, he and Kristen made a striking pair. "So is the party over?" Alex asked.

"No, it's not over!" Heather grinned at him. "You just want Kristen all to yourself."

"My present isn't even opened," Aunt Margaret said with a laugh. As Gloria picked up the large rectangular box, Margaret added, "Careful. It's fragile."

Gloria placed the box in the middle of the table for Kristen to open. As she lifted the lid, she grinned. "Wow!"

"Hey, I want to see," Heather said impatiently.

Kristen gasped. "My goodness, Aunt Margaret, I've never seen such a...*big*...cake."

"And probably not as unusual a cake either," Alex mused with a cough as Kristen pulled it from the box.

Heather had to laugh and join the oohs and aahs at the sight of the rectangular cake emblazoned with a frosting portrait of a romantic couple in an embrace—a blonde woman in the arms of a dark-haired muscular man who looked like a pirate.

Oddly enough, though the man was dressed

in historical garb, he reminded Heather of Rick...

Alex laughed. "Where did the cake-maker get such inspiration?"

"From an old historical romance novel I've kept for decades," Aunt Margaret told him. "It's amazing what they can reproduce on cakes these days."

"Apparently," Alex said with a chuckle.

"You weren't even supposed to see it," Aunt Margaret informed him. "This was something for the ladies to enjoy."

Heather laughed. "You can choose your own cake, Alex—any kind you like—for your bachelor party. C'mon, Kristen, let's cut a piece."

Kristen started with the hero-decorated half, giving each of the women a giggle along with their serving.

Heather's piece was a shoulder and part of a well-muscled arm encased in a billowing thin white shirt. As she took her first bite, she couldn't help thinking about Rick, who had muscled arms to match those from the romance novel cover.

Or The Terminator, she thought with a grin.

CHAPTER SIX

ONE OF THE surveillance cameras went off in the middle of the night, the alarm waking Rick, who'd left his laptop on the table next to the bed. To his disappointment, the culprit wasn't human, but rather a couple of raccoons foraging for grubs in the lawn, where it had been ripped apart for new gardens.

Before going back to bed, he hadn't been able to resist watching the video of Heather again that he told himself he was going to delete.

Really he was.

Just not yet.

Watching her fuss with her hair, make faces for the camera and pucker her lips in an air kiss, he couldn't help but grin. He'd seen movement in the dark, but he hadn't been able to make out what was going on—the camera needed to be adjusted because he should have been able to see more clearly. Only when Heather turned on the light did he realize she'd changed into that dress. And wearing it, her hair fancied up, her lips luscious with a swipe of lipstick, she looked amazing.

Maybe that was the reason he'd dreamed of her.

Of them.

Together…

Awake now, the dream still pricking at the edges of his mind as he left his coach house quarters to find the housekeeper, he faced reality. Heather Clarke was more than an attractive woman that he would like to get to know better. She was a mother with two young girls, one of whom probably hated him after the dog incident.

He didn't need that kind of complication in his life.

That decided, Rick tried to shove Heather out of mind and entered the mansion through the kitchen. He'd expected to find the housekeeper having her breakfast, but no one sat at the big table near the kitchen windows.

"Have you seen Cora?" he asked Kelly.

The chef was preparing some kind of fancy egg dish in a glass baking tray. And she'd set out a platter of mixed fruits, too.

"You'll probably find Cora in the drawing room," Kelly said. "She's waiting to have breakfast with our only guest so he doesn't have to eat alone, but that won't be for a short while yet."

Remembering Cora's excitement at Mr. Guildfren's arrival, Rick suspected her having breakfast with the man spoke to a more complex motive. A romantic one? Though he hated interrupting them, he needed a minute to speak with her.

"Thanks, Kelly."

But he didn't get as far as the dining room before Gina Luca greeted him. "Rick, are you here for breakfast this morning?"

He wasn't much of a breakfast person, usually just slogged down some coffee with a piece of toast. "Actually, I'm here on business. I need to see Cora for a moment."

"Maybe I can help. I *am* the concierge here," she reminded him. "I book the clients, make plans for them, give them advice and directions on places to eat or have fun."

"Thanks so much, but I need to talk business with Cora specifically."

Gina shrugged. "Well, if you change your mind…"

Rick proceeded to the drawing room.

The Phillips family had kept the public room just as it had been for many decades—old-fashioned but elegant. The room had a fireplace and a fancy crystal chandelier hanging from the middle of the ceiling, with cherubs dancing around the base. Several couches and even more chairs were upholstered in pale creams and yellows and blues.

Cora and her gentleman sat in upholstered chairs in a bay looking out to the lake. David Guildfren was leaning over the table toward Cora, his hand on hers. Whatever he was saying in a low tone was making her smile. Seventy-some years or not, she looked radiant, transformed by her apparent feelings for the man.

Rick's gut tightened. No woman had ever looked at him like that.

What if Heather Clarke did?

Reminding himself that he had a job to do, he shook away the thought and cleared his throat loudly enough that he got their attention.

"Rick," Cora said, the smile fading on her lips.

"I need to speak to you," Rick said, "just for a moment, I promise. It's about my work here."

"Of course." Cora withdrew her hand and stood. "Excuse me, David. I must see what our handyman needs."

"Don't worry, I'm not going anywhere."

Cora quickly joined Rick, who led her away from the open doorway, just in case anyone was around to hear.

"Do you have the information I need?" He'd asked her for a list of all employees, both full and part time, and for their Social Security numbers so he could run a security check on each of them.

"Yes." She slipped her hand into her trouser pocket and pulled out a folded piece of paper. "Though I just can't believe anyone working here has anything to do with our intruder."

"Hopefully, you're right."

Taking the paper from her, he slipped it into his own pocket.

"In addition to Kelly and Gina, we have three day maids, two kitchen helpers, a server and a boat man for the season. They've all been working here for years."

"No one is new?"

"Kelly started last summer, and Gina was hired at the holidays, but the day workers have all been here for at least three years. One of the maids as long as eight years."

Not that length of time proved anything, Rick thought. But because Cora seemed so distressed by the idea that one of the people working for her could be dishonest, he nodded encouragingly.

"I'll let you know what I find out."

Cora glanced back in the direction of her breakfast companion. "I was in the middle of a new tale about Red Flanagan, and I've left Mr. Guildfren midstory. So, is that it?"

"Not exactly. I wanted you to know I have security cameras in place on all sides of the house, inside the coach house and inside the boathouse. They're all triggered by movement and once they go on, they send a digital signal to my computer system where the action is recorded."

"Good. Good."

"Did you see or hear anything unusual last night?"

"Why? Did you get something on one of those recordings?"

"Actually, I did." Not that Rick would tell her about catching Heather in the boathouse. That was his secret. "Raccoons."

Cora gave a relieved laugh. "Oh."

"I just thought I would check with you to see if the cameras missed anything."

"Not that I can say."

He nodded.

She frowned. "Is there something you're not telling me?"

"Nothing definite, but I have an idea how someone got in one of the tunnels."

"How?"

"I'm looking for an entrance that either

wasn't blocked or, more likely, was reopened by a previous owner—"

Just then, Kelly approached and entered the drawing room. "Breakfast is served."

"Ah, good! I'm starving!" they heard Mr. Guildfren say.

Cora looked from the doorway to Rick, questions in her gaze.

"It can wait," he murmured. "I still have to check out my theory. Maybe tonight I'll have something to report." He intended to do a little exploring at the end of the day after Heather and her work crew were gone. He didn't want any interruptions. "Go see to your guest."

She flushed a little. "All right. Later, then."

He suspected the secret entrance was somewhere in the coach house, but he hadn't yet found it. He simply needed more time.

Even as he left the mansion, the EPI crew arrived, Tyrone and Amber in the truck, Heather in her SUV. His phone practically burned a hole in his pocket, and it took a great deal of willpower not to take it out and view the footage again.

Instead, he helped Heather's crew haul out more landscaping materials from the truck and took the time to admire her in person. She was a hard worker and an amiable boss. It was obvious that both Tyrone and Amber liked her, if not in quite the same way as he might.

"Thanks for helping us," Heather said as they loaded bags of mulch onto the cart. "And I didn't even ask."

"No problem. I wasn't doing anything anyway."

Of course he had something to do as soon as he got to his computer.

Not that he was in a rush to leave her.

"And, um, Rick—" she looked around as if making sure they were alone for the moment "—about yesterday…"

Okay, here it came. She undoubtedly wanted an explanation.

"Listen, I'm sorry if I overstepped my bounds."

"No, no! *I'm* sorry. When I cooled down, I realized you were trying to keep my girls safe, which is what I want, of course."

"You're apologizing to me?"

"Yes! Taylor can be quite a handful. And even though she claimed you hurt her, I'm sure that was her frustration talking."

The attraction he already felt for her curled through his stomach. His lips softened into what had to be a loopy grin as she gazed into his eyes.

"Oh, my gosh, I forgot!" she suddenly said. "Don't leave!"

Rick put up his hands. "Okay."

Heather ran back to her SUV and opened one of the rear doors, reached in, then slammed the door and ran back toward him, waving her hand.

"My sunglasses!" He immediately slipped them in place. "I forgot where they were."

"Addison mistakenly took them with her."

"No problem. I'm just glad to get them back." Seeing that Tyrone and Amber were joining them, he grinned and said, "Gotta keep up the image, you know."

Heather laughed, and the warm sound whispered through Rick, making him back up. He needed to get a grip when he was around her. He could hardly think of anything else.

"What now, boss?" Tyrone asked.

Amber slugged him in the arm. "The retaining wall, remember?"

"Oh, right."

"I'll let you get to it," Rick said. "I have some work to do myself. See you later."

He whipped around and headed for the coach house. When he got to his quarters, he'd make a fresh pot of coffee and then get down to those security checks. He should be able to make a good start on them today.

If he could put Heather out of mind long enough to do his work.

THE MORNING WENT by quickly. Rick's stomach rumbling made him check the time. Lunch. Having gotten through a couple of the part-time employees in just a few hours, he left the computer in hibernate mode.

So far, Sam Johnson, the former handyman, was the only person who rang any bells. The man had been arrested a couple of times, first after getting into a fray with one of his neighbors and then being involved in a bar fight. And Rick knew Ben Phillips had let Johnson go when he'd gotten into a verbal altercation with one of the guests over the holidays. Could Johnson be trying to exact some kind of revenge?

He was probably going to have to do some digging in person to find more personal information on the man, he thought as he crossed to the main house.

Just then, his phone vibrated in his pocket. Stopping to see if he needed to take this right now, he was shocked when the caller ID read *Keith Murphy*. His pulse thundered as he picked up the call.

"Murphy, how are you?" He was hoping his old teammate hadn't gotten hurt again.

"I'm great, Slater, how about you?"

Relieved, Rick sucked in some air. "I'm adapting."

"That doesn't sound promising."

Not wanting to be forced to justify his decision to leave the army, Rick asked, "What's up? Where are you?"

"Stateside on a short leave. Right now I'm visiting family. But I thought I would take some time and visit my old buddy, too."

"I'm on a security job." Rick lowered his voice and added, "Undercover 24/7."

"So you're not in Milwaukee."

"Close. In Kenosha."

"Hey, even better. That'll save me an hour behind the wheel. I'm in Michigan, straight across the lake. I thought about spending a couple of days in Chicago for a little R & R. I was going to invite you to join me."

"Not an option for me, unfortunately." He could use some time with an old friend. Someone who had shared the same experiences, good and bad.

"Got it. So I'll head up north to see you before my leave is up. If you can find time for me in your schedule, that is."

"Don't worry, I'll make the time."

"We, uh, have a lot to talk about," Murphy said.

Rick's built-in antenna went on alert. He had good reason to believe Murphy wanted to do more than relive the good old days.

"What's on your mind?" Rick asked.

"It can wait until I see you. I gotta go. My sister is waiting on me."

He knew it. He wasn't going to get anything out of his old buddy until Murphy was ready to talk. "When?"

"Not sure yet. I just wanted to give you a head's up. Maybe next week sometime. I'll give you a call when I know for sure."

"Sounds like a plan."

Rick couldn't believe how good it had been hearing an old friend's voice. Part of him longed to be part of a unit where everyone counted on everyone else. As it was now, he was alone. Not that he didn't have people he could talk to. But he didn't have anyone he could count on, someone who would watch his back.

Thoughtful, he entered the kitchen. "Smells good," he told Kelly, who was placing a pot on the center island where she set up the buffet so the employees could help themselves to lunch.

"It's just chili."

"One of my favorites. Let me help you set up."

"That's nice of you. You could get the bowls and spoons while I cut up the cornbread."

"Anything else?"

"There's a pitcher of iced tea in the fridge."

"Where is everyone?"

"Looks like it's just us for now."

"Okay with me. When everyone eats at the same time, the noise in here makes my head spin."

Kelly laughed as she cut a pan of cornbread into squares. "Probably because you're the only guy right now."

"Did my predecessor like being the only guy?"

"Sam?" Kelly's smile faded. "Truthfully, I don't know that Sam liked much of anything."

"Not the friendly type, I take it."

"Well...sometimes he was too friendly, if you know what I mean. But he certainly wasn't congenial."

"I know he was fired because of some argument with a guest."

Kelly sighed as she set the cornbread on the buffet. "That time the guest complained."

He set the pitcher of iced tea next to the glasses on the island. "So there were other times?"

"Not that I witnessed. But so I heard from various staff members. You know you don't want to think badly of people, so you just put it off as gossip. Only this time it wasn't, and Ben said Sam had to go."

"Did he give Ben a hard time about it?"

"It wasn't Ben who gave him the bad news. Cora had to do the actual firing, and Sam didn't take it well."

"He threatened her?"

"He said she would be sorry. And that Ben would be sorry. The usual threat."

As he ladled chili into a bowl, Rick wondered if it was a bluff or if there was something to this lead.

He picked up his bowl and said, "I think I'll get some air."

Rather than going directly to the coach house, he headed for the terrace, where he quickly demolished his food.

He looked around and saw Heather in the distance, working on that retaining wall. Seeing her reminded him of the video. The one he'd promised himself to delete.

Stopping in the shade of an old growth maple, he pulled out his phone. He couldn't resist. He wanted to watch the playful moment he'd captured one more time before deleting the footage as he'd intended all along. It showed such a different side to Heather and he was truly intrigued. She was simply charming. He was watching her play with her hair and make all those faces when the skin crawling along his neck made him realize someone was behind him. He shut down the phone and slid it into his pocket as he turned to see a wide-eyed Tyrone staring at him. Uh-oh. Rick feared Tyrone had seen and only hoped that, if he had, he would keep his lips locked.

"Tyrone, did you need something?" Rick asked.

"Um, that lady who runs this place, the young one, wants me to move the bags of stone we stored over there, next to the terrace. She says it'll be an eyesore for the guests."

Young one. *Gina.* Not that she ran the place, which was Cora's job. Gina merely serviced the guests. But she did have a point. And although David Guildfren was the only guest at the moment, more were scheduled to check in on Friday or Saturday.

"Gina does have a point if the area isn't cleared by the weekend."

"Any suggestions about where I should move the bags?"

The coach house was the logical place, but if Tyrone stacked all those bags inside, they might interfere with Rick's search for the hidden tunnel entrance.

So he said, "How about at the side of the coach house?"

"On the plants? That's a nice little garden. Stacking bags of rock would kill them."

"How about in back of the building then?"

Rick amended. "On the asphalt pad. There's some room opposite the garbage containers."

"Okay, I'll go get the cart." Tyrone nodded and gave him one last odd look before heading off.

About to delete the footage as he'd meant to do, Rick stopped when he saw Cora coming from the mansion.

"Oh, Rick, there you are. I need you. One of the window blinds is stuck all the way up. And there's a loose baluster on the staircase that needs to be secured."

"Sure. I can take care of that right now."

Though being a handyman was only a cover, he had to make it look real. And because part of the job was to make the small repairs required around the estate, he picked up his bowl to drop off in the kitchen and followed Cora back inside.

Deleting the footage of Heather could wait until he was finished with his chores.

CHAPTER SEVEN

IT HAD BEEN a long, hard but rewarding work day. Thankfully, Brian had volunteered to take care of Kirby until she got home. *Dog,* she reminded herself. She had to stop personalizing. Had to stop thinking of him as if he could be part of her family. Heather was grateful that she hadn't had to deal with the dog at work today, no matter how cute he was. Her brother had promised to put up signs for her around town this morning, and hopefully the dog's real owner would see one of them and call her this evening.

And if not? What then? She didn't want to think about it. How long would it take before there was room at the local shelter? Either way—owner or shelter—Taylor's little heart would be broken when she had to give up the dog. Having a pet would give her girls a sense of responsibility and a deeper appreciation for animals, but Heather simply couldn't afford to take care of an animal right now. Licenses and shots and other vet bills, food and toys—all that would bust her budget.

If EPI offered her a full-time job after this internship, she could rethink the pet situation. Considering no one was home all day, though, a cat probably would be easier to deal with than a dog.

She shook away the problem and stood back from the completed retaining walls for the two rain gardens so that she could take in the whole picture with the mansion as the backdrop. The retaining walls not only looked great, but they also appeared to have been there forever thanks to the stone she'd chosen.

Tomorrow the plan was to cut a path from house to gardens through the grass and tunnel into the soil. That way, they could bury the extensions they'd attach to two of the house's downspouts. Rain would come down the slope on its own, and the extensions would further divert it from the area around the building itself. Then they would create the pathway from the house, snaking it between the rain gardens and ending at the start of the beach. They had to remove more sod, pour sand as a base, then install stone that matched the retaining walls.

Next week, they would begin planting the rain gardens and then the dunes area, all of which needed to be completed before moving on to another stage of the landscape renovation.

Things were starting off quite nicely, and it was only the first week. Heather couldn't be more pleased.

"Looks great already, doesn't it?" she said to Tyrone as he stopped to stand beside her.

Tyrone cleared his throat and grinned. However, something in his tone made Heather think he was uncomfortable when he remarked, "Lots of things around here look great—some kind of unexpected."

An odd reply. And he was staring at her oddly, too.

"Unexpected?" Heather frowned at him. "What are you talking about?"

"Loosening up. Showing the real person inside."

"All right, Tyrone, stop dancing around whatever it is you want to say and just *tell* me."

His expression conflicted, he said, "Look, I didn't mean to see it or anything. It was an accident."

"Tyrone!"

"Okay, okay. Rick was watching this video of you earlier, and I, um, happened to get a glimpse of it. I didn't realize you two had something going on."

"Something going on?" Heather asked, at a

loss. Then she reacted to the rest of his statement. "Video? *Of me?*" Warmth crept up her neck.

"Uh-huh. In the boathouse."

Though she'd had a feeling that's what he'd meant, Heather still gaped at him. Rick had a video of her and had been entertaining himself watching it? What in the world had he seen?

"It's okay. I won't gossip or anything."

"Well, I should hope not because there's *nothing* going on!" she nearly shouted.

Tyrone seemed even more uncomfortable. He took a step back. "Well, sure. Sorry I brought it up."

Heather could only sputter, "And I don't know why he…how…"

Without another word, she stalked away from Tyrone and headed for the mansion. She'd seen Rick go inside with Cora a while ago, and he hadn't yet come out.

"Heather, wait a minute!" Tyrone called, but she ignored him and swept past Amber, who was just returning to help clean up.

"Hey, Heather, do you…" Amber started, but her voice faded off when Heather kept going without looking back.

Her face heated, Heather knew she was probably beet-red. She was focused on one thing—giving Rick a piece of her mind. She wondered how she could have been so wrong about him as she opened the back door and entered the kitchen. She'd thought he was such a nice guy. She could hardly believe he would secretly record someone. *Her.*

Kelly was standing at the island, chopping vegetables. "Hi. Can I help you?"

Heather took a deep breath to get herself under control and sweetly said, "I need to find Rick."

Kelly pointed to a doorway. "Through the hall and into the rotunda. He's working on the staircase."

"Thanks."

Heather swept by her and zigzagged into the round, central, two-story room. She barely saw the details as she looked around. The rotunda was empty, but she followed the sound of wood being hammered and found herself at the bottom of the staircase. Rick was at the top, adjusting one of the wooden rails. Heather wanted to yell at him, but the breath caught in her throat. She was still trying to find her voice when he looked down and saw her standing there.

"Hey, looking for me?"

"Who else?" she asked stiffly.

"Give me a minute. I'm done here." Rick

dropped something inside his toolbox, then fastened it.

He took the stairs down to her two at a time, and her pulse picked up with each step. He wasn't wearing his sunglasses, and she took the opportunity to lock onto his gaze.

"You have some explaining to do," she said when he reached ground level.

His eyes flicked with something like guilt, and his mouth tightened. "About?"

Holding Rick's gaze, she didn't let him off the hook. "I just had an interesting chat with Tyrone about you, and it wasn't about your being The Terminator."

"What did Tyrone tell you?"

"What do you think he told me?" Even though no one was in sight, she lowered her voice but still kept her tone rightfully indignant. "That you were watching a video of me in the boathouse!"

He kept his voice low, too. "Look, I wasn't trying to get footage of you. It was an accident. Let's get away from here, and I'll explain."

"If you think explaining is going to—"

"Please."

She swallowed her anger for the moment and managed to nod.

He led the way to the kitchen, empty for the

moment, then set his toolbox down, out of the way, before continuing outside.

Heather's adrenaline was crashing. She tried to remember she was angry as she followed Rick to the terrace, where they took seats on cushioned chairs.

Rick immediately said, "Look, I'm sorry you got caught, but part of my job was to install cameras around the property for security. They all have motion and light sensors, and they are wirelessly rigged to digitally record anything they catch. That camera would have gone off no matter who went inside the boathouse."

Wondering what might have been going on at the estate to warrant increased security, Heather realized everything he said sounded reasonable. But…

"I was in the boathouse *yesterday,*" she said, still wondering exactly what he'd seen of her. "You were watching the footage *today.*"

He sighed. "I meant to delete it. I shouldn't have watched it again. I'm sorry. I didn't mean to infringe on your privacy. And then, when I realized Tyrone was there, I put the phone away, hoping he hadn't seen anything."

"Okay, what is 'anything'?" she asked.

His lips quivered but he kept a straight face.

"You messing with your hair, making faces at your mirror."

"That's all?" she asked.

"I couldn't actually see you until you turned on the light."

Even though she said, "I'm not sure I believe that," her pulse steadied.

"Then let me show you."

He pulled out his phone and played the file for her from the beginning, when she first entered the boathouse. All she could see was a blur of movement through the room. Then when she'd left the main room, the recording stopped and only started again when she re-entered it. Rick had been truthful about not seeing anything clearly until after she'd turned on the light. Warmth crept up her neck as she watched herself playing with her hair and puckering into the mirror after putting on her lipstick.

Still, she said, "I look like an idiot!"

"I don't know, those faces you make are kind of cute…"

Her face grew hot. "I demand that you delete it."

"Of course."

"And I'm at a loss as to why you still have the footage." Why in the world would he have wanted to watch such silliness more than once?

"Well, um…" Rick had the good grace to appear uncomfortable. "I've been busy. I kind of forgot."

Heather narrowed her gaze.

Still seeming uncomfortable, he said, "Look, I'm going to do it right now."

He let her see the screen as he quickly hit Delete. "Again, I'm truly sorry."

Finally, the warmth in her neck and face started to fade. From all that had been said, she believed Rick. Still, she asked, "Where else have you put security cameras? Just in case. I'd like to know."

"Well, not where people usually need privacy. I placed them around the buildings. Anywhere a stranger might be where he shouldn't."

"You think someone might be messing around in the boathouse?"

"Boats can dock there. You never know these days. Lake Michigan is a highway of sorts. People forget that. In Red Flanagan's day, whiskey was unloaded right out there." He pointed in the direction of the dock.

Heather was beginning to understand. "Yeah, I've heard stories about boat runs back in the old days of prohibition."

"You want to hear a funny tale about Red Flanagan?"

"Sure." She could use a laugh.

"One time the cops were alerted to a bootlegger's arrival by boat and they roared out here to the mansion, sirens blaring. Red and his men got busy in the meantime and threw heavy rocks into the whiskey barrels and dumped them in the lake. The cops found nothing, and Red and his group pretended they were having a nice hoity-toity tea party with cookies and such."

Heather smiled at the vision. "I'm sure they enjoyed the finger sandwiches."

"Everything was okay until Red threw a stick into the lake for his poodle to fetch. It took the dog a while to find it and when he came back out of the water, he was staggering from the alcohol he'd ingested."

"Aw, poor dog." Heather couldn't help but think about the dog Taylor wanted to keep.

"Don't worry—he was okay. And the cops didn't suspect anything because one of Red's men scooped up the poodle and took him inside to dry out."

Heather smiled. "That's some story. Where did you hear it?"

"There's an archive of newspaper articles in the library and other materials on Red in the roaring twenties and dirty thirties, as they call them. Mr. Phillips collects them."

They talked and laughed some more before

Heather realized quite a bit of time had passed and she needed to go pick up the twins. She felt a little guilty about yelling at Rick. "I'm sorry I got upset. I'm sure a place like this needs security cameras."

"You don't have to apologize. I, uh, guess I deserved it." It was his turn to look a little embarrassed.

Heather glanced over to the work area and saw that Amber and Tyrone were almost finished cleaning up. "Tomorrow we're going to cut a curving pathway through the lawn down to the beach."

"So the sod cutter is still working okay?"

"It's working perfectly, thanks to you."

Rick was a nice guy. And Heather was getting the idea that he was attracted to her, which was probably why he'd watched the footage of her before deleting it. With his looks, he could get any woman he wanted. Not that she included herself in that package. Despite the fact that she was attracted to him, she couldn't forget about the possibility of Rick re-enlisting, which put him off-limits.

She remembered when Scott had been set on taking a second tour, and she'd asked him to think of her and the girls. He'd told her they were all he thought about—he wanted the world to be a safer place for them. How could she have argued with that? So Scott had returned to Iraq. And had never come back.

Unwilling to go through such grief a second time, she knew Rick wasn't right for her, no matter how much she respected his dedication.

But what about someone else?

Like Priscilla.

The thought had occurred to her the night before at the shower, but she'd tucked it away. Now it came back at her full blast.

"Are you doing anything Friday night?"

His eyebrows arched. "Friday night? No. No plans."

"Priscilla Ryan, an old high school friend of my sister, has a new artisan cheese shop in Sparrow Lake. That's the town where I live, about a fifteen-minute drive from here. On Friday she's having a grand opening with a cheese tasting. Everyone's invited."

"I'd love to come."

"Great." Wanting to focus on Priscilla, Heather said, "I'm certain she would love to meet you."

"What time do you want me to pick you up?" Rick asked.

"Oh, you can just meet me at Priscilla's Main Street Cheese Shoppe. The tasting starts at seven."

He appeared surprised. Then he shrugged.

"All right. Seven it is, then. How do I get there?"

No sooner had she given him directions than Heather realized her workers were gone for the day. She checked her watch and got to her feet.

"Sorry, but I have to pick up the twins."

Without waiting for a reply, Heather rushed off toward the parking lot. She felt a little weird at playing matchmaker, but it was all for the best.

RICK WATCHED HEATHER run from him like she had wings on her heels. Was she that late? Or was she simply freaked out after asking him for a date?

He grinned, thinking about it. A little down time with Heather would give him a lot to smile about. The more he got to know her, the more he liked her. Odd, though, that she hadn't wanted him to pick her up. So was meeting your date at the event typical these days? He'd been out of the loop far too long. Or did Heather have a specific reason for wanting to meet him at the opening?

Hmm, maybe she didn't want Taylor to see him after the dog incident. Rick and her mom going out together might set off the little girl again. That was the only reason that came to mind, and it bothered him.

Did he really want to date a young widow with a built-in family? Considering how he'd failed his men, he wasn't certain he was up for that kind of responsibility. Then again, it was only a date, he told himself. No big deal.

Shrugging away his uncertainty, he headed for the coach house. Plenty of time to think things through later. Right now he had other concerns.

Dinner wouldn't be until seven, so no one would be looking for him for a couple of hours. While there was still daylight and everyone left on the property was occupied, he could start searching for that tunnel entry. He'd already made one attempt to find it after seeing the damage on the sod cutter, but he hadn't had much time. Once it got dark, finding anything on that ground floor was nearly impossible.

Not to mention he might warn the intruder if the man was on the grounds.

The element of surprise was essential.

Rick made sure he closed the garage doors once he was inside. No need to alert anyone, even if it was too early for the intruder to be around.

He flipped on the lights and entered the shop area, where he took one of the battery-operated utility lanterns from its shelf. The powerful beam would let him inspect the dark paneling in detail.

His initial target was where he'd found the damaged sod cutter. He inspected the paneling closely and ran his fingers over the entire area, including the chair rail circling the room. Nothing to find there.

He continued his search, inspecting every inch of wall as he went.

Nothing…nothing…nothing…

Until…

He got to the paneling alongside the staircase that went up to his apartment. Adjusting the light, he took a closer look at the chair rail. The molding didn't quite match up. And when he moved his open hand over the area, he swore he felt a shift in the air. This had to be it. Of course. It made perfect sense. A secret entrance under the stairs. Hidden stairs below the visible staircase.

Now the question was how to access it.

He pushed. He pulled. He slid his hands along the paneling.

There had to be some kind of catch release. But where? It wasn't on the side wall below the staircase.

What about the staircase itself?

Rick reached up and ran a hand over the balusters as he made his way down to the newel post. Nothing moved. Not until he touched the ornate brass top of the post. He pushed harder. Felt it give a little. Heard a click.

Glancing back at the wall, he saw that the panel had opened. The doorway was low, but he ducked and went inside, flashing his light over the stairs and beyond. A tunnel. So the Feds hadn't blocked off every access point. Maybe they hadn't thought this one was important. Then again, probably one of the half-dozen former owners in the past eight decades had found and re-opened it.

He felt for a switch on the wall and turned on a couple of lights—bare bulbs that faintly revealed the tunnel's length. He calculated the path would take him directly under the mansion. Hearsay had it that, via the tunnels, Red Flanagan had built secret rooms both to hold his shipments and to hide some unspecified treasure.

Rick assumed the intruder was looking for the supposed treasure. If Rick found the treasure first and Phillips released that information to the media, the would-be thief would have no reason to come back. It would end the intrusions right there. So Rick's focus was to try to find the purported secret rooms.

Even though he spotted the release on the tunnel side of the door, he jammed a piece of wood near the bottom to make doubly certain the panel couldn't close and lock behind him. He hated going underground and couldn't help being paranoid that he could be trapped.

Again.

This is my job, he told himself. He had to get over his feeling of dread. *This isn't Afghanistan.*

Taking a deep breath to bolster himself, he went down the stairs and set off along the tunnel. A gust of air from his right—lakeside— made him think there was another branch. Perhaps from the boathouse?

Wanting to see where this part of the tunnel led, he went straight forward in the direction of the mansion. He'd only gotten a few yards before the lights went out. His pulse surged, and not wanting to be surprised by a possible intruder, he froze in place and listened hard. He could stand here like this for hours. Had, in fact, been forced to do so more than once when on dangerous missions.

But that was before...

The invisible walls closed in on him, and his stomach clutched as he waited in the dark in what was feeling more and more like a tomb.

He focused his mind and listened intently. Nothing. No one moving around down here. Only when he was certain that he was alone, that the lights had, for some reason, given up on their own, did he manage to take an easy breath. He turned the utility lantern on and swung the beam around for another check. Lots of loose rock on the floor. And sand had sifted in from somewhere, reminding him of those caves in Afghanistan.

Nothing more ominous, so he put his paranoia in check and went on.

Two minutes later, he'd reached a split. He must be directly under the mansion, the tunnels leading to separate exits into the building. He took the left fork and went on another ten yards before coming to a second split and a staircase.

The walls closed in on him even tighter. The climb was narrow and steep, then turned to the right midway, the passageway filled with cobwebs and things that skittered in the dark. And at the top of the stairs, the exit was sealed with cement. Someone would need tools to break it open.

Rick took the steps back down and tried the other branch, only to face the same situation. Another flight of steps. Another blocked exit.

Back down he went to the original split. The right fork toward the mansion was wider, and the tunnel looked as if it had been constructed at a different time. Wood beams and cross braces were exposed. He was halfway down this branch when he felt moving air.

Stopping dead in his tracks, Rick concentrated to identify the source—an unobtrusive door in the middle of the wall. He ran his light all around it and found the catch on a wooden beam. Part of the wall clicked open to reveal another set of stairs half as high as the other one he'd tried. This must lead to an entrance on the ground floor. Either the Feds had missed this door, or one of the previous owners had already unsealed it.

He went up the several steps and found another latch. This time when the door opened, the tunnel flooded with light so bright it was almost blinding.

The conservatory!

He stepped inside the giant, glass-paned room filled with tropical plants and wondered if the intruder had found his way inside through this entrance.

CHAPTER EIGHT

HEATHER ENTERED THE Main Street Cheese Shoppe a little before seven on Friday evening, the first person to arrive. Low strains of classical music welcomed her into the shop, which was large enough to have several small round tables with chairs amid the displays of cutting boards and knives and packaged munchies, including the spiced nuts Priscilla had brought to the shower. The tables were covered with colorful fabric and decorated with small sprays of flowers and lit candles.

"Hey, Heather," Priscilla called. She was stationed behind the counter with several large wheels of cheese.

"Very inviting."

"Thanks!"

Heather was on tenterhooks thinking about seeing Rick at any minute. To calm her nerves, she volunteered to help Priscilla, who looked amazingly calm for a woman opening a new business.

"Okay, you can help by arranging a nice display of cheeses and crackers on these boards. I'm going to put them out over there."

Priscilla nodded to a long table set with a colorful cloth, matching small paper plates and cups. Several bottles of red wine were already opened to "breathe," Heather guessed.

"No problem," she assured her friend.

Priscilla was currently cutting Wisconsin cheddar into bite-size pieces. She'd already sliced several other kinds, and a couple of spreadable cheeses were out, too.

"What fun," Heather said of the mice-shaped cheese boards and spreading knives.

She thought her friend looked pretty tonight, with her hair pulled up in a fancy clip. If only she would dress herself as colorfully as she did her displays. Tonight Priscilla was wearing gray trousers and a pale gray shirt. Hmm. Was Rick a man who noticed women's clothing? She wouldn't want him to pass up a nice woman like Priscilla because she faded into the woodwork. Well, other than her bright red hair.

Thinking again about Rick watching the footage of her, she flushed and got to work setting up the cheese trays. By the time she was done, two couples had arrived. Heather set the trays on the long table as Priscilla approached the guests to introduce herself.

"Welcome. I'm Priscilla Ryan, and this is my store. If you have any questions, I'm here to help you. In the meantime, please try some samples." She indicated the table, which looked festive now.

Heather thought Priscilla handled herself professionally and was a welcoming presence. Surely Rick would appreciate that about her. Suddenly realizing that thinking about the man had knotted her stomach, Heather took a big breath.

"We're thrilled you opened this shop," one of the customers was saying. "My husband and I appreciate all kinds of cheeses and we've had to go into Kenosha to find imports until now."

Priscilla spoke to them for a moment, then came back to the counter to pull a pitcher of iced tea and a couple of bottles of white wine from the refrigerator.

"I'll have a glass of the pinot grigio," Heather said.

"Sure." Priscilla poured a glass for each of them.

Heather raised her wine in a toast. "To your success."

"Thanks."

They clinked, and then Heather said, "So I invited a man to the opening."

"A date? Good for you. Why didn't he come with you?"

"He isn't my date. He works at Flanagan Manor."

"Oh, that's nice."

"I remembered you saying that if any of us knew an eligible man we should invite him."

"Wait a minute!" Priscilla lowered her voice. "You're fixing me up with him? *Tonight?*"

"No, I didn't say anything like that. I just told him to meet me here. I figured it would give you a chance to meet each other, see if there's a fit. Assuming he shows."

Heather checked her watch. Seven minutes after seven. Rick was late. But other people were entering the store, taking Priscilla's attention. Heather sipped her wine and talked to a woman who was a customer at Sew Fine, and then the door opened to reveal Rick Slater.

And what a revelation!

Dressed in black trousers and a black shirt, mirrored sunglasses hiding his eyes, he practically filled the doorway.

Heather swore she heard a few gasps, one of which whispered through her own lips.

Next to her, Priscilla murmured, "Is that the guy?"

Heather nodded.

"Wow!"

Removing the sunglasses and slipping them into his shirt pocket, Rick looked around until he spotted Heather. She took a deep breath as he came straight at her.

"Heather, sorry I'm late."

"The party's just getting started." Heather stepped back slightly and pushed at the small of Priscilla's back so she would take a step toward Rick. "This is the owner of the shop, Priscilla Ryan. Priscilla, meet Rick Slater."

Priscilla held out her hand. "Welcome to my store. I'm so pleased you could stop by and see what I have to offer."

He shook her hand and gave her a polite smile. "Nice to meet you." Then he turned back to Heather, his gaze roaming from her eyes to her lips. He put his hand on her shoulder, making her aware of its warmth. "Is there anything you want?"

Suddenly self-conscious, she said, "Uh, I suppose I could use some of that cheese."

"And if you have any questions about any of my offerings, just ask," Priscilla told Rick in what Heather thought sounded like a flirtatious tone.

"Sure. Thanks." Rick turned to Heather again. "Actually, why don't you come with me so you can choose whatever you like?"

"All right." Heather gave Priscilla a little shrug before following Rick.

Was there something about Priscilla he didn't like? she wondered. Then she thought about his keeping that footage of her to watch—was it simply that he preferred being with *her?* The idea made Heather's pulse quicken. She had so little experience with men that she'd never learned to read them very well.

The place was crowded now, and the sampling table had a short line.

When they stopped, Rick said, "This seems like a nice little business. I hope your friend has great success with it."

Heather nodded. "Me, too." She tried another pitch. "Priscilla is such a nice woman. Smart. Ambitious. She and my sister, Kristen, went to high school together, which means she's several years older than I am. You know, closer to *your* age."

He sailed right past the prompt. "She *must* be pretty ambitious to open a small business in this economy."

"I'm sure she would love to talk to you about it."

"I'd rather talk to *you*." His smile flooded her with warmth. "You know, so we can get to know each other better."

"Of course."

"Isn't that why you invited me?"

Suddenly flustered, Heather looked beyond him and realized the sample table was clear. "Oh, it's our turn now."

Okay, no doubt about it. Rick came tonight because he wanted to get to know *her* better. He thought that's why she'd invited him.

And then it hit her…

Oh, boy, had he thought she'd invited him out on a *date?*

If so…and he'd accepted…how was she supposed to feel about that?

When they stepped up to the cheese table, the lump in her stomach made her say, "I've changed my mind, but you go ahead and get whatever you want." It was suddenly a little hard to breathe.

"Okay." Rick picked a single wedge of cheese and a glass of wine and said, "Let's mingle."

Mingling meant standing. The place was packed. Seeing Gloria and Shara struggling through the crowd toward her, Heather was relieved. Maybe she could neutralize the situation until she could get her bearings. As soon as they reached her and Rick, she introduced the women.

"Rick works at Flanagan Manor where I'm doing my internship," she told her friends, who were looking him over like he was eye candy. "And Gloria and Shara used to work for me at Sew Fine," she told him as he slid a proprietary arm around her shoulders. She loved his touch but felt more than a little self-conscious.

And she could tell both Gloria and Shara noted the gesture and were nearly bursting to say something.

Before either of the women could speak, Heather cut in, "Sew Fine is, uh, my Aunt Margaret's quilting shop. I managed it while I was going to school for a while. Now Kristen is in charge." Realizing she hadn't seen her sister this evening, she said, "Kristen is always on time. I wonder what's keeping her."

"Maybe she's waiting on Alex," Shara said.

"Alex doesn't usually run late, either."

"Maybe he has a case to solve," Gloria said.

"Case?" Rick's curious gaze locked onto Heather's.

A little thrill she couldn't deny shot through her. "My sister's fiancé is the Sparrow Lake police chief."

She tore her gaze away from him and noted Shara's smirk.

"Looks like romance in your family is contagious. Kristen and Alex. Margaret and John." Shara grinned. "And now you and—"

"Oh, look, Marcus is here," Heather interrupted as Shara's husband came through the door followed by even more people.

"Ah, he found a parking spot. Talk to you later. C'mon, Gloria."

Gloria arched her eyebrows meaningfully at Heather before following.

The press of guests was becoming as uncomfortable as Heather's growing uncertainty. Left alone with Rick again, she felt awkward. At least he'd removed his arm to help himself to more cheese.

Rick glanced around. "Wow, what a turn-out."

"Great, isn't it?"

"Yeah, just too crowded. Think it's okay to leave?"

Heather frowned. "You want to go already?" Not that she wouldn't have enough company if he left. She knew at least half the people here.

"Well, there's nowhere to sit, and you and I can hardly have a conversation with so many people making so much noise."

Oh. He meant *they* should leave. Heather's stomach did a little dance. "Seems like the whole town is turning out. Where did you want to go instead?"

Rick leaned in close, his breath feathering her ear, sending waves of warmth down to her toes. "I thought maybe we could take a walk or something. Go someplace where we could talk. But only if you're okay with that."

Was she? The way Heather's pulse was ticking, she couldn't deny it. "Sure. I don't think anyone will miss us in this crowd."

Maybe her sister. If Kristen ever made it to the opening.

As they zigzagged their way out of the shop, dodging customers, Heather was aware of the light touch of Rick's hand in the middle of her back.

Once on the sidewalk, Rick asked, "Which way? Is there someplace we can sit outside?"

"Sure. Down by the lake. It's just a bit more than a block from here."

"Sounds perfect."

The late spring evening was indeed perfect. The promise of summer was warming things up. In more than one way, Heather thought, grateful for the errant breeze that cooled off her cheeks. Rain had been predicted for this evening, but a glance up at the sky made her think it wouldn't be any time soon.

"So what would you like to talk about?" Heather asked.

"You know a lot more about me than I do you," Rick said, "so why don't we start there? Tell me about yourself."

"Wait a minute. I know you were in the

army and moved around a lot and that now you work at the estate. And you know that I'm working on an internship to finish my degree, that I have two daughters and a temporary dog and that I used to manage my aunt's quilting store. Sounds like you know more about me."

Rick laughed. "You're right. Okay, I'll go first. What do you want to know?"

"What made you decide to follow in your dad's footsteps?"

"I didn't enlist just because Dad was an army man, but because it gave me the sense of belonging to something important—protecting this country."

Heather swallowed hard. Practically the same thing Scott had said when he'd gone on his second tour of duty. A reminder of why she shouldn't be out here with Rick.

"But with all the moving around because of your dad's job, did you even know this country?"

"Of course I did. Though we lived in other areas of the world later, when I was a kid, Dad was mostly stationed stateside at different bases."

"Did you like moving from place to place?"

"I did. I always got to see something new. To learn about another way of life. New customs."

Did... "And now?"

"I don't know," Rick admitted. "I think I would like having a place I could call home. I'm trying out a different lifestyle. We'll see how it goes."

Which meant he could be around forever… or for hardly any time at all, Heather thought, which was a very distinct possibility that she needed to keep in mind. She told herself she didn't need a romance in her life at the moment. She'd expected to be on her own until the twins got a little older, anyway.

"What if you get bored staying in one place?" she asked.

"It's not the places that attract me." He was looking directly at her when he said, "It's the people. Up until now I had my men. We were a team. Good friends."

He looked away from her and she got the feeling there was something he wasn't saying. "Almost like a family," he went on, staring ahead at the water. "Maybe I'm looking for something else to fulfill me."

Like a family of his own?

Whoa…she wasn't ready to go there. She hadn't even meant to be on a date tonight. Ironic that she'd thought she was trying to give Priscilla a shot at him. She reminded herself that Rick wasn't the right man for her. Better to think of Rick as a good friend than someone with whom she could form a closer relationship.

They'd reached the lake, making her glad for a reason to change the conversation.

"This is one of the public access points," she said, indicating the sloped pathway down to the water's edge. "We can go down to the shoreline and walk around the lake, or we could find a place to sit."

"Let's find that place to sit. I think it's a little late in the evening for walking around the lake. It'll be dark soon."

It was already dusk. The moon was glimmering in the distant sky, and a handful of streetlights made the area around them glow softly.

"We can sit on the grass closer to the water," she said, "or we can walk a little farther and grab one of the benches along the path."

"Your preference?"

"I'll leave it to you."

"Considering your choice of profession, I would guess grass would be *your* choice. And mine," he quickly added. "Don't worry, I haven't been mowing around here."

They laughed together, a good sound that lifted her mood. Heather couldn't have too much laughter in her life.

"Hmm, you know me better than you

thought." She pointed to a flat grassy spot above the water line. "How about right over there?"

"Looks perfect."

They sat a yard or so apart. Although there weren't any boats with motors on the lake, a sailboat still skimmed the water. And in the distance, along the opposite shoreline, Heather spotted a couple of rowboats, too. Undoubtedly dedicated fishermen who might have been out there all day. The wind was picking up now, and another glance at the sky revealed dark rain clouds rolling in.

"You like the water," he observed.

"Love it. My mother always said I was a water baby. She had to keep an eagle eye on me whenever we visited Aunt Margaret because I would head straight for the lake."

"Then you must enjoy working at Flanagan Manor."

"Being right on Lake Michigan is a big plus. But I would love the job even if it was inland. It's taken me so long to get to the place where I can be paid for what I want to do. And now I can. It doesn't get much better than that."

"It is great that you can be paid for doing something you love."

"What about you? Do you love what you do?"

Thoughtful for a moment, Rick finally said,

"Being a handyman? It's okay for an honest day's pay. I've always liked working with my hands."

"But you don't love it."

"Not exactly."

An odd reply, as if the answer were more complicated than he let on. She studied his strong features for a moment. Darkness was descending, and his face was half in shadow, half illuminated by a nearby streetlight. It made him seem…mysterious. She could sense he was holding something back.

"What about the army?" she asked, her throat tightening. "Did you love that?"

"The work itself? Not always. It can be a tough life. Scary at times. I guess what I loved about it—other than the people—was that I felt like I was doing something not only necessary but important. I must have inherited some kind of protector gene from my father."

"Protecting what you love *is* important." Heather's mood grew more serious. "But sometimes it can be devastating."

"You lost someone…?"

"My husband. He felt it was his duty to keep his country and his family safe. Twice. In Iraq. He didn't come back the second time."

"I'm so sorry. When?"

"Three years ago." She plucked at the grass

next to her leg. "Sometimes it seems like yesterday."

"So you've been raising two little girls, working and going to school at the same time."

"Welcome to my life. The internship is the last of school for a while."

"For a while?"

"I learned a lot about commercial landscaping and naturalizing areas. Lots of green thinking. I want to help make the world a better place for my kids. For everyone. That means I have to learn more. Someday I'll go on to get a four-year degree."

"Considering your circumstances, you've accomplished a lot in a short time." Rick slid his hand over hers and squeezed. "You're an impressive woman, Heather Clarke."

And he was an impressive man. His support warmed her inside. As did the touch of his hand, which she squeezed in return.

"Everyone should do work they love, Rick." Including him. She was certain he could do anything he wanted if he set his mind to it. "If you weren't working as a handyman for Ben Phillips, what would you want to do? What would make you happy?"

He stared at her for a long moment, and she swore she saw longing in his eyes. "Maybe I'm doing what I want to do for now."

Did he mean holding her hand, or his job at the estate? A little flustered, she pulled her hand from his and shifted positions so she was facing him more directly.

"There's nothing wrong with being a handyman." Though she couldn't imagine he made enough money to have that place he wanted to call home. "And living on the estate gives you the opportunity to try out civilian life without having to commit yourself to anything permanent."

"Right."

He seemed as if he wanted to say more.

She asked, "So why does a handyman install security cameras?"

"I told you, it's just part of my job."

"Hmm, I was thinking it might be more than that."

"Don't know what you're talking about."

His words told her one thing, his expression another. There was something more going on at the estate than she knew. But Rick wasn't talking. Even so, she was wondering now about those cameras he'd set up.

"I was just concerned about what might have been going on around the estate to require surveillance."

"Nothing to worry about. Cora saw someone on the property at night, and one morning there was a broken window. Just a precaution."

Rick was trying to make her believe it was nothing, but Heather's antennae were up. She'd had plenty of experience sorting truth from fiction when dealing with the twins.

"Why would someone be casing the place? Or trying to break in?"

"Maybe it was vandalism. Kids…" he said, still not being direct.

She fished for more information. "Does the house have something that someone would want to steal?"

"Antiques, I guess." He laughed. "Unless Red Flanagan actually left behind a treasure somewhere on the property. But that's nothing but a rumor. The Feds cleaned the gangster out and sold his house."

"But someone might believe in the treasure story. Or maybe you're right about the antiques." She suddenly made a connection. "Could an intruder have been responsible for what happened to our sod cutter?"

He shrugged. "If he stepped on it."

Heather's mind was racing. "And minor incidents like that are enough to require security cameras?"

The way he was looking at her, as if he remembered the recording that had so amused him, made Heather flush. And when Rick leaned forward, cupped her cheek and grinned at her, the warmth spread down to her toes. He looked like he wanted to kiss her.

Her eyes widened as he dipped his head closer.

He really was going to kiss her...

She sat frozen, not knowing what to do.

His lips brushing softly across hers made her head go light. This wasn't supposed to be a date, and here he was kissing her. And she wasn't objecting.

When he pulled back, she stared at him in confusion. Before she could decide what to do if he made another move on her, Rick kissed her again.

This kiss was more deliberate, and her body felt light. In contrast, her heart sped up and she could feel her pulse along with other pleasurable sensations. Her lips were tingling sweetly when he pulled back and stared into her eyes. Her heart was thumping even harder when he suddenly started, backed off and stuck his hand in his pocket.

"Sorry." He pulled out his phone and touched the screen several times. Then, frowning, he lunged upright. "I can't believe it."

She remained still, breathless.

"I'm so sorry. I have to get back to the estate."

Something serious was going on. She couldn't see the phone's screen clearly, but they'd talked about how it was hooked up to the security cameras. "What's the matter?"

"Oh, probably just raccoons again." He sounded casual, but his stance was alert and his closed expression reminded her of why her crew had called him a spy.

"Raccoons?" Heather scrambled to her feet. "Where?"

"Near the boathouse."

"Can you see them?"

He shook his head. "I'll walk you back to the shop."

"That's all right. I'm safe here. If you have to go right away, I understand."

His expression regretful, Rick nodded and jogged back to wherever he'd parked.

Heather didn't immediately follow. She thought about his quick reaction to the alert. A few raccoons wandering onto the property wouldn't prompt such concern. Again, she thought about the broken sod cutter and the intimation that an intruder could have damaged it. Would a handyman be responsible for doing something about an intruder? Surely he would just call the authorities. Something didn't add up here.

The wind was picking up, tearing at her hair, and fog was rolling over the water's surface. No sign of the sailboat or fishermen. Getting up, she headed for the shop. She should leave, but Kristen would no doubt be looking for her. Besides, she needed to talk to Priscilla, to apologize for leaving with Rick. She hadn't meant for this to happen. The turn in the evening had been a complete surprise to her.

Along with the surprise that mysterious activities might be happening at the Flanagan estate.

That put a different spin on her view of Rick, and she realized she could easily have something romantic going on with him. Her emotions buffeted her as strongly as the wind. Whether or not she'd planned on it, whether or not she wanted it, no matter the reasons she shouldn't get involved with Rick, her attraction to him was real and growing by leaps and bounds.

What now? she wondered as she re-entered the cheese shop.

Kristen had arrived and was the center of a small group, including Gloria and Shara and her husband.

Thinking she would talk to Priscilla first,

Heather spotted her chatting with a cute dark-haired guy and giving him her card. Hmm. He smiled at Priscilla and backed away, then headed for the door.

Heather took the opportunity to get to Priscilla before another customer did. "Hey, can I talk to you for a minute?"

"Yeah, sure. C'mon." Priscilla indicated Heather should follow her around the back of the counter. "I need to replenish the trays."

Priscilla didn't seem annoyed with the way things turned out. "I'm glad your opening is so successful," Heather said.

"You and me both." Priscilla pulled a couple chunks of cheese from the refrigerator. "Everyone told me I was crazy to start a small business in this economic climate, so such a great turnout gives me hope."

Heather took one of the pieces from her. "And, um, I'm sorry if I led you on about Rick."

Priscilla did a double take. "Sorry that a guy who looks like that is interested in you?"

"Seriously, I didn't know he was."

"Well, now you do."

"He sort of thought I asked him on a date," Heather admitted.

Priscilla laughed. "Wow, you got your wires crossed. No problem, though. Things worked out, anyway. That guy I was just talking to? Let's hope he calls."

Heather was relieved that Priscilla had such a good sense of humor about the situation. Now she just had to figure out what *she* was going to do about Rick.

CHAPTER NINE

As was the case most evenings before bedtime, Cora was curled up in the library, a good book in her hands. The only problem was her lack of concentration. She was no longer reading. Had she heard something out of place on the grounds, or was her imagination playing tricks on her? Maybe it was just the wind that had picked up and whistled along the lake.

The estate had been quiet for the past few hours. Kelly had left after dinner to meet her daughter Natalie in Milwaukee for the weekend. Cora wondered if it would be a fun weekend for the cook, or if her daughter simply needed money again. Gina had complained of a headache, had taken some aspirin and had retired early. And Mr. Guildfren—David—had not yet returned from his play at the Center for the Arts.

She was virtually alone.

So why did she imagine she heard a noise coming from the direction of the lake?

The book slipped from her fingers to the

floor. Pulse fluttering, Cora rose from the chair and went to the windows, which rattled when a gust of wind hit them. As if she could see anything in the dark.

There it was again, another noise that had nothing to do with the now howling wind. Or so she thought.

A slammed door?

The sound came not from the mansion, but from somewhere near the water to the south.

She hurried to the desk set in an alcove and turned on the computer there. Rick wasn't on the grounds tonight, but he had given her the URL and password for a private internet site that would show her feeds from any of the cameras on the grounds. She brought up the site and scanned the series of small frames on the monitor to match each camera. All were black but one—the boathouse.

Someone was in the boathouse!

Some*one* or some*thing*.

She clicked on the boathouse frame so the picture opened to fill the monitor's large screen.

Movement held her frozen for a second. Not a figure. Not a person. Floaty, that's what it was. Weird looking.

Floaty and out of focus, like something trying to materialize!

Heart pounding, hands shaking, Cora turned off the computer, went back to the windows and stared out into the dark night for some time. Fog was rolling in, and a light rain began to fall. Several minutes passed. Nothing to see. Nothing at all. She didn't want to face it, but she'd suspected it for a while.

Flanagan Manor really was haunted...

Soft footsteps along the hallway made her knees buckle. She stopped herself from falling by clinging to the window ledge. Turning, she set her back against the frame, felt her heart jump up into her throat and waited to see whatever was about to confront her.

David Guildfren entered the room, his lined face softening when he saw her. "Ah, there you are, Cora." He stopped short and frowned. "My dear, you look so pale. Is something wrong?"

She sagged with relief. "Oh, thank heavens it's you!"

"Well, of course it's me. Who else did you expect?"

"No one." She shook her head. "No one at all."

"Come. Sit. Let me get you something to drink."

Cora sat gingerly in one of the wingback chairs, but protested, "No, nothing, but thank you."

Touched by David's concern for her, Cora wondered if he would ever express more than friendship. He'd been coming to the mansion for several years now, and he had always sought her company. Now that she was no longer alone, she felt her breathing slow.

Noticing he seemed distracted, she asked, "Your play—did you enjoy it?"

"Yes, yes, of course."

But he didn't look like he had.

"Though it might have been better if…"

"If what?" Cora asked. "I think I should be asking you if there is something wrong."

"Oh, it's nothing." He sighed and shook his head. "My mind is simply on my business. These economic times are proving to be more difficult than I ever expected."

"When you were here for the holidays in December, I thought you said you were thinking of selling."

"I was until I came to grips with reality. An antique store is not as viable a business as it used to be. I need to hang in a while longer so I can fund my retirement properly." He gave her a sad smile. "Otherwise, I wouldn't have enough money for my little sojourns to this lovely estate."

"Oh, that would be a crime."

"Indeed." He shook his head. "My dear

Cora, I fear I'm off to bed early tonight. Perhaps we can play cards tomorrow night?"

"Of course."

He nodded. "Until then." And left the room.

Cora sighed. She and David had spent many an evening playing cards. He always made her feel like the center of his attention by encouraging her to talk about her work and the history of the estate. She suspected he was as attracted to her as she was to him, and she wondered if he would ever attempt to take their relationship a step forward.

Thinking about the fright she'd had a short while ago, Cora decided she would rather dream on that possibility than on what she'd seen on the computer.

DESPITE THE FOG and rain, Rick arrived at the estate in record time. He only hoped it was fast enough to catch the evasive interloper.

Had the man found an entrance to the tunnels in the boathouse? He'd been messing with the canvas covering one of the boats.

The question was why?

Rick wondered if the man had found whatever he was looking for, and if so, whether he intended to remove his booty in one of the boats via the lake.

Jumping out of his truck in the parking

lot, Rick ran past the mansion and across the lawn. He'd nearly reached the boathouse when he heard a motor come to life. He sped up but barely got in the door as one of the boats moved out of the building and onto the lake, the fog masking the man's identity.

"Hey!" he yelled, though he knew his shout was no use.

Swallowing his frustration, he started the mechanism to lower a second boat into the water while he removed the canvas covering. He jumped in and undid the lines as he started the motor. Less than two minutes behind the intruder, he took the boat out of the building and into the fog.

He stopped to listen, the fog moving about him like a thick veil. Another motor was rumbling to the south so he headed straight for it, but between the fog deadening the sound and the noise of his own engine, he couldn't keep a bead on the other boat.

Still, he refused to give up so easily. He zigzagged through the area for as long as he could hear the other motor. When he shut his down to listen, and all he detected was the sound of waves hitting the rocks, he realized it was no use. The man had gotten away.

Frustrated, he headed back for the boathouse, where he spent too much time trying to get in without crashing his boat against the wall. Wet and discouraged, he tied up the craft, lifted it back out of the water and went straight to the coach house.

If he had only been here when the alert came in, he would have caught the intruder. As it was, nearly twenty minutes had passed before the person made his getaway. What had he been doing?

Rick regretted not being able to stop him.

But he didn't regret being with Heather. He liked her. More than liked her. He thought about her sweet face, about his lips brushing hers…about the aborted deeper kiss he'd like to have shared with her. Spending the evening with her had been the best time he'd had since becoming a civilian.

Entering his quarters, he stripped off his wet clothes. He needed a hot shower. But first he was going to check the recording on his laptop so he could get a better look at the guy.

Another disappointment.

He mostly saw canvas fluttering. And a man's back. Then nothing. The recording ended. But another one followed when the man returned to the boathouse. More of the same, only this time, it looked like he was carrying something that he stowed in the boat. He'd undoubtedly had enough time to set up the boat before taking the tunnel into the conservatory and stealing something from the mansion. But why one of their boats? He must have walked onto the property and whatever he'd stolen had been too heavy to carry back out on foot.

Rick looked at the time codes on both recordings. Eighteen minutes apart. Yep. About the same time it had taken him to return to the estate from Sparrow Lake. It seemed the intruder had prepared the boat, then had gone to get whatever it was he'd come for.

Watching the second recording again, he hoped to see something that would identify the man, who was dressed in dark clothing. His hair, spiked weirdly as if he'd slept on one side, wasn't dark, but Rick couldn't discern the color without more light. The man hadn't turned on the overheads and the camera needed adjustment.

Something he would do first thing in the morning. That and look for another tunnel entrance in the boathouse itself. Plus, he needed to talk to Cora. She'd be the only one who would know if anything had been taken from the house. Too late now. She'd been having trouble sleeping and he didn't want to wake her if she'd gone to bed early.

Too bad he couldn't look forward to seeing Heather in the morning. He had the whole weekend to miss her company. He should have gotten her phone number before leaving. Chances were he could get it, but maybe he should keep things low key for a while. She was definitely a little skittish, and he didn't want to scare her away.

Good thing he was a patient man.

RICK WAS ON Heather's mind all the way home. Despite her objections that he wasn't the man for her, she was definitely attracted to him. Having been alone for three long years, perhaps she was ready for something new in her life. Something other than work. Someone special.

But what if Rick decided to re-enlist? If she got involved with him and he went back to the army, that would break her heart. And she had the twins to think of. What about their little hearts? They'd lived half their lives without a daddy, and if they got attached to Rick and he left…

Dashing through the rain to her front door, she was grateful when it swung open without her having to stand there getting soaked while she unlocked it.

"Forget your umbrella?" Brian asked.

"I was in such a hurry to get out the door, I simply didn't think about the weather." She kissed her brother on the cheek as she passed him. "Did the girls behave for you?"

He closed the door. "For the most part."

"What?"

"Nothing terrible. Go take a look."

Heather went to the twins' room and peeked in. Both girls were in one bed. And the dog was sleeping between them. Taylor had her arm around him, and his front paws were pushed up against Addison's chest.

Heather smiled as she closed the door. "What am I going to do about that dog?" No one had responded to the flyers that Brian had tacked up everywhere in town for her.

"Nothing if you don't want to."

"What does that mean?" she asked as she made her way into the living room, where a fairly large cage sat in the middle of the floor. "And what is that?"

"A kennel for Kirby. Look, sis, don't kill us, okay, but Kristen and I talked about you keeping the dog."

"Brian, that's just not possible right now."

"We want to make it possible. Kristen said she would pay for the vet and license and food until you could afford it. And I said I would take care of the guy while you're working. You know, come over and walk him midday.

At least until school starts again at the end of summer. And after that, whenever I can."

"You didn't promise the girls—"

"Of course not. We weren't sure you would agree."

She indicated the kennel. "You must have been pretty sure."

"Well, until you find a home for him, you need a way to make sure he doesn't get into trouble around here when he's left alone. Kirby is such a cool dog, Heather. Let us do this for you and the twins. And for him, poor guy."

Heather laughed at the way her brother was laying it on so thick. "I'll think about it."

"Good. Then it's time for me to get out of here."

"Yeah, I still have some work to take care of on the computer tonight." Unfortunately, she had a couple of tasks to do for Sew Fine before she could go to sleep.

"Don't stay up too late."

"Now who's thinking he's the older sibling? I used to tuck you into bed."

Brian just laughed as she walked him to the door, where she gave him a big hug. "Thanks."

After he left, she thought about how in the past year he'd straightened out and grown into a responsible young adult. He was someone they could count on, and that was a good feeling.

Having a man she could count on was a pretty good feeling, too.

Rick…

What was she going to do about him?

She was so conflicted.

She could still feel the brush of his lips on her own. Could feel her heart speed up when he kissed her more thoroughly. She wondered what it would have been like if they hadn't been interrupted, if he'd kept on kissing her.

Only one man had ever really kissed her before.

She removed a scrapbook from a lower shelf of the side table and sat on the couch with it. This was her and Scott's story. The memories they'd made together. Photos of them dating in high school. Of their wedding. Of Taylor and Addison as babies.

They were only three when their father was taken from them.

Remembering the DVD Taylor had been watching the other morning, Heather picked up the controllers from the coffee table and turned on the television and the DVD player.

There they were, Scott stooping to smooth Taylor's hair…

"You're Daddy's little girl," he said, kissing

her on the cheek. *"You'll always be Daddy's girl."*

"Forever and ever?"

"Forever and ever. Cross my heart."

Heather put the DVD on pause the way she'd done with her heart since learning the love of her life had been killed in Iraq. Forever and ever—that's the way it should have been, but he hadn't been able to keep that promise.

He'd been gone from her life for so long.

He could never hold her or kiss her again.

Scott wouldn't want her to be alone forever.

He'd want her to be happy.

Could she forget the only man she'd ever loved and make new memories with someone else?

With Rick?

CHAPTER TEN

"THAT WASN'T A ghost you saw," Rick assured Cora the next morning after he got her alone in the library to talk about the break-in.

Driving rain hadn't stopped several new guests—a newly married couple, a retired couple and a youngish couple with a teenage girl and a little boy—from checking in. Rick had found Cora talking to them in the dining room, where they'd been about to have breakfast, so he'd asked her to join him in the library for a few minutes. He hadn't expected this nervous, uncertain version of the woman he'd deemed competent the moment they'd met.

"I don't know," Cora muttered. "That wasn't the first time I wondered about the place being haunted by Red Flanagan himself. I saw something on the balcony, too. And those noises in the wall—"

"Were made by the intruder, who found his way into the secret passageways," Rick said, stopping at the window to stare out at the continuing storm. The rain hadn't stopped, and now the winds had picked up, so the fog had lifted, leaving the lake itself turbulent. Waves beat against the shoreline, pitching up several feet in the areas lined with rocks. "I assure you that was a flesh-and-blood man you saw in the boathouse, Cora. I chased him out onto the lake."

But Cora didn't look convinced. "Where he disappeared into the fog, right?"

"He *and* the boat he took out. A ghost wouldn't be able to do anything with a boat. Besides, I saw him, Cora, just not his face. Flesh and blood."

She closed her eyes for a second and let out a sigh. "You must think I'm a foolish old woman."

"No, I don't. You've had reason to be spooked. What I think is that you're someone I can count on."

Her eyes flashed open. "To do what?"

"To figure out what he took, for starters." Rick looked around the room, filled with books and some memorabilia of the 1920s. "If anyone knows what belongs in this house, you do. Something is missing. The man's a thief. He uncovered the boat, then disappeared for eighteen minutes then reappeared with his booty. That was enough time for him to get into the house, take what he wanted, then get back to the boat. Unfortunately, I couldn't tell what he was carrying."

"Are you saying he broke in? Where? Is there another window that needs repair?"

"No, no, take it easy." This situation was getting to the poor woman. Cora looked on the verge of nervous collapse.

"He used a tunnel—probably the one to the conservatory. I found the entrance from the coach house yesterday. He must have known the tunnels were there." And the intruder apparently had enough time—and the right equipment—to get through, if the cement rubble inside the tunnel were any indication.

He hesitated a moment. "Any idea where he could have found out about them?"

"Absolutely none." Cora sighed. "Since you arrived, I've done a lot of thinking about this. I recall that Mr. Phillips told me once that he had a partial map of the tunnels. It took him quite a bit of research—and time and money— to find it. The federal government had them sealed off back in the thirties."

"Did Phillips show the map to you?"

"No, he just talked about it."

"Could he have shown it to anyone else?"

"He sometimes shares historical information with those who appreciate it, like David."

"Guildfren, huh?"

She looked dismayed. "You don't think David—"

"I'm looking at everything and everyone," he stated honestly, though he certainly hoped her gentleman friend had nothing to do with the situation. To get her mind off that possibility, he said, "I could use a copy of that map myself."

"I'll call Mr. Phillips and ask him where he's keeping it. I know he has a personal wall safe."

"Which means he will have to be present to open it."

"Yes, and he's in New York on business at the moment."

Rick nodded. Okay, the map would have to wait. "This morning I ransacked the boathouse until I found an entrance into the main tunnel there, too."

He'd also adjusted the camera so that next time—if there was a next time—he would get a better look at the guy. He would have secured both entrances, but he wanted to catch the intruder in the act. And he didn't think the man was done with the estate.

"Oh, my," Cora said softly.

Rick could tell she was still worrying about her friend. "You said David—Mr. Guildfren— came in from an evening in town after you saw the footage of the boathouse."

"Yes."

"So why don't you ask him if he noticed anything out of the ordinary?"

She nodded slowly. "I can do that."

Rick thought for a moment. "Also, I know you trust your workers, but is there anyone who is worried about money for some reason?"

Cora shook her head and then her expression shifted. "Well, not for herself."

"Who are you talking about?"

"Kelly. Her daughter Natalie has gotten into some financial trouble."

Kelly, the cook, who lived at the mansion. "Natalie lives in Kenosha?"

"No, in Milwaukee. That's where Kelly is this weekend. She's visiting her daughter before the summer season gets into full swing next weekend. Then she won't be able to get away until fall. Her summer assistant is doing the cooking until she returns."

"What about this Natalie?" Rick asked. "What kind of financial trouble is she having?"

"I—I don't like to gossip."

"Cora, I need to know anything that could give me a lead to the intruder."

"Oh." The color drained from her face. "I—I didn't realize…" She took a deep breath and said, "Natalie was passing bad checks last year.

Kelly basically has been supporting her until she finds a better job."

Which made Rick wonder about the daughter rather than Kelly herself. Maybe this Natalie was going beyond taking financial advantage of her mother and getting someone to steal valuables from Flanagan Manor. He wouldn't say such a thing to Cora, though. She obviously was uncomfortable with the subject.

"I need to get back to those security checks I was doing on the employees," he said instead. "And you'll look around to see what might be missing?"

Cora nodded. "All right. I will give the house a thorough once-over. I'll start with the butler's pantry right this minute." She clucked to herself as she headed in the direction of the kitchen.

And Rick headed for his quarters and his laptop.

As he raced across the grounds through the rain, he looked out at the areas that the EPI crew had been working on. He wished it weren't the weekend and that it wasn't raining, so he could watch Heather with her team. Not even a day since he'd seen her and he missed her already. Missed her smile. Her laugh. Her outrage when she was challenging him.

Thinking about the footage of her that he'd

deleted, he couldn't help smiling all the way to his quarters in spite of the weather.

Still…Monday seemed a long, long time away.

MONDAY MORNING DIDN'T come soon enough for Heather. Thankfully, the rain had stopped midday on Sunday. She hoped the ground wouldn't be too wet because she'd scheduled planting for today. She arrived at the manor at the same time as the EPI truck, which was filled with pots of grasses and perennials, plus several flats of flowering annuals for instant color. Her team had worked so hard last week and Heather was looking forward to the planting.

And she was looking forward to seeing Rick again.

All weekend she'd wondered what he'd found when he'd hightailed it back to the mansion from Sparrow Lake. She was anxious to learn whether or not he'd solved the mystery. And if he had, would he even tell her about it?

To her disappointment, he didn't seem to be around. Probably better for her focus, she thought as she helped Tyrone and Amber transfer the plants from the truck to the cart and then from the parking lot to lakeside.

They were on the last load when Rick finally appeared.

"There's the man," Tyrone said.

Amber waved. "Hey, Rick."

While Heather stood silent, her pulse accelerated with each step that brought him closer to her. He was staring at her, making it impossible for her to move.

When he stopped in front of her and said, "Heather," in a tone that curled her toes, she grinned up at him. "Rick."

Tyrone cleared his throat. "So what do you want us to do with this load, boss?"

Heather looked at him in confusion for a second. "Oh, the plants. Put them with the others."

Tyrone was grinning at her.

Amber playfully punched her coworker in the arm. "C'mon, give them a minute."

Give them a minute? Was Amber aware of the nondate date?

Good grief. Nothing like having everyone know her business.

"Did you have a nice weekend?" Rick asked.

"Lovely. I spent it taking care of some paperwork for Sew Fine's online store. But never mind what I did. What happened here Friday night after you left? Did you nail those pesky raccoons?"

"I wish." Rick looked around as if making

sure no one would overhear and then said, "Lost them in the fog."

"That's too bad." Really, it was. So why didn't she feel bad? In fact, she had to laugh. "Okay, look, I know we're not talking about raccoons. Did you figure out who set off the security alert?" For a moment, she thought he wasn't going to tell her. "C'mon, Rick."

He gazed at her for a second. "Since you've made some pretty good guesses, I want your word you aren't going to tell anyone else."

He looked so solemn, she became serious, too. "Of course, you have my word." A little thrill went through her. "Was it vandals?"

"A thief. He took something from the mansion. Cora spent half the weekend scouring the place to determine what was gone."

Heather became concerned. She had intuitively felt the security issue must be serious, but she hadn't expected a real robber to be stalking the estate. "What was stolen?"

"Cora finally figured out a candelabra is missing. Antique silver. And it belonged to Red Flanagan."

"Didn't just about everything that's old here belong to him at some point?"

"This candelabra had special significance. It is in the portrait of Flanagan in the rotunda."

Heather had never seen the portrait. Or the

rotunda. She'd been in the kitchen once, talking over her plans with Ben Phillips, but she hadn't had reason to tour the house.

"Was the candelabra valuable?" she asked.

"According to Cora, it was a Tiffany with seven lights. She estimates its worth at fifteen thousand dollars."

"Yikes, I'll bet Mr. Phillips wasn't too happy."

"No, but it was insured. We made a report with the local authorities, so it will be covered."

"The police?" she asked.

"This isn't the first time I talked to Detective Morse about the situation. I told him there have been multiple incidents, break-ins, over the past several weeks, but this is the first time anything was stolen."

Multiple break-ins? No wonder Rick had been installing security cameras. And he was definitely more than a handyman, Heather thought.

"But the candelabra was part of the house's history," she said. "I doubt there's a way to insure for that sort of loss. Is there any way you can get it back? The thief might have a hard time selling such a unique item."

"The police took a detailed description and are going to keep an eye on the local pawn shops and antique stores. They also dusted for fingerprints one afternoon when the guests were out. We're keeping it quiet."

"Yeah, a theft like that can't be good for business."

Just then, Tyrone yelled, "Hey, boss, you want us to get started here?"

Heather's pulse jumped.

"I'm coming!" Her gaze locked with Rick's as she backed away. "I need to get to work, but I'll keep an eye out for anything out of place. I'll also keep my mouth shut." He'd trusted her enough to confide in her and she wouldn't let him down.

"Thanks." He smiled. "Talk to you this afternoon."

She would be looking forward to that.

Ten minutes later, Heather was hard at work. First she checked the soil by grabbing a handful and forming it into a ball that easily crumbled. Perfect. If it had stayed clumped, they would have had to wait to plant to avoid compacting the soil.

She and Amber were placing plants on the first rain garden site, mixing and matching, creating a flow that, when mature, would look like natural drifts. Tyrone had gone to the coach house to load the cart with planting tools.

Wondering what was taking him so long, Heather stepped back to get an all-inclusive view of the area they were working on. "What do you think?" she asked Amber.

"I think it already looks great," Amber said. "I'm glad you got gallon-sized plants instead of plugs."

The seedlings grown in trays would have taken far longer to gain maximum growth. "We'll have to use plugs and even seeds on some of the bigger areas on the other side of the terrace." Otherwise the cost of a project this size would be prohibitive to her fairly generous budget. "But it made sense to use plants with some maturity this close to the house. People won't trample over them, and they should fill in by the end of summer."

"And next year, they'll double in size."

"Let's get in the Little Bluestem first." Heather loved the bronze-kissed blue-gray foliage that would turn to a gorgeous purple-bronze in fall. "If we ever get our tools." Frowning, she looked around for Tyrone and finally saw him coming from the coach house with the cart. "Ah, there he is! I wonder what took him so long."

"He probably got a call from his new girl-friend," Amber said with a snort.

Heather shrugged. If Tyrone had a little romance in his life, then good for him. He was a hard worker, so she wasn't going to give him grief over taking a few minutes for himself.

But when Tyrone stopped at the edge of the garden, he was scowling. "You won't believe this, but one of the new garden shovels is gone."

"What do you mean gone?" Heather asked.

"Disappeared…vanished…maybe borrowed by someone who didn't return it."

"Uh, oh," Amber mumbled. "The Terminator strikes again."

Heather shook her head, thinking about the conversation she'd had with Rick. "I doubt it."

"Whatever you say, boss." Tyrone sounded skeptical. "So what do you want me to do?"

"Start digging with the shovel you have. The two of you keep working on the first bed and I'll finish setting up the other one."

Which meant arranging the plants in the second rain garden in a mirror-image of the first. Tyrone and Amber got to work.

Heather got to work, too, but she was thinking about the missing shovel. She really didn't believe that Rick would borrow it. Could the same thief who'd stolen the candelabra have taken off with the tool? But why?

And should she be concerned about the

other equipment EPI left on the estate every weekend?

Certain Rick would have a theory, she would tell him about the missing shovel at the first opportunity.

HALFWAY THROUGH THE afternoon and most of the way through his security checks, Rick stopped when Keith Murphy called to tell him that he was in Chicago and wanted to drive up to Kenosha to meet for dinner. Though Rick agreed, the idea of seeing his best friend—of being reminded of the last mission they'd shared—put him on edge. He told himself not to dwell on it, but he was so unsettled inside that he left his laptop in the midst of a search.

He needed some fresh air.

Not wanting to face anyone at the moment, he stayed to the back of the property and walked past the boathouse to the southern end of the estate. Though the storm had abated the day before, the lake was still restless. He climbed on the wall of broken rocks that stopped the lake from eroding the land and sat down on one of them. He concentrated on watching the waves come in so he wouldn't see what he didn't want to—the tragic photograph burned forever in his mind.

He'd been in charge of a special ops team

assigned to find and rescue military hostages in Afghanistan. His informant had told him three men who'd been taken the week before were being held in a cave deep in the mountains. She'd even drawn a map for him.

Rick had had no reason to distrust the woman, who'd given him good information several times before. But he'd been duped. He and Murphy had gone in first, through a tunnel that had taken them to the cave. No hostages. Suddenly, the tunnel behind them had blown to smithereens. Nothing had been left of his two men to bury.

If not for Murphy, he might have lost it. Murphy had forced him to keep fighting, to find a way out.

That had been nearly nine months ago, but he could still see every detail as if it had happened yesterday. He couldn't stop thinking that he should somehow have known it was a trap. He'd been responsible for his men, and he'd trusted the wrong person and now he had to live with the guilt.

Raised an army brat, Rick himself had served for fifteen years. Since childhood, he'd been aware that soldiers died in battle. He'd *known* soldiers who *had* died. But this was different. This had been personal. This had been ugly. These men had been his friends. He and Murphy had been lucky to survive and escape.

Afterward, he hadn't been able to get what happened out of his head. Or, worse, out of his dreams. When he'd started avoiding sleeping so he wouldn't be confronted with that nightmare, he'd known he had to try something else, something away from a combat zone. Murphy had stayed in to fight the good fight, while Rick was trying his best to settle into civilian life. He had to admit that he missed the good parts of his old life. Being part of a unit was like being part of a family. As it was, he was alone too much. People were around him, of course. But not people he knew well. Or people he cared to know well. All except for...

"Rick, are you okay?"

...*Heather*.

He glanced up at her worried expression. His mood immediately lightened simply at the sight of her.

"Yeah, sure."

He was about to get to his feet when she dropped down beside him.

"I called you several times, but I guess you didn't hear me."

"Sorry. I was just thinking." Oddly enough about her. He was glad for the interruption, for the respite from the memories. "So, you need me to help you with something?"

"Not exactly. I was waiting for you to come outside so I could speak to you. Alone. I think the thief has been at it again."

Not expecting that, he asked, "Why? What's missing?"

"Nothing expensive like that silver candelabra. Just one of our new shovels. When Tyrone went to fetch the planting tools, he couldn't find it. He said he looked around the coach house, but it was gone. I'm assuming you didn't borrow it."

"Nope. Not me." His mind was already whirling. "What in the world would the thief have wanted with a shovel?"

A smile hovered on her lips. "To dig for buried treasure?"

Rick couldn't help but laugh. "I don't think Red Flanagan buried his booty. Legend says he had a hidden room where he kept a secret stash. If that's true, I haven't found it yet." He'd asked Mr. Phillips about the partial map that had been made of the tunnels, only to be told it was here in the safe as Cora had suggested. So much for that. Phillips hadn't been willing to give him the combination.

"So you've looked for it?" Heather inquired. "The treasure?"

"Not exactly." He'd been busy making more small repairs around the estate in addition to the security checks.

Her brows pulled together over her now serious blue eyes. "I can't believe someone is creeping around here at night. And messing with our stuff, too. First the sod cutter was damaged and now one of my shovels is missing."

"You know what? I'll replace it."

"That's very generous of you, but it's not your responsibility."

"It went missing on the property, and I have a discretionary fund for supplies and equipment. Don't worry about it."

"Um, okay, I guess."

"I can get a new one when I go into town a little later," he said, adding, "I'm having dinner with an old army buddy."

"Oh." She frowned and looked away. "I'd better get back…"

"Later."

Nodding, she jogged off, obviously in a hurry for some reason.

Rick sighed. If only he could be going to dinner with her.

CHAPTER ELEVEN

TAYLOR STRUGGLED OUT of the booster seat in the neighbor's van when they got to where Mommy worked. She jumped to the ground while Mommy helped Addison.

Why did they have to come here after camp? This was the place where that big man stopped her from having a good time with her dog.

"Mrs. Sola, thank you for driving them here," Mommy told Zooey's mother.

Addison waved to Zooey in the backseat, and their friend waved back.

"No problem," Mrs. Sola said. "I live practically across the street."

"We're not going home yet," Mommy said. "We have just a couple more plants to put in. Then we have to spread mulch and put away our tools."

Taylor sighed. "How long?"

"Maybe fifteen minutes. You can sit on the terrace and wait for me…" she pointed to the side of the house that had that glass place with plants inside "...or you can walk around as long as you stay together."

"Yay! We get to see the lake!" Addison shouted, already running.

"Stay away from the water!" Mommy yelled.

As if seeing the lake was some big deal, Taylor thought, when all she wanted to see was Kirby.

Taylor followed her sister, stopping short when she saw Addison talking to that man. Tyrone had told her he was The Terminator. She wasn't sure what that meant, but she would call him that, too. Right now, he was bending down and staring at Addison through those dumb sunglasses.

"So how is your dog?" he asked.

"He's great!" Addison said. "Now he lives with us."

"Your mom is going to let you keep him?"

Addison nodded. "He was a stray and he needed a forever home. He's *our* dog now."

Taylor scowled. Kirby was *her* dog!

"Yeah, I know what it's like to have nowhere to call home," The Terminator said. "I'm something of a stray myself."

Taylor moved away from them. Mommy said they could walk anywhere, so she walked around the house, stopping by the glass room, where she peered inside. So many plants. And flowers. Mommy said it was too early for most flowers now, but there were tons of them on the other side of the glass.

It looked like a cool place to hang out.

Why not?

No one was going to miss her, anyway.

"OKAY, READY TO GO," Heather said when the tools were safely locked up in the coach house. She was being extra careful about them now.

Addison was entertaining Rick, if the smile on his face was any indication. While she watched, the little girl made expansive gestures, Rick nodding like he understood everything.

"Hey, Addison," Heather called. Rick looked in her direction. "Gotta go," she told him.

"I'll walk you to the parking lot." He was talking to Addison, but Heather realized his attention was focused on her.

"Have a nice night," Amber said as she and Tyrone headed for the EPI truck.

"You, too." Heather realized she didn't see Taylor. When Addison took her hand, she asked, "Where's your sister?"

Addison shrugged. "She ran off somewhere."

Heather looked to Rick. "Did you see where she went?"

"Sorry, no."

"Taylor!" she yelled. "We're going now!"

But no little blond head poked out from anywhere.

Thinking that Taylor was playing a game with her, she called again. "Come out, come out, wherever you are!"

And got exactly zero response.

Now she was getting a bit concerned. "I'd better look for her. Addison, are you sure you haven't seen your sister?"

Addison's little face puckered as she shook her head a second time. "I was talking to Rick."

Realizing she was scaring her daughter, Heather gave her a quick hug. "I'm not upset with you. I'm sure Taylor is just hiding on us. You can get in the SUV and wait while I find her, okay?"

"'Kay."

Heather made sure Addison went straight to the vehicle and climbed in the back before taking her eyes off the girl. "I don't know whether to be annoyed or worried."

Rick told her, "I don't think there's anything to worry about, but I'll help you look for her."

"Thanks."

Heather was pretty sure Taylor wouldn't like Rick getting in the middle of things, but she didn't care at the moment. She didn't appreciate her daughter trying to scare her like this. Truth be told, it was working.

They set off over the grounds, heading south toward the boathouse. Heather's worried gaze continually flicked out to the lake, though she'd cautioned the twins over and over not to go near the water.

"Taylor, honey, it's time to go home!"

She tried keeping her voice normal, as if nothing was wrong.

What if Taylor decided to play at the shoreline and a big wave swept her out into the lake? But surely she would have screamed and someone would have heard her.

"Taylor, where are you?"

With each passing minute, her fear that something had happened to her child grew, making it harder and harder for Heather to breathe normally.

"I'll check inside." Rick indicated the boathouse.

"Wouldn't your cell have warned you the camera went on?"

"I'll check, anyway. You keep going, and I'll catch up to you."

Heather swallowed hard and nodded. She kept walking, calling out for Taylor every few seconds. A few minutes later, she was at the property fence line, and Rick jogged over to her.

"The boathouse was empty. No sign of anyone having been in there. Sorry."

"Rick, where could she be?" Heather was fighting tears now. "I was only gone for—"

"Hey, don't blame yourself." He put his arms around her and rubbed her back. "Taylor's a little kid. Something got her attention, and she probably went off to investigate."

Heather leaned into him, appreciating his attempt at comforting her, even if wasn't working. "But why isn't she answering when I call her?"

"Come on." His arm around her shoulders, Rick led her back toward the house. "Maybe she can't hear you."

"You think she wandered off the property?"

"Not necessarily."

He didn't let go of her until they reached the terrace, where a couple of the guests sat talking.

"Have you seen a little girl wandering around here?" Rick asked.

"No," the man said.

"I hope she's all right," the woman added.

"Thanks." Heather swallowed hard.

Rick examined the ground as they walked closer to the house.

"What are you looking for?"

"Footprints. The rain might have stopped yesterday, but the ground is still damp."

Heather looked, too, but Rick was the one who spotted the prints in the garden area outside the conservatory.

"Made by little sneakers," he said, then turned his attention upward. "And someone opened the conservatory door."

Heather could see the door hadn't quite latched properly. She never would have noticed if Rick hadn't pointed it out.

"Thank goodness. She's probably inside."

Rick opened the door and indicated Heather should go first. As she met his gaze, she hoped he could read the depth of her gratitude for his help.

The conservatory was warm and humid and filled with tropical plants. Greenery and bromeliads and bird of paradise. But the orchids were most spectacular, several cultivars in different colors dotting every area in the large room.

"Taylor, are you in here?"

No answer.

"Taylor, come out now!"

Assuming her child was hiding from her, Heather started searching the conservatory, taking a small pathway into a jungle-thick area. Rick searched in the other direction.

When it became obvious Taylor was no-where to be found, Heather asked, "Can she get into the house from here?"

"She can if the door is unlocked." Rick was already heading for it. "I'll check." He jiggled the handle, but the door didn't budge. "Nope."

"Where else could she be?"

She noticed him running his hand along a wall.

"Wait a minute. You said there might be se-cret rooms…"

"There are hidden passageways here and there in the house. Tunnels."

"Tunnels?" Heather's heart beat faster. Was there no end to the mysteries around here? She fought back her rising panic. "Could Taylor have found her way into a secret passageway?"

"I doubt it. The entry spots are concealed and not easy to open." He slid his hand under a potting bench. Heather heard a sharp click and part of the wall popped open. She moved to join him and saw a dozen stairs leading down-ward into darkness.

"There's no light?"

Was her child down there? Heather was quickly losing her sense of equilibrium, her breathing rapid.

"It'll be okay." Rick pulled out his phone and turned on the flashlight app. "This is good enough for me to take a look. You stay up here and watch for her."

"All right."

Remaining in the conservatory, Heather walked over to the windows to look outside but turned at a noise behind her. Taylor stood there, barely a yard away. Relief flooded her.

"Rick!" she called. "You can come back. I found her!"

"Are we going home now?" Taylor asked as if nothing was wrong.

Heather could finally breathe again. The little girl looked just fine other than some streaks of dirt on her clothes and skin. She and Addison used to love to hide in tiny spaces, but Heather couldn't imagine where she'd done so in here. Under one of the tables? Or behind a large potted palm?

"Where were you?" Heather demanded as Rick came up behind her.

Taylor's expression suddenly darkened when she saw him. "Nowhere."

"Never disappear on me like that again! You scared me." When her daughter didn't say anything, Heather added, "Taylor, do you hear me?"

The little girl shrugged. "Yes." Her mouth tightened.

She was being Taylor-impossible, as only she could be, Heather realized. No sense in having it out here. Besides, she wanted to wait a bit, so she could first reasonably explain why Taylor should never scare her like that again. She turned the girl toward the door.

"You and I are going to have a talk when we get home."

Glancing back, Heather saw Rick staring after them, his expression thoughtful. She silently mouthed *thank you,* and he simply nodded in acknowledgment and waved.

Taylor remained sullen all the way to the parking lot, but once inside the SUV with her chatty twin, she seemed to be in a better mood. She left the girls to themselves on the ride home, while she calmed down. She'd never had a scare like that before. She was beginning to feel a little creeped out by the Flanagan estate. Thieves and now secret tunnels. She hadn't even asked Rick if the intruder had gotten in via a secret passageway or broken a window. They hadn't had time to talk.

"That house is like a castle," Addison told Taylor, "from one of our books. And you were like a princess kept there by a dragon. That's why we couldn't find you."

"A big ugly Rick dragon!" agreed Taylor.

"Oh, he isn't so ugly," objected Addison.

"He's mean!" said Taylor.

"No, he isn't."

"Girls, girls," said Heather. How did they manage so often to make things into an argument? "Rick is not a dragon." Though she had no idea if one might dwell in the mansion's secret tunnels.

Addison leaned forward. "But Taylor is a princess."

"Well, I can agree to that. You're *both* princesses."

"And we're in a punkin."

"Uh-huh, this car is a pumpkin," Heather agreed, enjoying the imaginative play. "And we're going home to our own little castle where I'll serve you sloppy joes for your royal supper."

"And then we'll stay up late and watch a movie!" Addison went on enthusiastically.

"I don't know about that." But Heather laughed. Then she started thinking about whether or not she wanted the twins to set foot on the estate again. Considering they were at camp nearby and needed to go home with her, she didn't have much choice. She was just going to have to be careful. She told herself that the thief who'd been haunting the mansion wasn't interested in children. She also assured herself that the hidden tunnels weren't easily accessible. At least that's what Rick had said.

She was glad to get home. When Taylor ran straight to Kirby's kennel, Heather said, "Addison, will you take Kirby out to the yard, please?"

Taylor protested, "But he's my dog!"

"He belongs to the whole family." Including Brian and Kristen, Heather thought.

"Why can't I walk him?"

Taylor was shouting at her, but Heather forced herself to remain calm. "Because you're filthy from whatever you were doing. You need to wash up and change into clean clothes. Right now."

Her little face screwed into an angry expression, Taylor left the kitchen. And Addison got the dog on his leash. He was wagging his tail and staring at the little girl adoringly.

Addison started for the back door but stopped halfway through the kitchen. "Kirby is so happy here in his forever home."

"He is, isn't he?" Heather said. "That's because he's not a stray anymore."

"Rick's a stray. Can we help *him* get his forever home?"

A stray. Heather had to chuckle, though she was touched that Addison wanted to help him.

"Don't worry about Rick, honey. He's not in any danger of going to the pound."

Addison considered that. "Okay," she said at last, and took the dog out the back door.

Leaving Heather leaning on the refrigerator to get her balance back. Both girls were basically good kids who got out of hand once in a while. Especially Taylor. Lately, she had become impossible at times. Heather vowed she would find a way to cope, as she always did. This was simply a new phase, one that Taylor would grow out of. Tyrone had called it the psycho sixes. At least Taylor hadn't broken anything.

She opened the refrigerator and pulled out a package of ground beef for the sloppy joes, vegetables to make a big salad and fruit for dessert. As she prepared dinner, she heard the water running in the bathroom, then a few minutes later, the television in the living room.

Needing to use the bathroom herself, she left the kitchen. Taylor was at the DVD player. Though she wanted to know what her daughter was up to, it could wait.

In the bathroom, she saw that Taylor had simply stepped out of her dirty clothes and left them in the middle of the floor. Shaking her head, she picked them up to put them in the hamper. Before doing so, she checked the pockets to make certain nothing was in them and pulled out a piece of paper.

A folded-up ten dollar bill.

A ten dollar bill that looked kind of weird. It had a gold seal and the words Gold Certificate. A closer look showed her that it had been minted in 1922, nearly a century before.

Where in the world had Taylor found this?

Her mind immediately went to Red Flanagan's secret treasure that Rick had mentioned.

Heather headed for the living room to find out where her daughter had gone when she'd disappeared.

Taylor was sitting on the floor, glued to the television, watching her favorite video. Heather stopped short.

"You're Daddy's little girl. You'll always be Daddy's girl."

"Forever and ever?"

"Taylor, I need to talk to you." When her daughter ignored her, Heather walked to the television and manually turned it off.

"Mommy! Don't!"

"You can watch it in a minute. First I want you to tell me where you got this." She held out the bill.

Taylor gave a big sigh. "Found it."

"Where?"

Her daughter shrugged. "Can I watch Daddy now?"

"All right. But I'm returning this money to the mansion tomorrow. You can't take something that belongs to someone else."

"I didn't take it. I found it!"

Taylor's face screwed up as if she was ready to cry, but then Kirby burst into the room and nearly knocked her over. She squealed and laughed and hugged him.

Leaving Heather feeling utterly defeated.

ANTICIPATION AND TREPIDATION warring in him at the thought of seeing Keith Murphy again, Rick walked into Captain Bob's Burger Bar at the marina. The place was decorated to resemble the interior of a wooden ship. Murphy was waiting for him at an outside table overlooking the water. The moment Murphy saw Rick, he stood and held out a hand. Rick took it for a shake and his friend pulled him in for a quick hug and a hard slap on the back.

"Good to see you again, Slater. It's been too long."

The trouble was, Rick didn't know if it was too long…or not long enough.

"I almost forgot what you looked like," he fibbed.

Who could forget a tall, skinny man with

muscles like steel? Not to mention the shaved head. Murphy came from a line of men who went bald before they were fifty, so when his hairline started receding a decade ago, he just shaved it.

Rick was glad to see him again.

"So how's civilian life?" Murphy asked, sitting.

Rick took the chair opposite him. "It has its ups and downs. I'm just getting into the swing of things."

"The job."

"And a personal life."

A waitress stopped at their table, and they ordered burgers and beers. The moment she walked away, Murphy resumed the conversation as if they hadn't been interrupted.

"You have a girl, I take it?"

Did he? It was too soon to tell. "Not exactly."

"Which means?"

"There's potential."

"And problems?"

"Heather is an army widow, left with two little girls. Twins."

"Uh-oh, built-in family. That's a tough situation to involve yourself in."

"Well, it's something to think about," Rick agreed.

It was a stumbling point for him, but not in

the way Murphy thought. Rick had failed his men, failed his responsibility, so how could he get involved with a young woman who already had two little girls? How could they rely on him? What if he and Heather got serious, and then he decided to re-enlist? What if he didn't make it out the next time? How could he put Heather through that nightmare again?

And yet…

How could he stop wanting to see her and not give them a chance?

Feeling more torn than he had when he'd left the army, he said, "Addison is a cool little kid, real chatty, real likeable. But her sister, Taylor, doesn't seem to care for me much." Which did bother him. He'd just been trying to stop her from getting hurt when she'd taken off with the dog, but now he feared he'd screwed up by interfering.

"Maybe you should end it before you get in too deep."

Rick started. Despite the reasons he shouldn't get involved with her, he didn't want to end it with Heather before he had a chance to get to know her better. Or to know what it was he wanted to make of his life. He still hadn't figured out what he was going to do. And Murphy telling him to quit before he had his answers didn't sound like the supportive friend he thought he knew.

"What are you trying to say?" Rick asked. "Why are you here?"

"I need a reason to have dinner with my best friend?"

Rick stared at Murphy for a moment and tried to read him, even as his friend made his expression go blank.

"Now I know you have an ulterior motive."

"Slater—"

"Murphy! Spill!"

"All right, all right. I was hoping that with a little encouragement from me, you would be ready to come back."

"To what?" Rick asked, his gut immediately tightening.

"The life. Your team."

"My team is dead." That photograph burned in his memory flickered through his mind.

"*I'm* not dead," Murphy said. "And *you* aren't. The guys I'm working with now need a real leader."

As if he could just walk back in and take over Murphy's special operations intelligence team. Part of him wanted a way to make up for his men's deaths. Reduce the guilt. But the other part told him to give civilian life a chance.

"You could be a real leader for them," he told Murphy.

Arriving with their food, the waitress interrupted once more. "Can I get you boys anything else?"

"I'm good," Rick said.

"Me, too." Murphy winked at her, and, flustered, she moved away from the table. Murphy turned his attention back to their conversation. "Tell me you don't miss it."

"Okay, maybe I do. Parts of the life were good." Rick shook his head. But the parts that weren't good—more specifically, the tragedy that had made him walk away—were horrible. "I never knew anything else but army life. That's what I'm trying to do now—find out if I can build a life on my own."

"You're fooling yourself, Slater. You've been out for nearly four months now, and you still don't know what you want. Maybe that's because you're forcing yourself into a life that's not for you."

Rick grabbed his burger. "Let's just eat." He took a big bite, filling his mouth so he didn't have to answer.

Deep inside, Rick feared Murphy might be right.

CHAPTER TWELVE

"Don't worry," Heather told her workers as she picked up gardening tools and set them in the wheelbarrow. "I'll take everything back to the coach house and put it all away."

She'd seen Rick earlier but he'd been so preoccupied that he hadn't noticed her. He'd been outside the coach house, looking at what might have been blueprints. She'd watched him as he'd glanced from the papers in his hands to the mansion and back several times. A few of the guests had come out of the house, heading for the terrace. Seeing them, he'd gone back inside.

Come on, whatever he was up to had nothing to do with a handyman's job!

Heather hadn't even had the chance to show him the ten dollar gold certificate Taylor had found when she'd disappeared on them. She'd planned on doing that today. She wanted to give Rick the old bill and maybe talk some more about the rumored treasure and the hidden passageways. So she'd stalled in finishing up her landscaping work for the day. She would send her team home and have a logical reason to stay behind.

"You're going to have to stay late," Amber said.

"Only a few minutes," Heather hedged. She wasn't about to tell Amber and Tyrone *why* she was working late.

"What about the twins?" Tyrone asked.

"Brian is picking them up today." And babysitting for a while because she had errands to do.

Both workers raised their eyebrows, but neither said anything.

Heat slid along Heather's neck as she said, "See you in the morning."

"Yeah, sure," Tyrone said, but when he made no move to leave, Amber grabbed his arm and gave it a jerk.

"C'mon, let's get out of here. I have plans for tonight."

As they walked off, Tyrone asked, "What kind of plans? You got a date?"

"Why? Is that so unbelievable?"

Their voices faded as they headed for the parking lot, where another car was pulling in. More guests.

Heather quickly finished loading the wheelbarrow and then rolled it straight to the coach house. Excitement motivated her. It was the gold certificate, she told herself, not the possibility of being alone with Rick.

He'd crept into her thoughts too often over the weekend, especially while she'd been on the computer catching up with her work for Sew Fine's internet site. She'd tried to convince herself that with his background, he simply wasn't the right man for her, yet whenever she thought about Rick—about spending time with him or just seeing him—it was with a sense of anticipation that she hadn't felt in a very long while. Though a big part of her still struggled with the idea that he might re-enlist, she'd given up fighting her attraction to Rick. If she was ever going to move on, she needed to see where that attraction would lead. Surely, the situation would work itself out for the best one way or another, and she didn't always have to be so on guard.

Once in the coach house, she locked up the tools in the shop area as Rick had suggested—he'd given her a key to the shop door after learning the shovel had disappeared— and turned out the light. But before she could leave the room, she heard footsteps on stairs. She glanced out the shop window and saw Rick coming down. Good. She'd have the opportunity to give him the strange-looking bill.

He bent down to pick up a bag that leaned against the staircase. What could be in it? And why did he seem so on edge? He had those papers in his hand again. If they were blueprints, what was he doing with them? Her suspicions about his being more than a handyman continued to crystallize.

She stood frozen, watching him through the window.

RICK SWUNG THE bag he'd loaded with tools from the shop and quickly found the lock release in the door to the tunnels. Going down the stairs, he acknowledged the lights had mysteriously come back on. There must be a loose connection somewhere. If he knew where the feed started, he might be able to fix it.

He was still on edge. He could definitely feel the prickle. After what he'd survived in Afghanistan, he would undoubtedly always be a little claustrophobic in underground spaces.

As he traveled through the tunnel, Rick sensed he wasn't alone. He stopped to listen and heard a feminine gasp and a noise that sounded like rock skittering. He whipped around and shone his utility lantern straight on Heather Clarke.

"What are you doing here?" he demanded.

"I was putting away our gardening tools when I saw you come down here."

"So you just followed me?"

"I was curious. I wanted to see what you were doing."

"And you couldn't call out to tell me you were here?"

"Um, sorry. So this is another part of the secret tunnels, right? What *are* you doing down here?"

She had the nerve to sound suspicious, Rick realized. "I'm doing my job."

"Your job as a handyman is to explore tunnels? Or do you actually have a different job? First the security cameras…then running back here the other night when a thief set off one of those cameras…now this. Doesn't sound like a handyman's job to me."

Oh, great. She'd figured it out. Why couldn't he have done the smart thing and deleted that footage of her in the boathouse right away? Now there was no talking his way out of it. He would need her promise to secrecy yet again.

"Okay, you got me. I work for Lake Shore Security in Milwaukee," he admitted. "Ben Phillips needed someone to secure the mansion and to figure out who has been intruding on the estate's property and why. Cora is the only employee who knows why I'm here.

It's important to keep it that way because it's likely an employee has something to do with what's been going on, so I trust you won't tell anyone else."

"No, of course not. I already gave you my word once before."

"Good. Now let me walk you to your car."

"I'm not leaving. It's kind of spooky down here," she noted. "I mean, the ceiling could collapse on you or something, and you could get hurt. You shouldn't be down here alone."

Reminded of Afghanistan, Rick clenched his jaw. He felt torn. On one hand, he could use some company. Someone who could keep him centered. On the other hand, he felt uncomfortable being responsible for another person's safety underground...again.

"It's better to have two people than one in a situation like this," she said.

"Yeah." He couldn't deny that. Considering Heather now knew what he was doing at the estate, he supposed it wouldn't hurt anything to let her tag along.

He wanted to reassure her, and, to an extent, himself at the same time. "The ceilings won't collapse. See those beams? They're stable."

"You shouldn't be down here alone," she repeated.

"I can't change your mind?"

"Nope."

He handed her his battery-operated utility lantern and started off.

"What are you looking for?" she asked as she quickly followed.

"What I suspect the intruder is looking for—the rumored treasure room."

Rick told her about his initial exploration down here, how he thought the intruder had gotten into the house through the hidden door to the conservatory. All the while he noted Heather was flipping the beam around, checking every crack and crevice and spider web as they walked.

When some dirt sifted down on them halfway to the mansion, she jumped. "What just happened? I thought you said these tunnels are stable."

"They are." The tunnels were nearly a century old, but they seemed solid enough to him. Still, it didn't hurt to be extra careful. "I heard an engine—car, truck, something. Maybe it came close enough to cause a little vibration."

"I didn't hear any engine."

"You're not trained to."

His whole team had been trained for stealth operations. A few critical times his acute hearing had prevented him from walking into a dangerous situation. That training had saved his team members' lives more than once.

Too bad his instincts hadn't been enough to save his men on that last mission.

"Relax," he said, pulling Heather close so that he could wrap an arm around her shoulders. She fit perfectly in the shelter of his body and just holding her like this made him feel better. "I won't let you get hurt." Of course, he'd said the same thing to people before...

"You won't... I mean, good!"

Just enough light allowed him to see every feature of her face, and the way she was looking at him made his chest tighten. He wanted in the worst way to kiss her again. The way he'd meant to Friday night before being alerted to the intruder's presence in the boathouse.

"This place is so creepy," she said a little breathlessly. "I just didn't think you should be down here by yourself. You know...just in case."

"Which was very generous of you," Rick said, keeping his amusement from his tone. "We should go on."

"Oh...of course." Obviously flustered, she pulled free of his arm and went ahead of him.

Even though he felt the loss of her warmth against his side, Rick grinned. He didn't mind watching Heather as she stalked down the tunnel. She had this cute little sway to her hips.

He suddenly remembered her saying, *Just in case...*

What had she thought she could do if something did happen to him down here? Or what would she do if he was in some kind of danger? Very brave of her to insist on being here, especially because he knew how much she'd stepped out of her comfort zone. Of course, if he'd thought there was the slightest chance that there was any real danger, he would have turned down her very generous offer. Truth was, he wanted to spend some time with Heather, and this was a start.

Thinking about how he had her off guard, he couldn't stop grinning all the way to the split.

Heather stopped. "Which way?"

"Let's stay to the left."

A few minutes later, they reached the first set of narrow steps. Rick led the way up and took measurements with a laser tool. After checking the blueprints, he was certain this was the way into the master suite, either the very large drawing room on the lakeside or the dressing room next to it.

"It looks to be an interior wall," Rick said. "Which makes sense if you want a hidden room to stay hidden."

"Our shovel!" Heather said, shining her light on the floor area at the sealed entry. "Broken."

Indeed, the wooden shaft had been split near the metal. The shovel lay in two pieces. Rick noted there were also a few big chunks of concrete around the damaged garden tool.

"Looks like whoever took it was using it to try to break in," he said, noting Heather looked anxious. "And don't worry, I really will buy you another shovel."

She nodded. "I'm sorry it's ruined, of course, but I'm just glad the thief couldn't get in."

"Not this way," Rick said. "But he obviously found the entry through the conservatory. Remember, he stole the candelabra the other night. I'll have to remind Cora to make sure that door between the conservatory and the house stays locked at all times."

"What about whoever takes care of the plants? I was wondering who that might be."

"I think someone from a flower shop comes in on a regular basis. But the watering is done automatically on a timer."

"That makes sense. There are so many plants it would take quite a while to water manually." Heather paused for a few seconds, then said, "But if someone from the outside is coming in to take care of the plants…"

"...maybe I should run a security check on that person," he finished for her.

"Right. So what do we do now?"

She looked up to meet his gaze, and he realized how close they were. Nearly kissing close. Oh, so tempting. Though nerves suddenly filled him with warmth, he didn't move. Neither did she.

Getting a grip on himself, he cleared his throat. "I hadn't decided what I was going to do until I saw the remains of your shovel, actually. But the fact that someone could break away that much cement with a tool that isn't even meant to do the job tells me that I can do better."

"So you're going to try to break through?"

"First, I want to go inside to see if we can find the easy way in. I'm pretty sure there is some kind of secret room between this tunnel and whatever room it leads to. And the entry to the master suite seems the likely place."

"Then what?" she asked.

"I'll report it to Ben Phillips, see what he wants me to do. In the meantime, I don't want anyone in the house other than Cora to know what we're doing. The intruder might not be working alone. He might have a connection to someone working in the house. I would rather catch him and turn him in to the police."

"If he comes back. He did get the candelabra."

"My guess is that's what he settled for. At the moment. But I would bet he's looking for the fabled treasure. Plenty of places can be robbed more easily than Flanagan Manor. And the intruder was searching the tunnels for entries into the house. Come on, let's see if we can find a way into the hidden room through the master suite."

He started down the stairs with Heather following.

HEATHER WAS GLAD they'd soon be out of the tunnels. They were creepy and scary. Not that she regretted following Rick and insisting on staying. She only hoped Taylor hadn't found her way down here or her daughter would be having some bad dreams. She had yet to get any further information from the little girl about her hiding place the other evening.

"Let's leave the utility lights here with the other tools," Rick said when they reached the concealed door that led to the conservatory steps, "or someone who sees us might wonder what we're doing inside with construction tools."

"I thought you said the door to the house was locked."

"But I have the keys."

Once inside the conservatory a few minutes later, Rick pulled out his phone, called Cora and asked her to meet them at the door. As soon as they were inside the mansion, Heather saw the housekeeper coming toward them. They met her in the library, an impressively large room facing the lake.

Appearing concerned at seeing that Rick wasn't alone, Cora asked, "Is there a problem?"

"We need to get upstairs. Heather has had some trouble with equipment being broken by our intruder. She's giving me backup. There may be something our intruder wants that's in a hidden area between the tunnels and one of these rooms. I want to see if we can find an entrance to a secret room from the master suite."

Cora was still giving Heather a sideways look.

"I think it's terrible that you don't feel safe," Heather said in a soft voice, hoping to put the housekeeper at ease. "Rick is going to figure out what's going on, and I'm going to help him."

Cora seemed to relax a little. "What do you need *me* to do?"

"Keep everyone occupied so no one sees us," Rick said.

"That should be easy enough. The maids are

gone for the day. It's just about dinner time, so that will keep both staff and guests busy for a while. Probably an hour, give or take."

"Are the guests downstairs?" he asked.

"Already getting seated at the tables," Cora confirmed.

"Good, you go first then, and make sure that no one is around the rotunda or staircase."

Cora nodded and went to do just that. When she poked her head back into the library and gave them the signal, they followed.

At the bottom of the staircase, Rick placed a hand in the small of Heather's back and gave her a little push to urge her upward. Her pulse fluttered. She assumed he wasn't saying anything lest he alert someone nearby to his presence. Two thirds of the way up, she glanced back to see Cora waving them faster. Having also noted the signal, Rick caught up to her and placed his palm on her back again to hurry her. Heather's pulse threaded unevenly and she nearly tripped. Rick caught her just in time so that she didn't lose her footing. She couldn't breathe for a moment until he let her go.

"Oh, Gina, surely you're not done with dinner yet," she heard Cora say.

"No, Kelly asked me to find you," came a throaty voice. "Apparently, she has a problem in the kitchen. What are you doing here, any-way?"

"I was just getting something from my room…"

From the way their voices faded, Heather realized the housekeeper had led the other woman away from the stairs. Still, she was glad to be out of sight.

"We're good," Rick whispered, passing her. "C'mon."

Heather followed him into a long drawing room, the size of the library and the entry-way downstairs combined. Facing the lake, the room had doors that led onto a balcony. And in the middle of the outside wall was a fire-place with an elaborate carved wooden man-tel that looked original to the mansion. The walls were split with wainscoting on the bot-tom half, like some of the other rooms in the mansion and coach house. The upper halves were loaded with wooden trim, too. She imag-ined the room looked much as it had a century ago when it was built. The furniture, however, was eclectic with modern couches and chairs with antique wooden tables and storage units.

Rick pulled out the blueprints and set them on one of the tables. "The entry must be on this wall." He indicated the interior wall opposite the lakeside doors and balcony and pointed to the doorway in the middle. "Probably between here and the outside wall."

Because she worked with the equivalent of blueprints for landscaping, Heather easily matched the document with the space. "What's on the other side?"

"A very large dressing room with the bedroom beyond it. It looks like there might be some space behind the back wall of the dressing room but not enough that anyone would notice unless they were looking for it."

Taking out his laser tool, Rick opened the door and then the one to the dressing room. Heather followed and watched as he took measurements.

"Just as I thought. This space is smaller than it appears on the blueprint. Much smaller, actually."

A thrill shot through Heather. "So the tunnel leads inside this wall?"

"Right. Now all we have to do is find the entry."

"Which could be from this room or from the dressing room."

"You're sharp. You'd make a good investigator."

Heather smiled. "The twins give me a lot of practice. I'm always having to figure out what they're up to or how they've disappeared on me when I only turned my back for a moment."

"My mother used to tell me she had eyes in the back of her head so she always knew what I was up to. She said all mothers had them."

They laughed together, a nice sound that warmed her inside. She'd never had such easy rapport with any man other than her late husband.

Splitting up, with her in the dressing room and him in the drawing room, they began searching for the secret doorway. The dressing room wall was divided between shelving and double racks of clothing. No matter how many surfaces or crevices or trim Heather pressed, nothing so much as budged.

"No luck, huh?" Rick asked a few minutes later.

She turned to find him in the doorway, his expression equally discouraged. "Not a clue," she said. "What now?"

"Now I go back into the tunnel and see if I can break through from that side. I brought along a sledgehammer and pry bar. They're with my tools downstairs. I'm hoping no one wanders this way, but just in case, I'm going to ask you to stay up here and keep watch."

A frisson of discomfort shot through her. "And do what?"

"Distract anyone who might wander up to this floor. I'll be making noise. Who knows how loud? Just try to keep them away from here."

"I'll do my best."

"I know you will." He gave her a slow smile that warmed her to her toes. "Hopefully, I'll get through fast and see you in a little while."

After he left, Heather walked over to the balcony doors and looked out over the lake. A few sailboats dotted the horizon. The sun was setting in the west behind her, drizzling the water with streaks of red and pink. It would be dusk soon.

She took a big breath and tried to chase away the squirrelly feeling in her middle. She wasn't built for subterfuge. Being alone in the mansion made her nerves jitter. And when she heard a voice drifting up the staircase, she tried not to panic.

Tiptoeing to the doorway, she peered out to see that one of the employees—Gina, the bossy one—was coming up the stairs, a cell phone glued to her ear. Heather could hear snatches of what she was saying.

"No, not right now…later tonight."

Gina came into view, and Heather backed out of sight.

"I'm telling you it's too early. It's still light

out." Her tone changed to vulnerable. "I thought you cared about me…"

Was she talking to a man? Heather wondered. A boyfriend, probably. Not wanting to hear the other woman's personal conversation, she grew even more uncomfortable.

"The sun hasn't even set yet," Gina went on. "Later would be better. You know I'm right."

Heather peeked around the doorway. Gina stood frozen at the top of the stairs.

"Oh, baby, I knew you'd come through for me…"

Gina suddenly pulled the phone from her ear and glared at it. "Cell phones!" she said, disgust ripe in her voice.

Apparently the call had been dropped, Heather thought, glad when Gina turned around and quickly headed back downstairs.

Relieved Gina hadn't seen her lurking so close by, Heather started when a sound from the interior wall got her attention. Pounding. Soft pounding, but audible nevertheless. Thank goodness, Gina was already gone. Now if only Rick would hurry! Moving in the direction of the sound, Heather followed it out of the drawing room into the dressing room, where it was even louder. She placed her hands on the wall, and the next strike sent a vibration down to her toes, making her jump back.

"You're so close," she muttered.

"Who's close?"

Heather whipped around to face a boy of eight or so.

"What are you doing in here?" he asked, looking from her to the wall.

Pulse pounding, Heather waited for the next whomp, but thankfully, there was silence.

"Looking for something," she said. Turning out the light, she left the dressing room, pushing the boy before her. "And you don't belong in these rooms. These are the private family rooms."

"You own this place?" He stopped dead in the doorway to the drawing room.

Heather waited anxiously to hear the slam of the sledgehammer again.

"I work here," she said.

Which was true. At least for the moment.

To her relief, Cora raced into the room. "Ah, there you are, Mason. You must be lost. Your room is on the other side of the staircase."

"I'm not lost," he protested, his expression belligerent.

"Well, you can't be in here. Come on." Cora waved him in her direction. "Your parents are looking for you."

The kid went reluctantly.

And as they left the room, Cora glanced over

her shoulder and shot a look of exasperation at Heather, who sagged against the doorway with relief.

Just as a muffled crunching noise came from the dressing room.

CHAPTER THIRTEEN

TRYING TO IGNORE the unsettled feeling that was jangling his nerves, Rick worked the pry bar behind the concrete slab until another chunk gave and dropped to the ground behind the sheet of heavy-duty plastic that would protect him from being hit by flying rubble or choking on a cloud of dust.

He hooked the pry bar behind what was left of the cement seal, then used the sledge to make a few good cracks. Within minutes, it was done. He ripped down the plastic and faced the original doorway that led from the tunnel into the house.

Though he breathed a little easier, he looked around, down the stairway and beyond. He couldn't shake the feeling that something was wrong. Only he couldn't see or hear anything unusual. He had no clue why his sixth sense had gone on alert the moment he'd re-entered the tunnel alone. Claustrophobia was getting to him again.

He grabbed the door handle and gave it a twist. The door easily opened and he stepped inside.

The utility lantern illuminated the narrow interior room, which was furnished. He took in the desk and shelves on one side, the cabinetry on the other. Every surface was thick with dust, and a spider had been busy creating one of the biggest webs he'd ever seen across the back wall.

"So where's the door to the dressing room?" he muttered, just before he spotted the lever at waist level.

Not knowing if Heather was still by herself, Rick decided not to take any chances. He pulled out his cell and called her.

A few seconds later, she answered. "Rick, where are you?" She sounded anxious.

"Everything okay? Are you alone?"

"I am now."

"I'm in." He opened the door to find her standing in the dressing room, looking straight at the wall of shelving that swung open. "So I was right about the interior room."

Her eyes were wide as they met his. "But did you find Flanagan's treasure?"

"I haven't looked yet. C'mon."

Rick waved Heather in, then closed the door

behind them. He didn't want anyone stumbling on them and discovering what he was doing. The room felt too tight for him. Too narrow, prompting a memory of being trapped, distracting him from his purpose.

Telling himself to calm down and get back on track, he flashed the utility light along the wall and found a light switch. That an overhead light and a lamp on the desk both went on when he flipped it surprised Rick.

"Wow," Heather said

"It works, but my guess is the wiring needs to be replaced."

Then her gaze lit on the huge spider web. "Eww."

"Don't worry, I'll take care of that." He stepped into the tunnel and pulled a clean pair of gloves from his sack—he hadn't removed his. "Here, put these on." Then he picked up the pry bar and pulled down the spider web. "You look through the desk and I'll take the cabinetry. Let's see whether or not there's anything worth finding."

Heather pulled on the gloves and slid open the center drawer. "Empty."

After clearing the spider web out of the way, Rick flipped open a cabinet door. "Empty here, too." He went on to the next one. "When I asked you about being alone, you said, *I am now*. Did someone see you?"

"One of the guests. A kid. He wanted to know what I was doing."

Rick glanced back as Heather opened a bottom drawer. "What did you say?"

She turned to face him. "Just that I was looking for something and that I worked here. Then Cora arrived, thankfully, and took him away."

"No harm done, then."

"No. Thankfully Gina didn't see me." Before he could ask, she explained. "She was on her cell, arguing with someone about tonight. Sounded like her boyfriend was trying to get her to see him now and she wanted him to wait until later."

Something to keep in mind. Opening the last drawer—empty—Rick said, "Looks like the Feds cleaned the place out before they sealed it. Makes sense, I guess."

"But they never found the supposed treasure."

"Or they never admitted to it." Rick thought about the complexity of the tunnels and entries he'd found so far. "I wonder how much more there is to Flanagan's underground world."

"You mean a room even a government crew didn't find?" Heather mused.

"Could be." He sighed. "Well, I'm disappointed but not surprised. And we've done enough for one night. Let's get out of here. Through the tunnel. Let me call Cora first to give her the all clear."

Heather nodded and slipped off the gloves.

Rick got Cora on the first ring. The housekeeper jumped on the call as if she'd been waiting to hear from him.

"Is there a problem?" she whispered.

"No. We're done for the day. I just wanted to let you know we were leaving so you could relax."

He updated her, told her they would leave through the tunnel and slid his phone back in his pocket.

Heather had already put her gloves and his pry bar back in the tool bag. He threw his own gloves in and slung the bag over his shoulder. About to head down the stairs, he froze. Again, he sensed something out of place. Had he heard a noise without its really registering?

"What's wrong?" Heather asked, keeping her voice low. Still, he picked up the slight catch that said she was nervous.

"I don't know. Something's off. Maybe me."

His awareness doubled, he made his way down, one slow step at a time with Heather so close behind him that he could feel her breath on the back of his neck. Reaching the bottom, he stood there for a moment. Frozen. Silent. Heather followed suit.

Nothing.

No sound. No movement.

So why did he sense they weren't alone?

"This is creepy," she whispered.

He flashed his utility lantern all around to make sure nothing was lurking in the shadows. "Let's get out of here."

They'd gotten only as far as the split when Heather stopped, saying, "Wait a minute. What's that?"

She was shining her light on a crack in the wall just ahead.

"Another entry?" Rick flashed his light in every direction to make sure no one was lurking nearby. "Stay back a minute."

He moved closer and the beam broke as it met the crack. Close enough to look inside, he took a quick glance then slid the hidden doorway open.

"An empty room," he told Heather before stepping inside.

THOUGH THEY WERE separated by a mere few feet, Heather felt exposed. She nearly jumped out of her skin when she heard a soft scraping sound behind her.

"Don't worry, it's probably just vermin," Rick said as he set his tools down on a big table in the center of the room.

"Rats?"

Rats were plenty bad as far as Heather was concerned, though not as threatening as a human up to no good. She glanced around, unable to see much in the darkness. For the past few minutes, she'd had the weirdest feeling, like someone had been watching them. Undoubtedly Rick's tension was affecting her imagination. She quickly stepped inside the room and shone her light around the dark recesses, slowly taking the beam in a big circle. The walls were lined with shelves. All empty.

"It looks like this was a storage room," she said.

"Probably where Flanagan kept his illegal stash." Rick walked over to the shelving as if to take a closer look. "His men could have brought kegs of whiskey or cartons of bottles onto the property via the lake and boathouse."

"If the size of the room is any indication, it looks like selling alcohol during prohibition was big business in this area."

"Flanagan's stock was Chicago mob related," he said. "I imagine this was his distribution center. He could have stored the alcohol in here, then to fill an order, his men could have brought it up through the coach house—"

"—where they would have a truck waiting inside where it couldn't be seen," she finished. "Now the multiple tunnel entries are making sense."

"What I need to know is how long ago the intruder was in here."

"You're sure the door wasn't cracked open all along?"

"I'm positive that it wasn't even open when we passed it earlier."

Heather's pulse quickened and invisible fingers crawled up her spine. "What are you saying?"

Rick frowned and swung back toward the opening. "That someone was just in here while we were in the tunnels. Let's get out. Now."

She stepped backward across the threshold, part of her thinking she felt a malevolent presence behind her...hot breath on the back of her neck. Before she could turn around, a heavy hand hit her in the middle of her back and shoved hard. She was flung forward, back into the storage room, right into Rick. The door slid shut behind them with a bang.

"What the…" That was all Rick said.

She clung to him, frightened out of her mind. "Someone pushed me! He was right behind me, Rick." It had been an aggressive, hostile shove.

"He's shut us in here."

She clung to Rick with all her strength. "What's going on? Is he going to kill us?"

Their hearts beat hard, nearly in unison. Rick cradled her against him.

Finally, he said, "My guess is we surprised him and he's just slowing us down. I knew something was off!"

"And we're locked in?" Heather also had felt danger in the air. Her imagination hadn't been playing with her, after all. Someone had been sneaking around after them.

"Let me see what I can do." Gently, Rick released her and felt around the door, pushed, tugged. But it stayed firmly in place.

"There's got to be a way."

As she held her lantern to light the area for him she saw his growing frustration as he failed to find a release. He slammed the flat of his hand into the metal panel. Then his expression tightened and froze like a mask. His breathing grew rapid but shallow. Unbelievable as it seemed, she thought, The Terminator was getting a little claustrophobic.

When he gave up the search and fell back against the wall, his head bowed, his hands tightened into fists, Heather fought her own panic. What was wrong with him? Being locked in here was definitely creepy, especially with some criminal type messing around outside. But Rick was a take-charge kind of guy and he looked ready to fold.

"You said the intruder was slowing us down. He's probably gone by now." Meeting up with the person who pushed her was her greatest fear.

"I'm sure he's gone. But we're still locked in."

He was definitely claustrophobic.

"Why don't we call for help?"

"Help?" he repeated, not seeming to get what she was suggesting.

"The housekeeper."

"Cora? She doesn't know how to get in here."

"You can tell her how. She doesn't have to come alone."

"Then everyone will know about the tunnels."

"Um, I know you were trying to keep your

activities down here secret because you feared one of the employees was working with the intruder, but that's kind of a moot point now, wouldn't you agree?"

Rick blinked a few times and his features pulled into a frown. "Of course. You're right. What was I thinking?"

What was he thinking? she wondered. *What was wrong with him?*

She might have asked had he not pulled out his cell that very moment. As he punched in a number, his hand shook a little. She was shaking inside herself.

Seconds later, he muttered, "I should have known!" His jaw clenched. "No signal in here!"

"Let me try mine."

But she couldn't get a signal, either. Biting her lip so that she wouldn't burst into tears, Heather returned her cell to her pocket. They were going to be all right, she told herself. They were just temporarily locked in. They would get out of here, and they would be fine.

Taking a deep breath, she talked herself into control, but, with his back still against the wall, Rick was clutching his phone like he would never let go. His gaze was focused on something internal. He no longer seemed to know she was even in the room. Sweat broke out along his hairline. A single bead was working its way down the side of his face.

"Rick," she said softly.

He didn't seem to hear. He was frozen by something she didn't understand. "Rick!" she said louder.

He blinked and focused on her. No answer.

"Rick, what's wrong?"

"Trapped. We're trapped."

His voice sounded rough. Forced. A chill shot through her. He was more than just a little claustrophobic. He was having some kind of panic attack.

"We're not trapped," she said evenly as she moved closer to him and put a reassuring hand on his arm. She had to keep *herself* calm so she could find a way to talk him down. "We're just locked in this room for the moment, but we're going to get out. It's going to be all right."

At least she hoped it would be.

His muscles had tightened with his building stress, but the human connection seemed to get through to him. He blinked and met her gaze. Then his expression softened, and he sagged a little and sucked in a deep breath.

"Hey, sorry."

"Don't be." Heather tightened her hand on

his arm reassuringly before letting go. "Are you all right?"

"Yeah, sure. It's just that…"

"Just what?" she asked.

"A bad memory. Being trapped." He pulled a hand through his hair. "I don't like tight places. Being underground."

The army…had to be. That had been his life until he'd decided to try out being a civilian mere months ago. But what in the world had happened to him? Heather wondered.

Not about to play that guessing game, she said, "Let's do something to get out of here. You did bring your tools with you." Even as she said it, he straightened and his expression shifted into something more familiar. "Maybe you can crash your way out of here."

"The pry bar." Rick pushed away from the wall and fetched his tools.

Heather took a relieved if shaky breath. Thank goodness. She couldn't help but wonder about that bad memory, but she wasn't about to ask.

When Rick set down the bag close to the door and pulled out the pry bar, she asked, "What can I do to help?"

"Just stand back." He maneuvered the tip at the door's edge. "I think I've got it."

He levered the bar, adjusted it and levered it again. The door didn't budge. He slid the bar lower until he couldn't move it any further and then tried again. The door whined and creaked, and with Rick's mighty shove, clicked open a crack.

"You got it!"

"I believe so." He reached a hand into the break, felt around and finally managed to slide the door open. "Yep. Got it!"

"Then let's get out of here." Heather started to go past him, but he held out an arm to stop her.

"Wait a minute." He replaced the pry bar in his tool bag, which he slung over his shoulder. Then he shone his utility lamp into the tunnel. "Looks clear. Whoever locked us in here is gone. Stay tight next to me."

Heart racing again, Heather did as he ordered. Even though Rick was himself again, she didn't relax until they got up the stairs and back onto the main floor of the coach house.

RICK COULDN'T BELIEVE he'd caved in to his fear, and in front of Heather of all people. She'd kept calm, despite her own fears, and had brought him back to himself, but what must she be thinking?

"What now?" she asked. "Do we call the police?"

"I'll call Detective Morse and tell him what happened."

"He needs to know that someone was down there and pushed me into that room with you."

"Thankfully, you weren't hurt."

"But someone had bad intentions."

"True," Rick grunted. And the situation had been enough to trip him up mentally. The therapist he'd worked with after the disastrous mission had told him this could happen, but he'd never felt trapped like that before.

"What if one of us had been harmed?" Heather asked. "What if I had fallen? Or what if the thief stole something again? Or maybe he's going to. He could think we're safely locked up, and he can do whatever he wants."

"Like I said, I think we surprised him and he probably took off. But I plan on checking the house and the entire grounds and telling Cora about the incident."

To his surprise, she said, "I'll go with you."

He'd expected her to leave the moment they got out of the tunnels. Had expected her to hot-foot it away from him and never look back. That she seemed to be offering him such support surprised him. Other than his mother, he'd never known such a generous woman. Or such a courageous one. She was supportive in spite of her own scare. Would he ever be able to give her such support in return?

"Thanks, Heather. Let me lock up the tools first."

Opening the shop area, he set the bag and utility lights on a shelf, then secured the room once more.

"Rick, I almost forgot about this." Heather pulled something from her jeans pocket and held it out to him. "I found it in Taylor's pocket last night."

He took what looked like a ten dollar bill from her. Frowning, he carefully inspected it and saw that it had a gold seal and the words Gold Certificate. He checked the date—it had been minted more than ninety years ago.

"Did Taylor say where she found this?" he asked.

"Unfortunately not. Do you think she could have stumbled onto the treasure room?"

He shrugged. "Maybe that's where she was when we were looking for her."

"I can try talking to her about it again. She was in one of her moods yesterday. Impossible."

"I noticed." Rick pulled out his wallet and

secured the bill. "As soon as I get back into my apartment, I'll put this someplace safe until I can give it to Phillips. In the meantime…"

They left the building and walked over to the mansion. It was nearly dusk, and shadows were already lengthening. They entered through the kitchen.

"Rick, you missed dinner," Kelly said, starting when she took a better look at them. "What have you two been doing? Rolling around in the dirt?"

Realizing they were not only dusty but streaked with grime, Rick said, "Something like that."

"That's pretty much my job, and Rick doesn't mind lending a hand," Heather added, covering for them.

"You want me to get you something to eat? I was just putting everything away."

"Thanks, Kelly, but I have to find Cora and then check out some things. It may take a while. I can nuke a dinner from the freezer."

Kelly made a sound of exaggerated horror. "I'll pack something for you and leave it on the island. You can pick it up on your way back to the coach house."

"Hey, thanks."

Rick indicated Heather should follow him as

he headed for the dining room, where the last of the guests were leaving their table.

"Cora's not here," Heather said.

"I'll call her." He was about to pull out his cell when the housekeeper stepped out of the rotunda, looking very concerned. "There she is."

When Cora saw them, her eyes widened. He indicated they should go out on the front portico, which was vacant. The housekeeper followed, but she seemed preoccupied.

"Cora, is there a problem?" Rick asked.

She shook her head. "I don't think so. It's just that David...uh, Mr. Guildfren...never came to dinner, and his car is in the lot, so I got worried and checked his room. But he wasn't there, either. I can't imagine where he's disappeared to."

"He's probably holed up somewhere, relaxing and reading or something," Rick said, glancing at Heather, who was, for some reason, frowning. "I'm sure he'll turn up."

Cora's expression cleared. "Yes, of course. You were looking for me? What is it, Rick?"

"Our uninvited guest was here."

"Where?"

"In the tunnels," Heather said. "He pushed me into a store room and locked us in there."

"You *saw* him?"

"No, but I felt him."

Cora's face blanched. "I've felt him, too."

"Which simply means your senses are well developed." Rick patted the housekeeper's arm. "But he's not a ghost, Cora, so take it easy."

"How do you know that for sure?"

"I felt a flesh and blood hand on my back," Heather said. "Believe me, this guy is plenty real."

Though he didn't say so, Rick thought he'd take a ghost instead of a dangerous criminal any day.

"I'm going to take a fast tour of the mansion, Cora, to make sure the thief isn't lurking around the corridors. If you see anything of value missing, you need to alert me right away so that we can make another police report."

"I'll do another inventory," she promised as Rick opened the door to get his own search underway.

Heather stuck with him as he toured the downstairs rooms, then checked each of the unoccupied rooms in the family wing. They walked the halls of the other wing, but Rick didn't knock on doors or open them and disturb paying guests.

"Well, that's it, then," he said. "The thief seems to be gone."

"Or hiding. I thought you wanted to check the grounds."

"I just realized it's dark enough that movement will set off the cameras. If he's still sneaking around, I'll know."

And he would collar the thief and deliver him personally to Detective Morse. He still needed to call the detective and let him know there had been another "incident."

"You must be hungry. I'm sure Kelly packed up enough food to share."

Heather looked torn. "Thanks, but I don't want my brother to feel like I'm taking advantage. Besides, I would like to spend some time with my girls tonight before they go to bed."

"I don't blame you." He'd want the same thing if he had a family. "I'll walk you to your SUV."

Heather nodded. "I appreciate that, considering the circumstances."

He waited until they were out of the house and headed for her vehicle before apologizing again. "Listen, Heather, I'm sorry I let you get involved in this situation."

"I was already involved, Rick. The sod cutter. The shovel."

"But I never should have let you go into the tunnels with me," he said as they started through the parking lot. "I had no idea I was putting you in danger."

"You didn't. And now that I've calmed down, I realize the guy wasn't trying to kill me, just get me out of the way. Besides, exploring the tunnels was my choice. I wanted to go."

Right. To watch *his* back. Which she'd had to do in spades. "Then I'm sorry about how I reacted when we were trapped."

Heather stopped and put a hand on his arm, reminding him of the way she'd done when they'd been trapped in that underground room, triggering a rush of something that made his chest grow tight.

"Rick, please, don't. I get it."

"Get what?" he choked out.

"When Scott came home between tours, he told me about how terrible war could be on a man. Not only physically. He had friends who were scarred inside and couldn't talk about what they'd gone through."

Rick had never been able to talk about it, either, not with anyone but the therapist who'd seen him through the aftermath, and that had been reluctantly. How could anyone who hadn't been there understand? He hadn't even been able to talk to Murphy about what had happened to them—how they could have ended up like the other two men—and Murphy had kept his own counsel.

Heather broke the silence between them. "Look, Rick, I'm not going to ask you what happened to make you leave the army. You don't ever have to tell me…unless you want to. Just know that I respect your choices and whatever you had to go through to defend our country."

Her words touched him. Considering she'd lost her husband in battle, she, of all people, had reason to resent anyone connected to the military. And the way she was looking at him…

Evening surrounded them with a deepening dusk, yet Heather's eyes seemed to glow as she looked up at him. An unfamiliar yearning claimed him when he gazed down into her sweet face. It was more than wanting to kiss her. And he *did* want to kiss her. It was wanting *her*. Wanting what she could give him. Her kindness and understanding. Her generosity and warmth.

Reaching out, he touched her cheek. She didn't move away. He hesitated a second, then using both hands, he cupped her face. Touching her felt like the most natural thing in the world. Her expression sharpened as if she was expectant.

Rick couldn't resist.

His heart was pounding as he dipped his head and claimed her mouth as his in the slowest...longest...sweetest kiss he'd ever known.

CORA COULD HARDLY breathe. It was nearly dark now and she stared out the library windows toward the lake, its waves washed with silver-blue by a full moon. She'd been standing here on watch for nearly a half hour now.

Where could David be?

Rick had set her imagination in motion when he'd asked about their frequent guest's interest in the history of the estate. David probably knew more about Flanagan Manor than anyone other than Mr. Phillips. *Or her.* She'd shared everything she'd known and then some, giving him access to the library.

Her eyes suddenly stung, and she blinked rapidly and clenched her jaw.

Had she simply been foolish in thinking a man might find her company attractive enough to book multiple stays in the bed-and-breakfast over the past several years?

A man who was an antiques dealer.

Who undoubtedly could find a wealthy customer willing to buy a Tiffany candelabra, no matter the cost.

Moaning, Cora shook her head. How could she have been so foolish?

So absorbed was she in her own disappointment that she almost missed the furtive movement over on the terrace. Almost. The man—of that she was certain—was sneaking toward the house.

Her pulse thrummed.

Was it David? Had he been hiding out somewhere until he deemed it safe to come back to the house with no one the wiser?

Cora rushed outside and headed for the terrace, yelling at the man in black whose brimmed hat hid his face. "What are you up to now? Did you think I was so stupid I would never know?"

Suddenly, the dark figure rushed toward her, a deep, angry sound emanating from his throat, hands outstretched as if to harm her.

A wide-eyed Cora froze.

And then a second figure came out of nowhere...

"Hey, you, what are you up to?" David demanded.

The dark figure—surely the thief, surely she

had been wrong!—turned and attacked David, punching him in the face. David grabbed onto him. The men were of a similar size and strength. Clasped close together, they moved across the patio like a macabre dance team from that television show Cora liked to watch.

Oh, dear, no! David might be hurt!

Unwilling to let that happen, Cora looked for a way to stop the fight before it got bloody. Needing a weapon of some sort, she picked up a small pot filled with purple pansies. Several feet from the men, Cora couldn't get closer because they kept twisting and turning. The thief's back was to her...now David's...now the thief's...

Catching her breath, Cora took aim, and when the thief turned toward her again, she pitched the pot at his head.

If the man hadn't ducked, she likely would have knocked him out cold. Instead, the pot smacked David on the slope of his forehead. His head jerked, and he went down like a sack of potatoes.

Cora cried out in horror.

Free now, the thief ran toward the parking area behind the mansion.

And David lay collapsed on the deck, moaning.

Cora ran to his side and got down on her knees. "Oh, my goodness, I didn't mean to hit you, David!"

Running footsteps made her think the thief was coming back, but when she looked up it was to see Rick racing from the coach house.

"What happened?"

"The thief was here and Mr. Guildfren tried to stop him." She pointed toward the parking area. "He ran off that way."

Rick took off after him, and Cora turned her attention back to the man who had tried to save her. The man who had her affections. The man she'd thought was guilty of theft.

Oh, dear!

Would he ever forgive her if he knew the truth?

CHAPTER FOURTEEN

"HE KISSED YOU!" Kristen repeated after Heather invited her over to the house the next evening.

Heather shushed her and nodded to the other room. She didn't want the twins to hear. She'd told them to play in their room because she and Aunt Kristen had to talk about plans for the wedding. In truth, she wanted to talk to her sister about what had happened between her and Rick.

"Actually, that was the second time. He kissed me the night of Priscilla's opening, too."

Kristen went on in a lower voice. "And you didn't think to stop him?"

"No. We had a moment, okay?"

"It sounds like more than a moment or you wouldn't be telling me." Kristen grinned at her. "It sounds as if you need approval. Is that why you asked me to come over here? Well, you have my approval. Heather, if you like the man, it's okay."

"Is it?" Heather had been in the moment the

night before—she had even smiled all the way home—but after another day of reality working on the estate, she wasn't so sure the kiss hadn't been a mistake.

"Scott was everything to you," Kristen said, "but he's been gone for three years now. He would want you to be happy."

"I know that. And when I'm with Rick, my past—and his—doesn't seem to matter. It's after, when I have time to think, that I'm just not sure."

"Maybe you simply need to give whatever might happen from here a chance. Give *him* a chance."

Heather had thought that, too. But after that kiss the night before—a kiss that could curl her toes—Rick had looked as stunned as she'd felt. And he hadn't said anything about…well, about anything. He'd simply seen her into her vehicle and stood there, watching her drive off.

"If Rick wanted a chance with me, he certainly didn't say so today. And he was around all day." He'd come by multiple times to see if her team needed anything, but he hadn't tried to get her alone other than to talk about the incident that happened *after* she'd left. "He did say that Cora—that's the housekeeper—saw the thief last night. And one of the guests got into an altercation with him. But the man ran off before Rick arrived on the scene. Rick went after him, but the guy got away. Again."

She'd told Kristen about the intruder before, but she hadn't revealed Rick's true purpose at the estate. Nor had she told her sister about the tunnels or their getting locked in that secret room. Rick had asked her to keep everything in confidence. Besides, she didn't need any lectures from a sibling.

Still, Kristen asked, "Oh, Heather, are you sure you're safe working there?"

"Yes. Please don't worry about me. The intruder has been haunting the estate at night only."

"What about the girls? The neighbor is still dropping them off at the estate after day camp so you can work a little later, right?"

"Right. My only other option would be to get Brian to go pick them up every day, and that's not really fair to him. They're only on the grounds for a short while—though, to tell the truth, I was a little concerned myself." But mostly because Taylor had disappeared on them. "When I said something about it today, Rick came up with a great idea. He suggested I buy the girls those special cell phones that are made just for kids. They have all kinds of parental controls. It's cheaper than if I had to pay for gas for Brian's car if he drove into

Kenosha to get them every day. My provider has refurbished models for practically nothing, and I can add the girls to my account for ten dollars a month." Not a huge expense and certainly worthwhile for her peace of mind.

"We're getting cell phones?" Addison asked excitedly.

"Yay!" Taylor yelled.

Heather hadn't even realized the twins were standing in the doorway. They launched themselves into the living room, Kirby following at their heels. Wondering how much of the conversation they had overheard, Heather braced herself as the girls threw themselves at her.

"Cell phones!"

"Thank you! Thank you!"

The girls were yelling, Kirby was barking and Kristen was laughing.

Heather had to laugh, too. She hugged the girls back, then said, "Okay, okay, calm down already!"

"Can I get a purple phone?"

"I want green!"

"Can we text?"

"When do we get them?"

"Wait until we tell our friends!"

"They'll be jealous 'cause most of 'em don't have cell phones."

"Then who are we gonna call?"

The girls were talking so fast, Heather was having a hard time keeping up with who was saying what.

"Calm down," she said again. "The phones are for safety. They'll be restricted. They have a button for emergencies—"

"But it had better be a *real* emergency if you use it," Kristen warned them.

Heather forced back a grin as she remembered an incident from the year before. Unused to dealing with kids, Kristen had been babysitting and had used the wrong shampoo on Taylor, who'd started crying when she got some soap in her eyes. Thinking her sister was in trouble and needed help, Addison had called 9-1-1.

Heather said, "And you'll be able to phone me."

"No one else?" Addison asked in a squeaky voice.

"Not fair!" Taylor's mouth turned down in a pouty frown.

"We'll set up your phone so you will have limited minutes a month when you can call friends, as long as I know who they are."

Both girls hugged her again and Kirby forced himself into the circle.

Heather kissed her daughters on the head

and gave the dog a pat. "Isn't it time for Kirby to go *outside?*"

The dog barked and then ran to get his leash from the container next to the door. He came trotting back with it hanging from his mouth.

"Just take him to the backyard. Don't go wandering off anywhere else. It's getting late."

"'Kay!" Taylor clipped the leash to Kirby's collar, then led the way back through the kitchen.

Sighing dramatically, Addison followed, dragging her feet. Heather felt sorry for her, the way Taylor had taken over ownership of Kirby. Heather didn't want the girls fighting over the dog, but sometimes she thought Addison should be a little more assertive with her sister.

Waiting just until the girls disappeared, Kristen said, "So, let's get back to Rick."

"I don't know what to do about him."

"Go out with him and figure it out as you go."

"He hasn't even asked me."

"Well, then you ask him."

"I'm not comfortable doing that." Heather was aware that women had been asking men out for a long time, but she'd never had any experience at it. Just thinking about it made her uncomfortable. "I mean...he already thought

I asked him to the cheese shop opening as a date. If I asked him out now...what would he think?"

"That you like him?"

Heather *did* like Rick. Maybe too much. She'd anxiously looked forward to seeing him that morning, and when she had, she'd been able to feel her pulse race, something that seemed to happen a lot when she was around him. And when she'd tried talking to him, her mouth had gone dry. The only other man who'd ever done that to her was Scott. A thought that reminded her of how she'd lost her husband.

"Rick is army, Kristen."

"What?"

"Was army. His dad was a lifer. Rick thought *he* was going to be a lifer." Thinking about the way he'd shut down when he'd felt trapped, she was certain that had been the result of a mission gone bad. "Then something happened to make him want to try civilian life." Something terrible that he apparently didn't want to talk about.

"Then he's not army anymore."

"Who knows? He doesn't. Maybe he'll want to go back. I would respect that decision, Kristen, but the idea that it could happen scares me. Living with worry only to see my worst fears come true was enough to go through once."

"Well, you don't know what he'll decide. Maybe he's looking for something that will keep him here. That could be you and the girls."

"The girls. That's another thing. Taylor doesn't like him."

"That can change." Kristen paused for a second. "You're putting the horse before the cart. You're worrying about possible reasons that a relationship won't work out...and you don't even have the relationship yet. I was kind of like that with Alex. I didn't want to get involved because I was certain I wanted a job like my old one and would move back to Chicago. Look at us now."

Heather grinned. "Only three more days, and you'll be a married woman!"

"And my stubborn little sister is planning to come alone."

"I don't exactly have a choice."

"Of course you do. You can ask Rick to be your date."

Heather was instantly caught up in an image of Rick by her side, his arms around her on the dance floor. She flushed at the thought. But if he wanted to see her, why hadn't he said so by now?

"Part of me would like to have Rick escort

me to your wedding, Kristen, but I can't ask him. I just can't."

Just then, she heard the outside door slam. Thinking the girls must have come in with the dog, Heather looked toward the kitchen and realized that Addison had been standing there in the hallway, maybe all along. Her expression was intent, and when she saw that her mother was staring at her, she whipped around as Kirby came bouncing down the hall.

Now what was that about? Heather wondered.

And again, how much had Addison heard?

"MR. GUILDFREN IS all right, then?" Rick asked Cora the next afternoon.

He'd found her in the music room arranging a vase of cut flowers on the fireplace mantel and thought it was a perfect place to discuss the flower pot incident away from prying ears.

"No concussion, thank heavens." Finished with the vase, she joined him at the lakeside windows. "We went to the emergency room to make sure. David objected all the way, saying his head was much harder than a mere piece of pottery." She laughed softly. "He likes to joke, even when he's hurting."

"Quite a trouper." Rick noted the warm tone

of her voice. Cora and Guildfren definitely liked each other.

"And here David was only trying to protect me and I was trying to help him. The bed-and-breakfast will pay for the emergency room, of course. Though I told Mr. Phillips it was my fault."

Rick looked out over the portico, where two of the guests sat in lounge chairs enjoying the breeze off the lake. The day, now late afternoon, had been a warm one. "What about the other guests?" he asked.

"I've told them about the intruder and the various incidents. I gave them the option of leaving, but no one decided to go."

"Hopefully there won't be any more incidents now that the guy almost got caught." Rick didn't have high hopes of that, though, considering the intruder had been hanging around for weeks. "Nothing else was stolen?"

"No, and I've gone over everything."

Rick couldn't help but think the thief was after something specific. He wished he had a clue as to what.

"If only I'd gotten a better look at him," Cora said with a sigh. "He was medium height and not a large man…but he was wearing dark clothing, so I can't be sure. I couldn't make out his face."

"At least now you know for sure that he's not a ghost."

"There's that." She looked thoughtful for a minute. "And then...well, for a moment, I wondered about David being involved."

Rick had had suspicions about the antiques dealer himself, especially considering Guildfren had so much knowledge of the mansion. "I'm glad we can eliminate him from the list."

"Do you really have a list?"

"Not exactly. Though I think it's likely that someone who stays or works here has something to do with what's been going on."

Rick hadn't eliminated the former handyman Sam Johnson yet, and he hadn't been able to pinpoint the man's current whereabouts. He had also learned that Gina left her last position under odd circumstances. Her employer, James Dodd, simply admitted that she'd been asked to leave but wouldn't say why. And Dodd had sounded uncomfortable. Rick wanted to press the man for more information, but because he had to go into Milwaukee on Monday, he decided he'd make a surprise stop at the hotel Dodd owned. If he were there, it wouldn't hurt to catch him off guard, so to speak. He didn't intend to worry Cora about all these details, however.

Suddenly, a small figure dressed in green

appeared on the other side of the window and waved. "Hi, Rick!" chirped Addison.

He waved back with a smile. "Camp must be over." And he hadn't yet had a chance to talk to Heather.

Taylor also appeared, holding something that got Addison's interest. Both twins scurried away.

"Those children are so darling," said Cora. "I can't tell them apart, though."

"Heather says there's some difference in facial structure." Plus, Taylor was usually frowning when she looked at him, Rick thought, whereas Addison was all smiles.

"You told Heather Clarke about the tunnels—and about the intruder, I assume?"

"I had to." Rick gave the housekeeper a half-truth. "She found one of the entrances to the tunnels when her daughter was hiding in it." He assured the older woman, saying, "She won't talk about it to anyone."

"Are you two dating?"

Were they? "Uh, well…we've gone out." At least that evening at the cheese store. They'd also shared an experience when they got shut in the tunnels the other night.

"I don't mean to pry," said Cora.

"That's okay."

"She seems like a nice young woman."

"She's a good person," he agreed. And a very pretty one. And he definitely looked forward to "going out" with her whenever he got the chance.

Cora turned. "Well, I'd better get back to the kitchen. I have to go over a few things with the staff before dinner."

Nodding, Rick left the house, intending to find Heather.

Addison came running up to him. "Look!" She slid a cell phone out of her pocket. "See what I got? And Mommy's gonna get me a green cover for it!"

Glad that Heather had taken his advice, Rick said, "Very nice."

"Mommy programmed your number in here. Can I call you?"

"Sure." He knelt down and examined the phone's directory. "If you get lost or get into trouble, you call me, okay?"

"Call you or call Mommy?"

"How about both?"

"Okay." When Addison saw Taylor suddenly appear, she yelled, "Come and have Rick check your phone."

"Mommy already checked it." Taylor gave him a slanted look before running the opposite direction.

Would Taylor ever like him? Rick wondered.

He asked Addison, "How's Kirby?"

"He's real-l-l good. He likes to live with us."

"I'll bet he does."

"He has to stay in a cage when we're gone. I hope he doesn't feel bad."

"I don't think a dog minds being kenneled," Rick said. "Plus you don't want him eating the couch while you're away."

Addison laughed. "He wouldn't eat a couch!"

"No, but he might chew on it."

"Kirby has lots of toys to chew on."

"I'm sure." What a chatty little urchin she was. Grinning, he gave the phone back and stood up. "Let's go see your mom."

He would ask Heather how things were going and see if he could help. And maybe there'd be an opportunity to suggest they do something more interesting together. Something away from work.

Addison skipped along beside him. "Do you like Mommy?"

"Sure."

"You like her a lot?"

He stared down at the intent little face. "Well, sure I do…"

Addison sounded so earnest when she said, "Mommy needs a date."

"Oh, yeah?"

Rick choked back a laugh. He had a feeling

Heather wouldn't want her daughter match-making. If she found out, he imagined she would flush with embarrassment.

"That's what Aunt Kristen said. For the wedding."

"The wedding, huh." Rick had just been wondering about the opportunity of seeing Heather and now here it was...

"Aunt Kristen and Uncle Alex are getting married," Addison explained. "They love each other. And Mommy is the matron of..." She frowned.

"Honor?"

Addison nodded. "But she needs a date and doesn't have one."

Well, she did now. Unless she objected.

"When is the wedding?"

"On Saturday." Addison gave him a pleading expression. "Will you take her...ple-e-ease!"

Though he wished Heather had asked him, Rick wasn't going to pass up this opportunity. "Sure I will."

"'Kay, I'll tell her right now!"

"Whoa!" Before the little girl darted away, Rick grasped her shoulder. "Let's slow down a bit." He didn't think Addison telling Heather was the best approach. "Let *me* talk to her, all right?"

"Promise?"

"I promise. You have to save me a dance, though."

"Yay!" Addison jumped up and down. "I love dancing!"

"I bet you do."

He watched her run off to join her twin, who was playing under one of the big trees on the lawn.

He thought about it for a moment. Heather had known about the wedding for quite some time. Maybe she thought it was too soon to ask him to a family event. For a moment, he wondered if he *should* ask to escort her, but his gut overrode his reservations. Any excuse to spend personal time with Heather was a good thing. Plus he had a little girl's expectations to live up to.

He looked around and saw that Heather and Tyrone were some yards away, standing back to admire their latest handiwork—another stone barrier for plantings.

"Hey," Rick said as he joined them.

"Hey, yourself, Mr. Terminator," joked Tyrone.

Heather merely gave him a big smile.

"About finished here today?" Rick asked.

Heather nodded. "We're ready to pack up. Tyrone, could you make sure the tools are put away?"

Tyrone agreed to do so, which meant Rick and Heather were left conveniently alone.

Seeing his chance, Rick took it. "I hear you're going to be matron of honor at your sister's wedding on Saturday."

Heather gave him a wary look. "Where did you hear that?"

"From Addison."

"She's quite a chatterbox."

"She does like to talk," Rick agreed, aiming the conversation in the right direction. "I'll bet she'll be popular when she gets older."

"She's popular now. Other kids give her their phone numbers."

"Uh-oh, you'd better be careful with that cell phone."

Heather nodded. "I know."

"She's a regular little social director. She asked me to escort you to the wedding."

Heather choked out, "She...what?"

"Of course I said yes."

"Uh..."

Rick grinned because, just as he knew she would, she blushed, which made her look adorable. Though she hadn't agreed, he didn't sense that she was displeased. He wasn't about to let her consider the offer too long.

"What time do you want me to pick you

guys up?" he asked smoothly. "As matron of honor, I assume you have to be there early."

He could sense her racing thoughts, could see a hint of panic in her expression before she quickly covered.

"Well, um, the ceremony is at a church in Sparrow Lake, and the reception is at my aunt's house." Then Heather gave him an intent look. "Are you sure you want to do this? There'll be a lot of family there."

"You mean you'll be ashamed to be seen with me?" he joked.

She laughed. "Of course I wouldn't be ashamed. But...you know how family things are."

"No, not really. But I've been to weddings." He winked. "I clean up pretty good."

"No one is questioning your presentability," she told him, then admitted with a smile, "Actually, I would really appreciate your company."

And, as she gave him the pertinent details, he realized that's what she'd wanted all along, only...

For some reason, she was afraid.

Normally Heather Clarke was a take-charge kind of woman, but her nerves had gotten the better of her. Was she beginning to realize she liked him as much as he did her?

Rick hoped so.

After their experience in the tunnels together, he had a new appreciation of the woman. She was strong and caring, and she'd shouldered tremendous responsibility for one so young. He was not only attracted to her, he admired her.

Rick was beginning to think that despite his own initial reservations, they just might be perfect together.

CHAPTER FIFTEEN

THE STRESS OF last-minute wedding preparations overrode any nervousness Heather might have about bringing Rick as her date. On the positive side, his presence meant that relatives would probably not talk about her late husband or ask, with pity, how she was doing. On the negative side, they were sure to make assumptions that were not true.

Such as she and Rick being a real "item."

They might be a *potential* item, but Heather didn't want to let her own expectations get out of hand because Rick hadn't asked her out on his own.

"I'm so glad you changed your mind about an escort," Kristen told Heather at the back of the church as everyone was being seated inside. She gave her a big hug. "And those flower girls are absolutely adorable."

"Yes, they are," Heather said. The twins had even gotten to dress in their favorite colors, pale green for Addison and lavender for Taylor. "Addison is the one responsible for my having a date. It was really cute how she prompted Rick into volunteering, but from now on, I'm going to be careful what I say in front of the twins."

They laughed together and hugged again.

The music drifting out to them told Heather it was time. Brian appeared, looking more grown-up than ever in his tuxedo. Since their father had been gone for many years, Brian would give away the bride.

"Ready, sis?" He held out his arm.

Kristen took it, saying, "Absolutely."

The church was a riot of pastel hues with magnificent sprays of summer flowers. The ladies of the wedding party resembled blooms themselves as they walked down the aisle— Heather in apricot, Priscilla in pale green, Gloria in melon, and Shara in lavender. Heather was so proud of the twins, who carried out their flower-girl duties without a hitch. Looking solemn as they paced down the aisle strewing rose petals from little baskets, the girls smiled sweetly when they reached the altar and the guests beamed. The twins even managed to behave through the ceremony, which ended with tear-inducing vows and a romantic kiss between Kristen and her handsome groom, Alex.

A few minutes later, everyone was outside,

throwing birdseed on the bride and groom as they ran to their chauffeured town car.

Rick joined her and whispered, "You're the prettiest woman here today."

Heather said, "You mean after the bride, of course."

"Of course."

But he was grinning at her, making her neck grow warm. She'd almost forgotten how nice it was to have a man compliment her.

Rick was definitely eye candy himself today—a tall, chiseled and slightly mysterious-looking man who cut quite a figure in his dark crisp suit, dark shirt and tie. Other women were giving him appreciative looks.

Heather's mother, having flown in from California, fought the crowd to get to them. Having already spent some time with her daughter before the ceremony, she looked to Rick.

"Well, hello. I'm Heather's mom, Isabel, and this is my husband, Mike."

"Mom, this is my date, Rick."

"I can see where Heather gets her good looks," Rick said, first taking her hand, then Mike's.

Isabel smiled, looking much prettier and happier than Heather had ever seen her. Her second marriage had obviously given her a new lease on life.

Realizing the bride and groom were gone and guests were getting in their cars, Heather said, "We should get going. Where are the girls?" She spotted the twins with some other kids. "Girls, c'mon, we're leaving for the reception at Aunt Margaret's now!"

"Yay!" Addison yelled as she came running. "I wanna dance!"

"I want cake!" Taylor added.

Both twins had birdseed sprinkled in their hair and on their dresses.

"Everyone will have cake after we eat the rest of the meal," Heather told them, flicking away the birdseed from their hair. "And everyone will get to dance, too."

They'd taken her vehicle rather than Rick's because it already had booster seats. Rick picked up Addison and put her in the backseat, then Taylor, who was so surprised she didn't have time to complain. The weather was beautiful, and the huge yard in back of Margaret's large, rambling, stone house was the perfect place for the reception. To protect guests from the sun, white, flower-bedecked canopies shaded the tables. The flower sprays and arrangements from the church had been moved to the reception. Along with the yard's own blooms and flowering shrubs, the surroundings were a gardener's dream. Sparrow Lake glistened nearby with mirrored blue calm.

As Heather had anticipated, many relatives and friends expected introductions.

The only embarrassing incident happened with Heather's great-uncle Fred from North Dakota. White-haired and in his late eighties, he gazed up at Rick and said, "Well, well Scott. Looking good, young man."

"It's not Scott, dear," murmured Fred's elderly wife, pulling on his arm. "This young man is Heather's date."

Uncle Fred looked confused even when his wife explained, "Scott was killed in action some years ago. You remember that."

Heather jumped in with a hug for the older man. "Nice to see you again, Uncle Fred."

Meanwhile, the twins were on the receiving end of dozens of hugs, kisses and head pats from affectionate out-of-town relatives.

Taylor finally wormed her way over to Heather. "Mommy, can we have some cake now?" she pleaded.

"Not yet. We have to eat lunch first."

The four-tiered wedding cake, decorated with swirls and flowers, was the centerpiece of the white-linen-covered buffet tables set up on one side of the large yard. "I'll be happy to take care of my adorable little granddaughters," said Isabel, taking their hands to lead them off.

"Make sure they get some salad along with the other stuff," Heather called after her. "They can sit at the children's table." She and Rick loaded their plates and ate at one of the nearby adult tables.

Afterward, Rick sat back, looking content. He gazed around, a smile softening his granite features. "Did you have anything to do with the landscaping here?"

"I worked quite a bit on the layout of the plant beds and shrubs for Aunt Margaret. And sometimes I help her with the upkeep. She doesn't like to admit it, but she's not as young or as strong as she used to be."

"Nice work. Not that I'm an expert on landscapes, as you know."

Rick grinned and she laughed.

"You just need a little guidance."

"I'll remember to ask you before I mow anything else down. So, did you always have an interest in plants?"

"I always loved nature. And being outside. I didn't think about pursuing an outdoor career, though...well, any kind of career until a few years ago. I was eighteen when I had the twins. They were only three when I was widowed. I was busy taking care of them."

"That must have been difficult."

She nodded. "Not that I regret a moment of my time with my girls."

"But it would have helped if you'd had a partner to help raise them." He hesitated a moment, then asked, "Were you and Scott high school sweethearts?"

Heather smiled. "Exactly. We went steady from first year of high school on."

"A long-term relationship. It's kind of unusual for one like that to last, I think."

"I agree. We were atypical, at least for these days when people usually don't commit to someone else until they're at least out of their teens."

"Scott must have been special."

"We believed we were soul mates." Many times they'd known what the other was feeling and even thinking. "I have to admit I wasn't too happy when he went off to the military." She added, "Not that I didn't respect his patriotism…and practicality. He thought that a military background and training would help him for our future. At the time we didn't have money for college for either of us." Or the grades to get a scholarship like Kristen did or a stepfather who was willing to help out, the way Mike did with Brian.

"And you had two children to support."

"Scott was doing well for an enlisted man," Heather said. "He liked the men he served with. And the army gave him incentives to sign up for a second tour. I was reluctant to tell him not to go."

"But he didn't come back," Rick said solemnly.

"I don't blame the military," Heather hurried on. "It was Scott's choice to serve. He knew what he was getting into, and so did I."

Rick nodded. "I know something about risks and loss."

Their eyes met, and Heather remembered his behavior when they'd gotten locked in that hidden room in the tunnel. "I'm sure you had some close calls."

"Like getting stuck in a cave and having the entrance blasted shut by the enemy."

So that's what had happened. "I can understand why you don't like tight places."

"Let's not talk about such grim stuff on such a beautiful day," Rick said, looking around. "It's nice you've got so many family members and that you seem to keep in touch. I envy that."

"You don't see much of your family?"

"I get together with my folks about once a year. Dad retired and they live in Florida. My brother is in Washington when he's not traveling the world."

He didn't go on with details. Heather figured that meant he didn't feel particularly close to any of them.

"In a way, the men I've served with are like my family," he went on.

"You've probably shared a lot."

"But soldiers come and go. Every couple of years, sometimes every few months, you have to get used to somebody new. Living in a town with family must provide more continuity."

"Probably," Heather agreed. "Things aren't perfect for anyone, though. Our father went off and left us, you know. We still don't know why or where he is or if he's okay. Or if he even cares what happened to us."

Rick seemed surprised. "I guess I didn't think about that when you said your mother was bringing your stepfather. I just thought she was divorced and remarried."

"Nothing that simple."

"Being abandoned must have been devastating."

"It was, for everyone. And we've all dealt with it in our own way. Maybe that's the reason I didn't mind starting a family so young," Heather admitted. "I wanted a warm and stable home life. And Kristen became a workaholic to prove she wasn't irresponsible like our dad. Brian acted out and got into trouble because he didn't have a real father."

"At least you guys seem to be doing well now."

"Well, Kristen is happy. Brian's settled down and in college. And I'm...well, I have a plan."

"Which I'm sure will be successful. You're a competent, gutsy woman. That's one reason I was attracted to you," he added.

"That and my ability to make kissy faces in a mirror," Heather teased, remembering the boathouse incident with the security camera. She wasn't the least bit uptight about it anymore.

They both laughed and watched Brian and some other young men move tables and chairs from the center of the patio. A band was setting up on a platform beyond the buffet tables. Kristen had said they would be playing soft rock oldies.

"Do you like to dance?" she asked Rick.

"I'd better like it. I promised Addison a whirl around the dance floor."

"Save one for me, too, okay?"

"I'll save *all* the other dances for you."

Just thinking about spending the rest of the afternoon in Rick's arms made Heather feel a little giddy.

IN REALITY, DESPITE what he'd said, Rick found he had a nearly full dance card before he even stepped out onto the patio. Besides Addison, who wanted him to take her hands and twirl her in a circle, Rick partnered up with a couple of other little girls, each of the bridesmaids, Isabel, and so many relatives and friends he could barely remember their names. Heather's family didn't seem to be shy. Even Aunt Margaret, someone Rick remembered by her bright red hair and colorful blue gown, managed to dance a number with him before returning to her own escort, a tanned outdoorsy-looking older man named John. Rick liked her, especially when she joked about his "Terminator" sunglasses.

"How do you know about the sunglasses?" He'd taken them off before he entered the church.

"Addison was wearing them one day."

He laughed. "I forgot about that." He also wondered if Heather had mentioned the nickname because she had made such a big deal out of wanting to see his eyes when they'd first gotten to know each other.

He was sitting down, taking a break with a cold cola in the shadow of the old rambling house, when Heather finally appeared at their table. She'd been busy helping the bride change into her "going away" outfit. "Sorry I left you here for so long."

"I've only been in this chair for five minutes. I think I've had at least one dance with every female at this wedding."

Heather grinned. "My, aren't you Mr. Popular?"

"Luckily I'm in shape," Rick joked, rising to offer a hand out to the dance floor.

The band was playing a slow tune so he swung her around gently and back into his arms. She felt good there. He breathed in the scent of her sun-streaked hair, which was piled into a soft updo with a flower nestled into one side. Her hand in his was firm but soft. They moved together effortlessly, perfect partners.

If not exactly soul mates. Like Heather and Scott had been. From snatches of conversation here and there, Rick had found out that Scott had been greatly respected, a truly fine young man. But what other kind of man would Heather have chosen? Rick didn't want to compare himself to Scott. For one thing, he hadn't known her half as long.

A lull came right after the next dance when the band took a break. At the edge of the patio, Addison continued to dance with a toddler and laugh, the picture of happy childhood. When Heather was called away to talk to the bride again, Rick sat down and had another sip of cola. He was surprised when Taylor suddenly appeared.

"Can I have some of that?" she asked, actually smiling at him.

"Cola?"

When she nodded, he quickly poured a little into another glass. Taylor had never asked him for anything, so he was pleased.

She gulped down the contents of the glass, then said, "More?"

"I can get you a whole can, if you want."

"Thanks!"

He rose and went to the open bar, picking up a cold can for the little girl and another for himself. Taylor didn't wait for him to pour her can into a glass but stuck a straw in it and took off. She also grabbed the second can of cola for one of her friends.

Rick shrugged. Maybe he'd made some points.

In the crowd, Rick didn't see Taylor again for a while, not until Heather returned and they'd shared a piece of cake. Then he noticed a veritable herd of kids—twelve or thirteen, at least—running from one end of the yard to the other. Taylor was among them, barefoot, having tossed off her shoes.

"You're *it!* You're *it!*" Taylor yelled, chasing a straggler, a boy somewhat smaller than her.

"Wow, I hope she doesn't ruin that dress." Heather stirred in her chair. "Maybe I should catch her and get her to change into shorts."

A few minutes later, they saw Taylor tackle the straggler and shriek like a banshee. In another moment, she sat on top of him and yelled, "I said you were *it!*"

Heather sprang to her feet. "Good grief!"

Rick got up from his chair, too, though he didn't know what he should do. Taylor was pummeling the little boy. Was it appropriate to stop the fight? Then Taylor would hate him even more.

He followed Heather as she rushed over to them on the lawn.

"Stop it!" Heather grabbed Taylor.

The little girl paid no attention, smacking the sobbing boy beneath her again. "He's *it* and he won't play!"

"Taylor, stop this right now! What is wrong with you?"

Heather somehow managed to get her daughter to let go and pulled her off the other child. Meanwhile, the boy's dad had appeared and got his son to his feet.

Both kids were sobbing.

"I'm so sorry!" Heather told the other parent.

"That's okay. I think they just went wild," said the dad.

Rick felt helpless, just standing and watching.

Tears streaked Taylor's little face and dampened her already matted hair. Her dress was bedraggled and stained by grass, her hands and feet dirty.

"You are coming inside for a time out, young lady!" Heather told her, leading her toward the house.

Rick still didn't know what to do. He didn't think Heather wanted his help, so he returned to their table. After some murmuring over the excitement, the crowd settled down. Finally, about twenty minutes later, Heather returned, a crushed cola can in her hand, her face stormy.

"Sorry about that," she told Rick. "Taylor is really getting to me lately." She showed him the cola can. "Of course, this didn't help. She had it at the kids' table. Actually, two of them!"

Uh-oh. "What's wrong with cola?"

"You don't give a child caffeine, especially with sugar. Taylor had three pieces of cake, several pieces of candy and all the cola she could put away. She was really flying. I'm going to have a talk with the caterers in charge of beverages. The kids were only supposed to be served milk or juice."

Rick stopped her before she flounced off. He might as well come clean. "I gave her the cola, Heather. She asked me for it."

"And you thought it was okay for her?"

"I didn't know it was bad. She took the one for me, too."

"*Two* colas?"

"She said it was for a friend."

Heather looked tired. "Caffeine and kids don't mix. Especially not for Taylor. Add sugar and you have a really volatile combination."

"I can see that now." He told her, "Look, I'm sorry. It's my fault. I just don't have the experience with kids."

"No, you don't." She sighed. "And Taylor knows she's not supposed to have sodas, too. She was intentionally being naughty."

And perhaps setting up Rick for her own purposes. No doubt this had spoiled the edge he'd been gaining with Heather. He would be angry if the culprit who'd done him in wasn't a six-year-old girl.

"Let's sit back down and try to relax," Heather said. "I checked on Addison. She's okay."

"We can do some more dancing."

"Sure. When the band starts up again."

But Heather looked like she'd rather head home. Once again, Rick was only too aware of the difference in their backgrounds. She had two little girls who were completely dependent on her, whereas he'd never been responsible for anyone except the men in his military unit.

Men he'd failed.

He wouldn't blame Heather if she decided not to see him again.

HEATHER FIGURED TAYLOR must have slept for the remaining hour she and Rick stayed at the party. Taylor yawned as she climbed into her booster seat when Rick got ready to take them all home. Both the twins were quiet, no doubt worn out. Still, Addison managed to tell Rick "bye" before going into the house. Taylor didn't say anything.

"I'd invite you in but I have to put the girls to bed," Heather told him, feeling like she wanted to collapse fairly soon herself.

"No problem. I'll see you Monday afternoon. I have to go to Milwaukee in the morning."

"Okay. Thanks for being my escort."

"Any time."

Heather wondered if he would want to see a tired mother who had two children, one of whom was so difficult. Other divorced mothers had told her how hard it was to find a man who wanted a ready-made family. And Rick had no experience with kids, but that was something he could learn…assuming he wanted to.

He leaned forward and kissed her, but it was more of a brush on the lips than a deep emotional kiss like the last one they'd shared.

He touched her cheek and sounded regretful when he said, "Good night."

"Good night."

Disappointed that the reception had made their date take such a left turn, she watched him until he climbed into his own car and drove off. Then she went inside.

Taylor and Addison were shrugging out of their dresses, getting ready for a bath, which Taylor especially needed. Heather turned on the water, then took the dog out in the yard herself. When Kirby was ready to come back in, Heather went straight to help the twins clean themselves up and get into bed.

Taylor was finished first and burrowed into the sheets while Addison brushed her teeth and told the dog in a singsong voice about her day. Heather sat down on the bed and took the opportunity to speak to Taylor alone.

"You know you're not supposed to have cola. You're a big girl."

Taylor's lip quivered. "Rick gave it to me."

"You asked him for it." And though she hoped Taylor wasn't intentionally trying to get him into trouble, she had to wonder. "You don't like him, Taylor, and there's no reason for it."

"He hurt me!"

"He stopped you from running so fast with the dog. But he was just trying to protect you. He doesn't deserve to be treated so badly. You are mean to him." She added, "I didn't raise my girls to be mean."

Tears pooled in Taylor's eyes and spilled out onto her cheeks. But her expression remained stubborn. "You *like* him!"

"So you're jealous? Is that it?" Heather leaned closer to touch her daughter's face. "Honey, I love you. You're my baby. No one, not Rick or anybody, is ever going to get in the way of that."

"Daddy wouldn't like him!"

Heather was struck silent. An image of Taylor watching the DVD of Scott flooded her thoughts. She tried to keep her voice from cracking when she said, "Daddy isn't here anymore, sweetie. He's in heaven."

Now Taylor openly sobbed and Heather couldn't help crying herself. She took Taylor in her arms, the little body shivering with emotion.

"He said he was coming back!" Taylor cried against her shoulder.

"He would if he could, sweetie…but he

can't." How did one explain the finality of death to a child?

"I'm Daddy's little girl!" Taylor said, sobbing.

"Yes, you are." Heather just held the child as if for dear life. "And you always will be. And you're my little girl, too." She tried to explain, "But…life goes on. Daddy wouldn't want us to be so sad about him that we never have fun with other people."

"I don't want Rick as a daddy!" Taylor insisted. "You *danced* with him!"

Was Taylor having anxiety about a father replacement? Heather suddenly realized the issue of dating and remarriage might be even harder than she'd already thought.

She kept Taylor in her arms but turned her face up to gaze down at her. "I'm not ready to get married right now, honey. Right now, I just want to have someone to go out with and have fun."

Someone who made her feel good about herself and made her feel like the young woman she really was. Someone she couldn't wait to see again when they were apart. Someone like Rick. She couldn't help liking him, wanting to be with him.

"Someday I might want to marry again." Rick's image came to her unbidden and she shivered a little. "You have to have room in your heart for other people."

Suddenly, Heather was enveloped by another pair of little arms. Addison said, "I love you, Taylor. I love you, Mommy, and it's okay if you want to marry Rick."

Kirby barked in agreement.

Heather laughed. "Don't rush me. Let me just date him for now."

"Yay!" Addison chirped.

"'Kay," Taylor mumbled.

Thinking that Taylor might come around yet, Heather made a silly face that had everyone giggling and Kirby barking while she tucked the girls in.

Getting ready for bed, she thought about Rick, about how much she did want to see him again.

Now if only he felt the same way about her after today.

CHAPTER SIXTEEN

ON MONDAY MORNING, Rick drove the thirty miles to Milwaukee to pick up some special batteries he'd ordered. Afterward, he found the Lakeside Hotel, where Gina used to work as a concierge, and parked nearby. He went inside to ask about Dodd, the owner, fully knowing the man might not be in that day. However, to his satisfaction, Dodd happened to be in his office and told him to come inside and shut the door. Rick did so and sat down.

Dodd was probably forty or so, had a receding hairline and was fairly ordinary looking. His expression told Rick he was still as uncomfortable as he'd sounded on the phone when they'd spoken.

"Sorry to bother you," Rick began. "I didn't tell you I was working as a security specialist when I phoned you."

"At Flanagan Manor?"

"Right. Where Gina Luca is employed. From what you said it sounded like you had to let her go."

"Well, yes. I didn't give her a bad reference, though."

Rick went on, "I wouldn't press you for further information, except that, well, some odd things have been happening at the manor."

"Odd things?"

Rick was reassuring, "No guests are in danger." David Guildfren had been involved in an altercation, but he had attacked the guy after all. "We've had some trespassing, someone who's found his way into the buildings on the estate." He wasn't going to tell the other man about the tunnels or the missing candelabra. "We're keeping my investigation low key. We don't want rumors spreading."

"I understand. People can get alarmed by very little. You have my word I won't say anything about it."

Rick hoped so.

Dodd looked thoughtful. "But I don't know how trespassing could have anything to do with Gina."

Rick probed, "Exactly why did you let her go?"

"I don't have to tell you that."

"No, you don't. But I would appreciate it if you did." Rick smiled, hoping to put the other man at ease. "And Gina can't sue you if what you say is true."

"Well, I've felt uneasy about the whole thing," Dodd said finally, with a sigh. "There seemed to be some discrepancies with…tips when Gina worked here."

"Tips?"

"Guests can tip the concierge for their help. And it's just that, well, Gina often received larger tips than I'd ever seen before."

"On credit card receipts?"

"Right. Still, I wouldn't have asked her about it except one of the guests complained. He seemed to think the amount he'd written in had been altered."

"Really?"

"When that happened, I talked to Gina." Dodd went on, "She got upset, claimed the guest was lying."

"That's not good."

"I wanted to believe her." Dodd sighed again. "When I pressed the guy who'd made the claim against her, he kind of back-pedaled, said he'd been distracted when he checked out of the hotel."

Rick merely nodded.

"But then something else came up," Dodd said. "One day Gina came to me and asked for a loan. She claimed she had a special situation and needed money, that her salary wasn't enough to cover it."

"You felt sorry for her?"

Dodd nodded. "But then it really got out of hand. Gina said if I gave her the loan, she wouldn't tell my wife about 'us.'"

"Whoa. Blackmail?"

"We had gone out to dinner a few times." Dodd explained hurriedly, "But I wasn't married at the time. My divorce had gone through. My ex-wife and I have remained friends and business partners. It seems Gina thought we were still together."

"That's pretty underhanded." And embarrassing. Rick could understand why Dodd was uncomfortable. Still, he also cautioned himself about only hearing one side of the story.

"At that point, I told her I didn't want her working for me anymore. I gave her a final check and told her to be on her way." Dodd stared down at his desk. "Never thought I'd hear from her...or about her, again."

"I'll keep this as private as possible."

"What about your employers?"

"I think it's only fair that they know about the credit card discrepancies," Rick told him. "But Ben Phillips won't fire someone out of hand. They'll probably just want me to keep a closer eye on Gina. As you say, her past actions and what's going on at the manor may have nothing to do with each other. She's obviously not the one trespassing on the estate. Her presence is accounted for."

But his gut feeling told him something was going on. Maybe Gina was working with somebody else.

They talked a few minutes longer about general security issues, and Dodd asked for advice, which Rick was happy to give. Finally, Rick thanked the man and left to drive back to Kenosha.

On the way, he thought about seeing Heather when he arrived that afternoon, wondering what kind of greeting he would get from her.

HEATHER THOUGHT ABOUT Rick as she and her crew planted native sea grasses in the area around the beach. Would he want to see her again, or had the incident with Taylor turned him off entirely? She really hoped not. Just the thought of seeing him today made her stomach twirl with anticipation.

The sandy ground was damp. It had rained a little earlier that morning but it wasn't wet enough to stop work. Heather dug in, enjoying the fresh smell of the earth and growing greenery.

Cora strolled along the lakefront with one of the guests, a silver-haired gentleman. "Good day, Heather."

Heather smiled. "Good morning."

She got the distinct feeling that Cora and the man had a more complex relationship than housekeeper and guest. Seeing the way he and Cora acted with each other made her smile.

Thinking about Rick, she realized she was standing still, staring off into the distance, distracted. She quickly made herself get back to the planting.

When lunchtime rolled around, Heather wasn't very hungry, so she kept going while Tyrone and Amber drove a few blocks to get some fast food. Around noon, Rick's sedan finally entered the courtyard. He parked, got out and headed directly for the house, seeming somber. Of course, that didn't mean anything in particular where she was concerned, Heather told herself. Who knew what he'd been doing? Still, she felt a little thrill of anxiety and just as quickly told herself to settle down.

He came outside again and approached her several minutes later with a big smile that warmed her from the inside out. "How's it going?"

"We'll be finished with this area soon and start on the next. By fall, the garden is going to look pretty good. By next spring, it'll fill in more and be fabulous."

He glanced around. "Where's your crew?"

"They went to get some sandwiches for lunch."

"Are they bringing something back for you?"

She shook her head. "I wasn't that hungry. I brought some yogurt I'll get to eventually." Because it had been on her mind, she added, "I had fun at the wedding. In spite of Taylor getting out of hand. I hope you had a good time, too."

"I enjoyed it, especially being with you." His sincere expression made her a little breathless. "Speaking of Taylor, did she ever say where she found that ten dollar gold certificate from 1922?"

"With the wedding and everything else going on, I haven't had time to sit down and grill her about it."

"I suppose she could have found it anywhere, maybe even lying on the floor. It may have been dropped there by someone else."

"The intruder?"

He nodded. "When he gets back, I'm turning the certificate over to Mr. Phillips. He said it's worth a lot more than its original value."

"Wow, that would be exciting."

"He says some of it should go to the finder as a reward."

"That isn't necessary. Taylor found it on someone else's property. I don't want her to think she can just pick things up in other people's houses and profit from it." She was curious. "Anything more going on with that intruder? He gave us quite a scare."

"Not a peep. Maybe *he* got scared off. I think I told you Mr. Guildfren—one of the guests—got in a fight with the guy."

"You did tell me on the ride to the wedding. Is he doing all right?"

"He's fine. He's getting a lot of attention from Cora for his heroics. I'm pretty sure that's making up for any discomfort he may have suffered."

They both laughed, and Heather said, "I saw them taking a walk together this morning."

And remembered thinking they'd found a little romance, something she could use in her life. With Rick.

So when he asked, "Are you sure you wouldn't like something a little more substantial than yogurt for lunch—I'm in the mood to eat in town," she said, "I'm up for that. As long as it's short enough for me to get back to work in an hour."

"No problem."

They headed for his car.

"Maybe we can talk about going somewhere this coming weekend. If you're available, that is."

She felt her heart speed up. "I'd like that."

Despite Taylor throwing a wrench into the wedding date, Rick wanted to see her again.

She couldn't stop smiling.

CORA AND DAVID had stopped in the rotunda of the manor to once again admire the mural on the ceiling.

"This is such a magnificent old place," said David.

Cora agreed, "I've always loved it."

"I think there's a growing interest in old places and things. I only wish society would appreciate people the same way when they age. To the younger generation, I'm a man who's past his prime. But in some ways, I feel I'm at my very best."

"I know what you mean."

"Not that I should be fighting trespassers every day." David grimaced. "But I couldn't stand by and let anything harm you, Cora. I would put myself between you and danger any time."

"Now that just about makes me blush." Cora felt her face grow warm.

"That's all right. You're very pretty in pink," David told her. "What was going on with that trespasser, anyway? Before I stopped him, he was heading right toward you."

"I yelled at him. Maybe he was scared and got defensive." She was never going to tell David that she had actually suspected *him* of being the intruder.

"Well, we drove him off. We make a good team, don't you think?"

"We are very compatible." She had always thought so.

"If you're ever afraid, let me know. Call my cell, even it's the middle of the night."

"I might take you up on that." Though she'd be more likely to call Rick, she appreciated the thought.

He paused, clearing his throat. "I, uh, I do want you to know that part of the reason I come here twice a year is…well, it's because of you."

She felt touched. "I look forward to your visits."

"I just haven't acted on my feelings, not as I would have when I was younger. It's been a long time."

Cora knew he was a widower. "We both have our past experiences." She had once been married for a short time herself. But she focused on the word *feelings*. "Are you saying you might—"

"Care for you? Yes, I am saying that, Cora."

She felt as tongue-tied as she had when she

was young and dealing with her first serious boyfriend. Finally, she managed to stammer, "I—I care for you, too, David."

"You do?" His face lit up. "Wonderful! Then we can be more open. I'd love to take you out. To dinner, a concert, a play, wherever you want to go." He said hastily, "Of course, you're probably coming up on the busy season here now. We don't have to rush things. I can come down for you any time of the year. I don't live that far away."

"I can always take an evening off, as long as we plan ahead."

"Then plan we shall." Beaming, he took her hands in his and gazed into her eyes. "And for now…may I just steal one kiss?"

"Oh, David. You can steal two or three."

THEY DECIDED TO try the fish and chips at a large restaurant along Kenosha's harbor, where sailboats were docked. Heather didn't care where they ate as long as she could be with Rick. But she had to admit the setting was beautiful, especially at their table near a bank of wall-sized windows opening onto the deck.

After they'd finished eating, they lingered over mugs of coffee, and conversation led back to the wedding.

"So how many dance partners do you think you had in all?" Heather teased.

"Too numerous to count." Rick grinned. "There were several five- and six-year-olds."

"They probably saw you with Addison and thought it was open season on the tall guy."

"They were lots of fun."

"Children can be fun as well as problematic." Heather again thought about Taylor acting out.

"Well, I like kids, but I have about as much experience with them as I do mowing lawns."

Did he want more experience? Heather wondered. Dealing with a surly kid was not fun, especially for someone who didn't have a long-term investment in the relationship.

"Now about this weekend," Rick said, shifting the conversation away from kids and onto them. "What would you like to do?"

"I enjoyed dancing with you." Especially when he had his arms around her.

"We could do that." He reached across the table and covered her hand with his. "There are plenty of clubs in Chicago or Milwaukee."

Aware of his touch, Heather swallowed hard. "Not the noisy kind, though. I like being able to hear the person I'm with." And have a romantic dance or two, she thought.

"You aren't into punk or hip-hop? And here I thought that would be to your taste."

Heather laughed. "My lifestyle has made me a little too mature for punk and hip-hop, I'm afraid."

"Good, I'm not into either myself."

"Where did you learn to dance?"

"There was often a dance in officer's quarters." He explained, "My dad was an officer."

"Did he want you to follow in his footsteps?"

"Yeah, but I passed on the West Point thing. I got my education and training elsewhere."

Curious, she asked, "Training in what?"

"Before I left, I was in a special ops intelligence unit."

That surprised Heather. She'd had no idea that he hadn't just been regular army.

"You're a little overqualified for security work at a bed-and-breakfast, don't you think?"

"Hey, I'm not too qualified. I haven't caught the bad guy yet."

"I'll bet your work in the army was important."

"They made use of me," he admitted.

He obviously wasn't going to offer more details. Intelligence…perhaps he couldn't.

Rick suddenly stiffened.

"Is something wrong?"

"Look who just came in."

"Uh-huh." Heather saw it was Gina.

"I was looking for her at the house." Rick placed a hand on her arm. "Don't turn around, okay? Let's just keep talking."

"Okay." Her eyes moved to check out the mirror on the wall behind their table instead. It was definitely Gina. And she wasn't alone. A man accompanied her, kind of a skinny, wiry guy. He had thick reddish hair, one lock of which stuck straight up. He sported a tattoo on his forearm and a surly expression. Gina was hanging on to that arm and looking around. She soon spotted Rick. And stared.

"Seems a lot of people wanted to have lunch here, huh?" Rick said to Heather, on alert but smiling as if there was nothing wrong.

Yet Heather could feel the tension radiate from his body.

Gina gave a tight smile and murmured something to her companion. Then she left him to make her way over to Rick and Heather's table. He, in turn, hunkered down in a chair behind one of the columns.

"Hi, Rick," said Gina with a bright-looking smile and a glance at Heather. "Ms. Clarke. Fancy meeting you two here."

Rick smiled in return. "Everyone likes to eat." He nodded toward the man sitting behind the column. "Your boyfriend looks familiar."

"Oh, really? Well, maybe you've seen him in town before."

"I don't think so. It was somewhere else. At the estate, I'm pretty sure."

Gina fidgeted, as if she were anxious to take off. "I don't think you saw him. Ernie... he hasn't been to the manor yet."

"I wouldn't mind meeting him," Rick said.

"Uh, he's shy." Gina appeared even more uneasy. "Well, I'd better get back."

They watched as she returned to her companion. Almost hidden by the column, Gina sat down for a moment. Then both she and her boyfriend rose to exit the restaurant even faster than they had entered it.

Rick jumped up. "We have to follow them."

Heather wasn't sure why but she respected his urgent tone. "I'll get the check."

"Too much time." He pulled his wallet out and peeled off a couple of twenties to throw on the table.

"That's a lot for what we ate."

"It'll make the waitress's day." He grabbed her arm. "Come on."

When they rushed outside, they saw Gina and her escort disappear into an alley across the street.

"Stay here!" Rick ordered, taking off. A car beeped at him as he sped across the street.

Heather stood there for a moment, then followed, though she was careful to watch out for cars. She was curious. Entering the alley where Gina, then Rick, had disappeared, she found nothing but Dumpsters. Another alley intersected the one she stood in, bordered by a fence belonging to one of the houses on a parallel street. Where had Rick gone? And what was going on?

Taking a few more steps toward the cross-alley, she met Rick coming back.

"Lost them," he said, obviously disgruntled.

"They could have gone anywhere, either on foot or by car," said Heather.

"Yeah. And I'm not sure what kind of vehicle Gina drives. I think it's a subcompact."

"Her companion could have had a car or truck, too."

"Blast!" Rick struck his hand on his thigh. "So close."

"So close to what?"

"Let's get in the car. I'll tell you on the way back to the house."

"All right."

Once they were headed for the manor, Rick explained, "Gina has kind of a checkered background, as I found out this morning when I spoke to her former employer."

"I wonder if she knows you suspect her of

something. She sure looked uncomfortable when you mentioned her boyfriend."

"And he wanted to avoid me. I'm pretty sure he's the intruder, Heather. I believe he's the one who shut us in that room."

Heather was surprised. "So he does know someone in the house!"

"And she's probably been watching out for him. Six-to-one she's not coming back to her job after I said her boyfriend seemed familiar. I bet she doesn't even pick up her stuff."

As Rick swung his vehicle onto the estate drive, Heather thought about the assumption he'd made.

"What made you decide that guy was the intruder?"

"He's the right size—I have footage of him in the boathouse, remember. But more than that, by his wild red hair. Doesn't it look a little familiar to you?"

"Familiar?" Heather couldn't remember seeing anyone on the estate with hair like that.

"The portrait in the rotunda."

And then it dawned. "Oh, my… He looks a lot like Red Flanagan!"

"Exactly." Rick parked but made no move to get out. "Spotting him in the dark, Cora imagined she was seeing Red's ghost."

"Poor woman! That must have scared her."

"She was so shook up she told me she mentioned the ghost to the mansion's staff one time, including Gina. Another reason Gina didn't want us to meet whoever that guy was."

"Ernie? Earnest?" Heather mused.

"Things are starting to make sense, especially my theory that the intruder is searching for that legendary treasure. And he looks like Red Flanagan. What if it's a relative who thinks he was robbed of his inheritance?"

"If that's true...how would you find out for sure?"

"I have my ways."

He grinned at her, making her pulse speed a little faster.

"You certainly do," she said, but she wasn't thinking just about his investigative skills.

Rick Slater had a way of adding excitement to her life.

CHAPTER SEVENTEEN

As Rick feared, Gina didn't return to Flanagan Manor, not even for her personal items. His attempt to flush the intruder into the open had gone a little too well. If only he'd been able to catch up with them when they left the restaurant.

A few days after the incident, he talked to Cora at the front desk. She was serving as both concierge and housekeeper for the time being.

"I've done this before," she said with a sigh. "But I had a bit more notice. Is there no answer at either of Gina's phone numbers?"

"One just rings and the other is disconnected."

"Do you think she's left town?"

"Probably. No one answered the door at her former address and the landlord says she moved."

Cora sniffed. "How convenient. You never know when you can trust people, I guess."

"How could you know? Her background

check was clean. We were lucky a former employer said something about her."

"But this means she was definitely involved in the shenanigans around here, right?"

"I'm certain of it," Rick said. "If nothing else, she's a person who wants or needs money and she's willing to do whatever she has to do to get it."

"But you still don't have enough proof for the police to become more actively involved?"

"I told Detective Morse about it, but just as I suspected, there's not enough proof of anything to make out a police report."

Cora mused, "I thought he was a ghost. But I only saw him in a lightning flash." Then she added, "Gina just took off and didn't return to work after you saw them together—isn't that suspicious enough for the police?"

"It may be suspicious, but it's also circumstantial. Morse said Gina could say she just decided she didn't want her job anymore."

"What I want to know is how she and that man found out about the tunnels."

That was just one of many questions, Rick thought, frustrated. He'd felt he was right on the edge of getting his hands on the intruder, but was now stymied. He'd asked questions around Kenosha, but only a few merchants remembered Gina, and none recalled anyone who looked like the mystery guy. But then, the town was mainly a bedroom city for both Chicago and Milwaukee these days, or a destination for tourists. It wasn't the type of place where everyone knew everybody else's business. Lots of people came and went. When Rick showed the owner of a hardware store a photo of Gina, the man said that she had been in there one time. That was it, and no one else offered any better information.

Rick's cell phone rang and, to his surprise, he saw it was Murphy. "Excuse me," he told Cora, moving away from the front desk. "I have to take a call. I'll get back to you later."

She sighed. "I'll probably be right here."

Rick switched on the phone. "Hey, Murphy." He left the rotunda and stepped outside. "What's up?"

"Hey, man, is this place yours?" Murphy asked.

"What place?"

"Flanagan Manor." Murphy laughed. "I'm out in the parking lot."

So his old friend had just dropped by unexpectedly. Rick said, "I live in the coach house out in back. Meet me lakeside on the portico."

A moment later, Murphy joined him, saying, "Nice digs here."

"Yeah, it's great. I have an amazing view of Lake Michigan."

"You about finished with this job?"

"Not quite." Rick wasn't going into detail.

They wandered down to the beach shooting the breeze, though Rick suspected Murphy had more important things to say.

"Whenever I'm at the edge of a big body of water, it feels like I'm at the edge of the world," Murphy said as he took in the expansive view. "Even though I know maps show otherwise, looks like nothing but sky and water as far as you can see."

Rick merely nodded.

Murphy went on, "And speaking of the world, guys like us are needed out there, Slater."

So that's why he had shown up. He'd wanted one last shot at getting Rick to change his mind. "You're trying to talk me into re-enlisting again."

"Our team needs a good leader. A decision will be made soon. The last guy didn't care about us—he just stayed long enough to get a promotion. Meantime, we're swinging in the breeze."

"I did my turn and then some."

"Yeah, but we miss you, man."

Who missed him? Murphy was the only one

he'd really been close to in the past several years. At least the only one who was still alive.

"I only wish Jackson and Mazurski could still miss me." For once, Rick put names to the faces that haunted his dreams.

"The enemy is going to pick off some-body—"

"Not on my watch!"

"It wasn't your fault."

"I led them into that cave on bad intel. I was responsible for all of you."

Murphy had nothing for that remark, but a few seconds later, he came back with "The only way you'll get over a loss is to get back on the playing field."

Was that the path back to redemption? Rick wondered, gazing out at the shifting waves and gulls circling overhead.

"Where's your sense of honor, Slater? One loss and you walk away? You, who was always going on about us doing our patriotic duty?"

"I think I did my duty."

"Of course you did, but then you gave up on us."

"More like I gave up on myself. The guilt was killing me." Something he had only told his therapist until now.

"Here's your chance to give yourself a break. To make up for whatever guilt you've been nurturing. Time you got that monkey off your back."

Part of Rick wanted to do just that. Wanted to make up for trusting the wrong informant. He'd been had. He'd led his men into that underground cave thinking they were going to find hostages. Instead they'd run into unexpected munitions. And enemies who'd tried to blow them all to kingdom come.

When he didn't say anything, Murphy went on. "I know if you contact General Stanley, he can pull some strings. Get you in again without so much hassle."

Again, Rick said nothing. He and Murphy had been through so much together, he couldn't find it in himself to refuse him outright. And should he? That was the question. Maybe if he went back for one last tour, he could make up for what happened, could dispel the ghosts that shadowed him.

So when Murphy asked, "Will you think about coming back?" Rick figured it was the least he could do.

"All right. I'll think about it."

"Good. At least that's something. Now I have to head out of here to catch a plane."

Rick shook Murphy's hand and they patted each other on the back awkwardly in a manly kind of hug. Murphy had turned and headed back for the parking lot when Rick noticed Heather standing some paces away. She looked visibly upset. He opened his mouth to say something only to have her whirl about and rush off.

What had she heard?

HER HEART FULL to bursting, Heather hurried around the side of the house, intending to return to the front yard where she'd been working. She thought she heard Rick behind her, so she quickened her pace. But his stride was twice as long as hers, and he quickly caught up to her.

"Heather, stop," Rick demanded, taking hold of her arm.

She pulled away. "I have to get back to work."

"We need to talk."

She knew it was useless but she told him, "I don't *want* to talk."

"Well, you obviously have something to say."

Her emotions surged. She cleared her throat, fighting back tears. She wasn't sure if she could form words in her turmoil. Finally, she managed to blurt out, "I know that working here as a handyman/PI isn't what you're used to."

"I agree. It's a lot less dangerous."

"And if you want to go back, you certainly have the right to." Even if it would break her heart. She kept her face turned slightly. She wouldn't look directly at him. She knew she would sob if she did.

"Who's going where?"

"I heard you, Rick. You're thinking about re-enlisting." Something she'd always feared, but she had allowed herself to get involved with this man anyway.

He took a deep breath. "I said I would think about it. I didn't agree to anything."

"Yet."

"I feel I owe a debt of sorts. I lost two men."

"Losing your own life won't bring them back."

"I don't intend to lose my life..."

She cut in, "Nobody intends to, Rick, but loss of life is a reality in war, a loss that affects the ones you leave behind." Feeling as if she were choking, she said, "Not that I can really count myself as someone you'd be leaving behind. I have no right to ask you to stay."

He pulled her closer. "You have a right."

She tried to shake off his grip. "Then, I'm sorry, but I can't stand it, Rick! I've already lost enough." She didn't want to even think about something similar happening again. Though she tried to be stoic, tears spilled down her cheeks, making her feel helpless. "I can't stand the possibility of losing another man I care about."

He reached for her, enclosing her in his arms. "Then don't think about it."

"You told me the army was your family, that you were just trying out civilian life."

"And it's had some unexpected benefits." He kissed her forehead.

Finally giving in, at least for the moment, she leaned against his chest. Was he just trying to make her happy now? She wanted to be happy, but she simply wasn't convinced that everything would be all right. He still hadn't said that he had no intentions of re-enlisting. In fact, he'd said he owed a debt.

"This isn't your home," she said. "You'll have to leave Flanagan Manor once your job is done. And I can't ask you not to do what you think is right."

"Don't worry, I always do what I think is right. I just need some time to know what that is for sure." He lowered his voice, "I really care for you, Heather."

Her heart sped up. Maybe he had been falling in love, too. But she forced herself to think about reality. "I have to do what's right for my children and what's right for me, too."

"Of course. Children are a big responsibility."

One that he didn't want? Heather wondered. While she admired Rick's sense of duty, she didn't know how she could continue to see him if he was going to leave. Losing Scott had broken her heart and had shattered her world. It had taken three long years to rebuild a life that would bring her some joy and give her girls the security they needed.

Wanting to stay close to Rick, to cling to his warmth, she made herself push away. "While you're thinking about your options, I'm going to think about mine."

"Heather..."

"You can't expect me to even consider going through all the grief again."

He seemed reluctant, but he let her go. "I understand."

They just stood there. Though there were only a few inches between them, it might as well have been miles. But Heather couldn't, wouldn't put her heart and her little family into a situation that was so fraught with danger.

Not knowing how long it would take him to make up his mind about the right thing, she simply turned and walked away.

TAYLOR HAD BEEN on her very best behavior. After they had heard there were going to be fireworks over the lake tonight the twins had begged Mommy to stay at the mansion. Cora, the white-haired lady, had invited them to a picnic on the beach. They told Mommy it was Friday and they didn't have camp tomorrow, so they could stay up later. Mommy, who looked tired and a little sad for some reason, had finally agreed.

The twins had helped Mommy and Cora spread blankets on the sand. Then Cora and her friend, an older man, had dragged some canvas chairs over to sit in.

"The little arts festival downtown was very nice," said the older man. "I enjoyed looking at the booths set up on the main drag. I even found some old picture frames for a good price."

"This area of Wisconsin is great for antiquing," said Cora, smiling.

Taylor didn't know what "anticky" meant and she didn't care. She shook her head when Rick, who had joined the small group when the food got served, offered her another piece of pizza. "Nope." Pizza was okay but she preferred chicken nuggets.

"No, what?" said Mommy with a sharp look.

"No, *thanks*."

Taylor sulked. She was finished with the food. Now she was sitting quietly on the blanket with Addison when she'd rather be running around. Mommy should be happy.

And Taylor still didn't like Rick. Despite what Mommy said, she was certain he didn't like her, either. He paid way more attention to Addison…when he wasn't paying attention to Mommy. Daddy should be here, not Rick.

Beside her, Addison flopped back on the blanket. "Look at that big star over there." Her sister pointed to a bright speck of light visible beyond the glow of the city.

"Hmmp," grunted Taylor. "Stars are boring."

"They are not," argued Addison. "They're made of fire. And we can count them."

"I don't want to count them." Taylor didn't want to get in an argument with her sister.

"Now, girls, you'll soon have something more fiery to look at than stars," said Cora.

"You'll like the fireworks, honey," Mommy told her.

Taylor *did* like the fireworks, which began a few minutes later. She caught her breath when a red blaze suddenly burst into spray above the water, accompanied by a slight whoosh and a boom.

"Oooh, look at that!" said Mommy.

"Gorgeous," said Cora.

More fireworks exploded in cascades of blue and green and yellow and icy white. Taylor stared but tried hard not to act too impressed. As lots more firecrackers lit up the sky and made cracks and booms, she inched off the blanket, got to her feet and started sneaking away. No one saw her but Addison. Taylor made a face at her.

The adults were still watching the sky as she hurried off, planning to disappear…probably like everyone really wanted. She was too much trouble.

She didn't even pause when she reached Rick's house, instead skirting it to make a beeline for the big mansion. She heard the sound of voices as she passed the terrace, which was full of people. But only one woman glanced up to notice her. Soon, Taylor opened the big glass door that led into the mansion and went inside, intending to find the big room with the plants and statues.

The hallway was long and filled with shadows that made her heart thump a little harder. When she reached the plant room, Taylor thought she heard footsteps behind her. Scared, she stopped and turned but saw nothing. This big old house was spooky at night. But she would find her safe place.

The door to the glass plant room stood open. She hesitated a moment. Was someone in there?

Snaking her way around a fern and along the side of the big statue of a lady with flowers, Taylor ran her hands along the carving on the pedestal. When she touched an indented place, the hidden door opened. She smiled in satisfaction. Inside there was just enough room for her to hide alongside some books and a bag of paper money, bills like the one Mommy had taken from her. She would hide there like she had the last time, and if Mommy called her cell phone, she wouldn't answer.

Taylor had crawled halfway in when she suddenly felt the presence of someone else in the room. She froze and glanced up into the angry face of a strange man.

"Hey, what are you doing here?" he asked, sounding mean as he grabbed her.

Taylor tried to shriek but he covered her mouth with his large hand. "No-o-o!"

"Shut up!" His voice was rough. Then he spotted the pile of stuff in her secret place. "What is this?"

He had to let go of her to grab a handful of the dusty bills. "Money?"

She took the opportunity to run away. But he caught her, gave her a shake that rattled her teeth and covered her mouth again. "Not one noise! Not one or I'll throttle you!"

Taylor didn't know what "throttle" meant,

but she was thoroughly scared. The man's hair stood on end and he had eyes that were glittery and small like a snake's.

He took a flashlight out of his pocket and shined it on the books and paper. "Old bills, hmm?" He took another big handful and stuck it in his pocket. Then another and another until he had it all. "Huh. Still no treasure, but I guess this is better than nothing." Then he glanced around and looked back down at her. "You're coming with me."

Taylor tried to object, but his hand covered her mouth again. He half carried her to an opening in the wall and started down a dark, scary staircase. It smelled musty. Taylor went stiff, remembering monster stories about bad things that lived under bridges and houses. She screamed through his fingers, and when the man tightened his hold over her mouth, she tried to bite his hand.

"That's enough of this!"

He didn't let go as he bent over and searched through a big bag at the bottom of the stairs. From it, he took a roll of heavy tape. Ripping off a strip, he placed it over her mouth.

Taylor could hardly breathe!

Throwing her over his shoulder, the man continued down a dark tunnel, only stopping to smack her behind when she kicked and hit at him with her fists. The blow hurt, and Taylor sobbed. The man stopped for a moment and let her down just so he could use more tape to bind her wrists together. Then he hauled her back up and continued into the darkness. Tears seeped from Taylor's eyes. Would she ever see Mommy or Addison again?

Finally they emerged into the darkness outside. The man continued carrying her, only putting her down when they reached a car. A woman who looked familiar was sitting in the front passenger seat. Didn't she work in the mansion?

When she saw them, she climbed out of the car. "What is this?" she demanded. "What are you doing with the kid?"

"She saw me."

"You've got her tied up. Just leave her. She's not going to follow us."

Hope sprang in Taylor's heart but was quickly dashed.

"There's a bunch of tourists running around," the man said. "One of them could find her and then they'd have the cops after us in a flash."

"Kidnapping is a federal offense, Ernie!" cried the woman, sounding upset.

"We'll leave her at a rest stop as soon as we're some distance away. Come on. Get back in the car. I found something I want to show you."

With that, he opened the trunk, grabbed Taylor and threw her inside. As he did so, she felt her cell phone slide out of the pocket of her shorts. The man saw it and picked it up. "Glad I found this."

Then he slammed the trunk closed, leaving Taylor alone in the dark. She sobbed and struggled against the tape holding her wrists. She'd wanted to disappear, but not like this!

She might never see Mommy or Addison again.

CHAPTER EIGHTEEN

WHEN THE FIERY show ended with a spectacular bloom of color across the sky, Heather turned, wanting to see the awe on the girls' faces. But only Addison sat looking up at the display. Where was Taylor and how long had she been gone?

"Taylor!" she yelled, jumping to her feet. She grabbed Addison. "Where is your sister?"

"I think she had to go the bathroom, Mommy." Addison gestured toward the mansion. "She went that way."

"Why didn't you say anything?"

"I don't know..."

"Plenty of guests are on the patio," Cora pointed out, no doubt trying to be reassuring. "She isn't totally by herself."

"And she may have gone into the coach house," Rick put in. "That's the nearest bathroom."

But that only calmed Heather a little.

What in the world was the matter with Taylor? She thought she'd gotten to the bottom of the twin's misbehavior when they'd had the talk about Rick after the wedding. Now Taylor had gotten "lost" a second time. It was too much. "I'll go and look in the coach house," Rick told her.

She didn't meet his gaze, hadn't said much to him all evening. If she'd known he was coming to the picnic, she might not have stayed.

Rick headed for the coach house while Cora and Mr. Guildfren accompanied Heather and Addison to the mansion to check for Taylor there. No matter what anyone said, what she told herself, Heather couldn't help worrying. At least the last time, it had been daylight. But in the dark…

A few minutes later, Rick rejoined the group. "Not there. I even checked the closets."

"I'm not surprised she isn't there. She's never visited your place." Heather had been alone with Rick the time he'd shown her around.

She yelled "Taylor!" but got no response.

When they passed the terrace, she glanced at a couple who sat on the terrace quietly conversing. Ahead, several people were bunched up near the door.

"Taylor!"

Heather kept calling out and Addison tightened the grip on her hand.

One of the guests gestured toward the mansion. "I saw a little girl like that one go inside a while ago."

"Thank you, Mr. Zucker," Cora told him. "I'm sure we'll find her."

They headed straight for the portico and entered through the music room. Empty.

"Let's look in the conservatory," Heather said. "She was hanging out somewhere around there last time."

"She's gotten lost in the mansion before?" asked Cora.

Heather sighed. "Unfortunately, yes, and I think it was deliberate."

"Children like to play," added Guildfren. "I'm sure she's just having a good time."

Heather wasn't going to offer details about Taylor and her problems with Rick, so she said nothing. As they entered the darkened conservatory, Cora turned on the lights.

"That helps," Rick said.

But the conservatory seemed empty, the plants barely moving except for a leaf or two quivering in a draft from the vents. The statues stood mute and still, keeping watch. Rick paused near one, an upright of a woman holding flowers.

"What happened here?" He looked down with a puzzled frown.

Heather stared, noting that the pedestal of

the statue seemed to have a panel. And it was standing open.

"I never saw this before." Rick squatted and felt around. "A secret compartment."

In which Heather could see a stack of old, dusty books and a dilapidated canvas bag. He picked the bag up to shake it, dislodging what appeared to be another bill.

Heather recognized the gold certificate, similar to the one Taylor had found. "Do you think this is where she got it?"

"Very likely. This would make a good hiding place for a kid."

"Wow," said Addison, who'd been watching. "A secret place!" She crouched down and started to crawl in herself.

Heather grabbed her, hard. "You stay out of there! I'm having enough problems with your sister."

Addison looked stricken. "'Kay."

Heather immediately felt guilty. "I'm sorry, honey." She hugged the little girl, knowing she'd been a bit rough. But her concern was growing. "I'm just upset. We have to find your sister." She looked around. "Where can she have gone?"

Addison's eyes widened. "Look! The wall is open!"

"What?" Heather followed the direction of her daughter's gaze, spotting the crack.

"The tunnels," said Rick. "Someone's been in there."

"Oh, no!" Heather cried. "Taylor went in the tunnels?" Where it was dark and dangerous?

"She can't have opened the door from this side, Heather," said Rick. "Someone else opened it from the inside."

Heather tried to wrap her mind around the idea. "The intruder? But...where is Taylor?"

"Maybe he scared her and she's hiding," Rick offered.

He opened the hidden door wider and Addison pointed at the purple barrette lying on the stairs. "That's Taylor's!"

Heather picked up the barrette, fighting hysteria. "Taylor!" she yelled again into the darkness, trying not to think the worst. "Taylor, please answer me!"

Silence. Heather's heart thundered.

Rick took out his cell phone. "I'm going to call her and see if she picks up." Meanwhile, he used his other hand to hold on to Heather and keep her from running down into the dark. "Wait, she might not be there."

"Remember? There isn't cell phone reception way down there!"

He kept listening to his phone, obviously getting no answer. Then he took it from his ear and punched in some numbers. "GPS." He traced a finger across the screen. "And it says the phone is not here, not even on the property. It's moving west..."

"West? What on earth?"

"Moving fast. Probably in a car."

"Taylor's cell phone is in a car? What..." Heather could only think of one awful explanation. "He's kidnapped her!" Oh, why hadn't she demanded that Taylor and Addison sit right next to her on the beach? Why hadn't she watched them more closely? "My baby has been kidnapped!"

"Hold on," said Rick. "We don't know for sure what is going on."

"Taylor is kid-napt?" said Addison worriedly.

"I'll go after them, using the GPS, and I'll notify the police," Rick said, heading for the door.

Mr. Guildfren offered, "I'll search the tunnels with you, Heather."

"I can't believe that someone took her!" It was every parent's nightmare.

"You keep looking for her here," Rick told Heather before taking off. "Don't worry, I'll find her."

"And I'll take care of Addison." Cora had the little girl's hand.

Heather was so numb, she stood stock-still. Then she took a deep breath and felt adrenaline course through her veins.

"We're going to need a flashlight," Mr. Guildfren said. He had used one when he and Cora left the beach and now took it out of his pocket, flicked it on and started down the steps. "Come on."

Heather followed. "I've been down here before. I kind of know my way around."

"Then stay close behind me and tell me where to search." Mr. Guildfren didn't offer to let her pass in front of him, probably because he knew she was beside herself. "Don't worry— it's going to be all right. Even if the thief has your child, he has no reason to hurt her."

Hurt her? Heather pushed that thought aside, not wanting fear to take over again.

Rick was cruising into the night and he would come back with her child. She knew Rick's capabilities. He might not be ready to settle down with a family, but he would always perform his duties. She could trust that he would do whatever it took to get Taylor back. She had absolute faith in him.

Focusing on that, she followed Guildfren down the stairs.

OUTSIDE, THE MOONLESS night seemed twice as dark after the fireworks had stopped. Rick drove fast, keeping an eye on the GPS tracking on his phone. When he encountered traffic, people wending their way home from the festival in town, he gunned the car down an alley and slid out the other side. Then he sped along less busy side streets, heading in an easterly direction. From the path it was taking, he realized the vehicle he was chasing was probably on Sheridan Road, the historical street that wound its way along the lakeshore and into Chicago.

He'd called the police and reported what seemed to be a kidnapping. Detective Morse assured him several squad cars were on their way. But Rick wasn't going to wait for them to appear. He had to find Taylor.

Why the intruder took the child he wasn't sure, but his gut told him the guy had her. Maybe she'd been in the wrong place at the wrong time the night the thief decided to return, perhaps because the fireworks and general uproar of the festival would cover his presence.

Heather was nearly hysterical and Rick could understand why. He could empathize, knowing what it was like to fear losing men who served under him. But losing an innocent child was twice as bad.

And Taylor was innocent, he thought, a good little kid, even though she acted not-so-sweet at times. She had loads of courage and energy and spice. She was a lot like her mother.

He would catch up to the kidnapper's car if it was the last thing he ever did.

His emotions had been churning all day, ever since he'd had the go-around with Heather. He just hadn't known what to say, but his heart was heavy when he realized all the pain he'd put her through, all the hurt he could cause her in the future. That, more than whether or not he wanted to rejoin the army, had kept him from committing to their relationship outright and reassuring her. Was he capable, could he be trusted to take care of a woman and two small children who would depend on him? He wasn't sure.

He pressed his foot down on the accelerator. He didn't want to lose Taylor, not any more than he wanted to lose Heather. In the space of a few short weeks, Heather had come to mean a lot to him. He had been telling the absolute truth when he said he cared for her. He more than cared…and the same went for her daughters.

When he finally turned onto Sheridan Road,

Rick caught the flash of police cars some distance away in his rearview mirror. Good.

He punched in numbers to call Detective Morse. "I just turned onto Sheridan Road. GPS says they're now heading south."

"In sight?" asked the detective.

"Not yet."

"I'm putting a couple of cars on your tail and sending another down the main highway to cut them off."

The state road ran parallel to the lake and Sheridan.

Rick sped on, his car's headlights cutting through the dark. The other car should be coming into view any minute. Was it Gina and her friend?

He had to slow when he came to an open area where encroaching fields made the road zigzag. When he came out the far side, he finally spotted a speck of red up ahead, then two. Taillights. He shoved his foot on the accelerator.

A couple of minutes later, everything seemed to happen at once. Rick saw a police car suddenly come into view on a side road up ahead and heard squealing brakes. The light-colored sedan whose taillights Rick had spotted careened sideways on the road. More flashing lights appeared behind him as he hit the brakes himself.

Parking and jumping from his car, he watched the police drag out Gina and the wiry guy he'd seen at the restaurant to line them up against the sedan.

Rick was focused on finding the little girl. He grabbed the guy and the police didn't try to stop him. "Where's the child? Where's Taylor?"

"In the trunk," said Gina. "I didn't have anything to do with it! It was all Ernie's fault!"

Rick paid no attention to her. He wanted to punch Ernie in the face but thought better of it. Instead he threw him back against the car. "Give me the keys."

Ernie dropped a set of keys on the pavement and Rick grabbed them. He ran to the trunk and heard muffled thumps, small feet kicking against the metal. "I'm coming, Taylor!"

Full of emotion, he quickly opened the trunk to find the frightened child inside. A piece of thick silver tape covered her mouth and a longer one bound her wrists. She gazed up at Rick with huge eyes.

"Taylor!" Rick was careful in removing the tape. As he did so, huge tears ran down the girl's cheeks. "Are you okay?"

Taylor sobbed and threw her arms around

his neck. When he picked her up, she wrapped her legs around his sides and clung to him like she never wanted to let go. He didn't want to let go himself. He cradled her against him.

"Don't worry, you're safe now, honey."

She finally managed to gasp, "It…it was dark. I was s-scared." Luckily, she only seemed shaken up.

"I know what it's like to be stuck in a dark place, and it's not fun." An enclosed space. That had been *really* scary, all right. And he'd been an adult. A trained soldier. Taylor was just a little kid. "But I've got you now." He hugged her closer.

Taylor tightened her grip on him. "D-don't let go."

"I won't." He got out his phone. "But I have to call your mom."

He suddenly knew he couldn't let any of them go. Not Taylor, not Addison, and especially not Heather.

LATE THE NEXT morning, Cora was hiding a yawn when Heather and the twins came downstairs at Flanagan Manor. They'd all been up until the early morning hours giving statements to the police, so Cora had insisted they stay the night.

"Thank you again for giving us that room

so I didn't have to drive home after all the upset. It was very comfortable." An unused guest suite with a queen-size bed for all three of them allowed Heather to hold both twins tight all night.

"No problem," said Cora. "Not after all the trouble we had. The room was available and I didn't want you to get on the road that late." She leaned down to look at Taylor. "How are you doing, honey?"

"Okay," Taylor told the woman soberly. "My arm is sore is all."

"She has some bruises," said Heather, who had checked her daughter over thoroughly. "That creep grabbed her and threw her around."

"He was a bad man!" said Addison.

"Yes, he was. I'm glad he's in jail now." Cora explained, "Rick's down at the police station finishing things up. He should be back soon. Meanwhile, why don't you sit down on the terrace and Kelly will bring you some breakfast?"

"Thanks, Cora."

Heather took the girls outside and walked them around to the terrace.

The moment Mr. Guildfren spotted them, he waved them over and rose to help them into seats at his table. "I bet you're still exhausted."

"It was emotionally draining," Heather admitted. As well as physically demanding. She and Guildfren had still been scrambling around in the tunnels when Cora called down to say that Rick had found Taylor. "I'm sure you're tired, too. I really appreciated your help last night."

"No problem," Mr. Guildfren said. "I had my own run-in with that scoundrel not long ago."

Heather could see that Cora and Mr. Guildfren had a nice give-and-take chemistry between them and were probably dating. It was never too late to find love.

At least she hoped not.

WHEN SHE THOUGHT about Rick, he filled all her empty spaces, including the one left in her heart when Scott had been killed. And if she hadn't already fallen in love with Rick, she would have after the way he'd rescued her daughter. The questions were: Did he feel the same for her? And would he be around much longer, or would he re-enlist?

Heather decided the second question no longer mattered. To love meant you might very well suffer loss one day. Most of the beautiful things on earth—a rose, a sunrise, a baby's smile—were ephemeral, fleeting. She loved Rick and wanted to be with him no matter what he decided. The heart simply wasn't practical. It took chances. Thinking about how quickly she and Rick had connected, how could she not be willing to take a chance on him?

Mr. Guildfren smiled. "In a few months… and for years to come…we'll remember last night as an adventure."

"I hope so," said Heather. Though it was impossible to think of nearly losing a child as an adventure. She was simply grateful that the night hadn't turned into a tragedy.

Ernie Reilly, the intruder who'd been haunting the mansion for weeks, was safely in jail. As was Gina Luca, the mansion's former concierge. No one was certain of their connection, though Rick might be able to tell them when he returned today.

Meanwhile, Heather and the twins had toast and jam and juice. Taylor asked if she could have some scrambled eggs, which Cora was happy to provide. Heather was happy, too. Taylor usually had an appetite in the morning and the night's excitement hadn't reduced it.

Rick arrived when they were finishing up their food. Taylor cried out and rose to greet him, making Heather smile. Then she insisted on sitting next to him, so Addison decided she had to sit on the other side.

"Hey, I'm popular." Rick grinned, giving one girl a hug, then the other.

Seeing them like this tightened Heather's chest. Together, they looked like a family.

"Do you know the details of what was going on now?" Mr. Guildfren asked Rick.

Heather was anxious to find out, too. They'd given their statements here at the mansion the night before, but Gina and her friend had been taken straight to the station.

Rick asked Kelly for some coffee. "I know quite a bit. It seems Ernie Reilly is a long-lost relative of Red Flanagan's."

Mr. Guildfren seemed surprised. "Really?"

"A relative?" Heather asked.

"He claims Flanagan was his great-great-grandfather," Rick told them. "He has a map of the tunnels, one of the few things he said he inherited."

"We wondered how he knew about them," said Cora, joining the group.

"And he was looking for Red Flanagan's mythic treasure," Rick went on.

"Mythic? There wasn't really a treasure then, right?" asked Mr. Guildfren.

"Well, the police aren't sure." Rick looked at Heather. "You know those books we saw last night…beneath the statue?"

Addison said, "The hiding place!"

Heather frowned at her daughter. "Where neither of you is ever going to set foot again."

Rick continued, "Those books are full of details about breeding special types of orchids, Red's passion. They might be worth something."

"Unique orchids are worth quite a bit to some people," Mr. Guildfren put in, "and I saw some of those in the conservatory."

"And then there was a stack of old currency," said Rick. "Gold certificates. They're worth a lot more than their face value, probably a few hundred thousand dollars after all these years. I wouldn't say that was considered treasure, though."

"That candelabra was worth fifteen thousand or so," Cora added.

"The candelabra was in the car," Rick told her. "So the Phillipses will get it back eventually."

Mr. Guildfren asked, "Did Gina and this Ernie fellow case out the place beforehand?"

"I'm not sure about that. Maybe they just hatched the plan after Gina got a job here." Rick took a sip of coffee. "They seem to have been connected romantically. The police say they appear to hate each other now, each one blaming the other for the mess they're in. One thing that probably is certain is that Gina had nothing to do with the kidnapping. It wouldn't have happened if Ernie Reilly hadn't insisted on coming back to search one last time and encountered Taylor."

"He was a bad man!" said Taylor, looking angry.

Rick slid a hand over her shoulder comfortingly. "Yes, he was, but you're safe now. I won't let anything bad happen to you again."

The statement churned up Heather's emotions. Rick had told her that he needed to think about re-enlisting in the army, and if he did, he wouldn't be here to keep that promise.

Cora asked, "Why did this Reilly fellow compound his problems with a kidnapping?"

"I guess he thought Taylor would warn someone about him. She saw his face," Rick added, "so she could have given police a description. He swore he was going to put her out at the nearest rest stop."

Heather frowned. "That's still dangerous. A child alone in a rest stop at night?"

Cora just shook her head. "Well, he was persevering in his search. I'll give him that. He kept coming back, to my dismay."

"The police say the guy is adamant about his great-great-grandfather's 'treasure' belonging to him," said Rick. "Gina could have helped him hatch a plan."

"I'm just so glad you caught him." Filled with conflicting emotions, Heather rose to kiss Rick on the cheek.

"Yeah, I'm glad, too." Addison quickly followed suit.

"I'm gladder!" piped up Taylor.

"We're all glad to get you back," Rick told the incorrigible twin.

Whatever the reason for the kidnapping, it seemed to have brought Taylor around. Heather was happy to see her daughter had warmed up to the man she cared for. Before they had gone to sleep the night before, Taylor, unbidden, had told her that she could make some room in her heart for Rick because he'd understood what it was like to be locked up in a dark place, and he made sure he got her out.

That had been such a sweet confession, it made Heather cry. She could almost cry now, too, not only for what happened to Taylor, but for the uncertainty of Rick being in their lives in the future.

Cora made a motion to rise from the table and looked meaningfully at Mr. Guildfren. "David, why don't we take a walk and give these young people some space?"

"Well, all right," Mr. Guildfren agreed. "We can take the twins with us."

"I want to stay with Rick," insisted Taylor.

"I've got something interesting for you to do," Cora said. "Kelly is making some fresh cinnamon rolls in the kitchen. Wouldn't you like to help her roll out the dough?"

"Yay! I want to help," cried Addison.

"'Kay," Taylor agreed, reluctantly pulling herself away from Rick.

As soon as they were alone, Heather sat down and gazed into Rick's eyes. "I can never repay you for saving my child."

"Yes, you can. That look on your face is pretty good payment."

"Oh, Rick."

She embraced him, kissed him, not caring if anyone else on the terrace was watching them. He kissed her back, a sweet, slow kiss that seemed to last forever. His arms felt so good around her she never wanted him to let go.

"You can also repay me with a real night out," Rick said, keeping his arms around her waist. "Just you and me. You realize, we still haven't had an actual date."

Her pulse thrummed when she saw how intently he was looking at her.

"If you're willing to go out with me, that is."

"I will date you whenever, Rick. No matter what. I've decided that I want to be with you, and if you do re-enlist, I'm hoping you'll come back to us."

His expression softened and he hugged her closer. "I had a lot of thinking to do. Soul searching. Wondering if I owed it to my men who died to go back."

Exactly what she'd feared. She couldn't help the way she felt. Not about his loyalty to his men. Not about him.

Rick went on, "But I was the only one who blamed me for those men's deaths. They weren't my fault, Heather. If there had been a way to prevent what happened, I would have done it."

"I know."

"I don't blame you for having reservations about getting involved with me," Rick said softly. "You've lost so much already."

Heather wrapped her arms tighter around his neck. "I'll stand beside you no matter what, Rick. You deserve that kind of loyalty."

"You mean it?"

She nodded.

"No matter what?"

"No matter what."

"Good, because I decided that I've served my country to the best of my ability for fifteen years, and there's no reason I shouldn't finally put personal concerns first. I'm not re-enlisting."

That made her so happy, she could hardly breathe. "Personal?"

He grinned at her. "Very personal. I love you, you know, all three of you."

She couldn't help but smile back. "Rick, I love you, too."

He kissed her, and Heather's heart sang. She suspected their future would hold lots of surprises, and she couldn't be happier.

EPILOGUE

"THESE INSECTS REALLY make a lot of noise," said Rick as he and Heather and the twins finished up some lemonade in her backyard. They'd eaten supper outside and were gathered around the small picnic table.

"It's the end of summer," Heather said. "August always sounds like this in a small Midwestern town."

Cicadas buzzed as the sun went down, crickets joining in with squeaks and chirps. Happy and interested by anything that moved, Kirby ran around chomping at leaves and sticks. He picked up a medium-sized twig and brought it to Rick, who threw it for the dog to fetch.

"Go, Kirby!" Taylor laughed with delight.

Perched on one end of the bench, Addison swung her legs. "One of our books says those bugs are singing a song."

"They are singing," Heather agreed. "They're singing about how you should be getting ready for bed."

"Oh, Mom, are not!" complained Taylor,

grabbing onto Rick's arm. She looked up at him for confirmation. "We don't have to go to bed now, do we?"

Touched yet again by her including him in family decisions, he laughed and gave her a hug. "I'm afraid you do, honey. It's going on 9:00 p.m. Your mom says you have school starting in a few days. You need to be ready for first grade."

Taylor pouted. "I'm not sleepy!"

"You will be by the time you get your jammies on," said Heather, making eye contact with Rick. He knew that meant she was looking forward to some adult conversation after the kids were tucked in.

Not that they had anything complicated to talk about. Heather had finished the landscaping at Flanagan Manor and had a week off before starting a new job with EPI at another site in Kenosha. Rick was still employed by the security firm and doing some consultations in Milwaukee. He'd rented a small bachelor apartment in Sparrow Lake. It would do for now.

"I don't want to go to bed!" said Taylor, scooting off her chair to stand with her arms crossed. She could be very stubborn.

Heather appeared annoyed. "I'm not going through this fight again tonight..."

Rick jumped in, "You need to go to bed, Taylor. You can stay up late when we go to the drive-in on Saturday." There was still an outdoor movie theater in Kenosha and it was showing a kids' film. "You'll like it. The screen is really big and we can sit in the car and have popcorn."

Taylor's expression softened. "Popcorn?"

"And maybe hot dogs, too," he assured her. "Go and jump into bed."

"Well...'kay," the child finally and reluctantly agreed. She flung herself at him for a hug. "Night!"

"Good night." He kissed her soft little cheek, then caught Addison as she ran up, giving her a kiss, too.

"Hey, you're getting pretty good, Mr. Terminator," Heather said softly, leading the twins toward the house.

Yes, he was, Rick thought. He was getting better with kids all the time. Feeling a cold nose nudge his hand, he glanced down at Kirby, who had another stick in his mouth. Rick had always been good with dogs.

"Throw me the leash, will you?" he called to Heather as she went in the back door. "I'll take Kirby for a walk."

Leash in place, he led the dog down the

sidewalk and up an alley. Kirby pranced and panted happily.

Rick laughed and ruffled the fur on his head. "You're just a happy, happy little guy, aren't you?"

Kirby yipped softly in return, as if he understood.

"No wonder, you've found a good home."

A forever home, Rick mused, thinking about the time he'd told Addison he was a stray himself. And now, if things worked out, which he had every intention they would, he'd found a "forever" home, too.

* * * * *

REQUEST YOUR FREE BOOKS!

2 FREE INSPIRATIONAL NOVELS
PLUS 2
FREE
MYSTERY GIFTS *Love Inspired*™

YES! Please send me 2 FREE Love Inspired® novels and my 2 FREE mystery gifts (gifts are worth about $10). After receiving them, if I don't wish to receive any more books, I can return the shipping statement marked "cancel." If I don't cancel, I will receive 6 brand-new novels every month and be billed just $4.74 per book in the U.S. or $5.24 per book in Canada. That's a savings of at least 21% off the cover price. It's quite a bargain! Shipping and handling is just 50¢ per book in the U.S. and 75¢ per book in Canada.* I understand that accepting the 2 free books and gifts places me under no obligation to buy anything. I can always return a shipment and cancel at any time. Even if I never buy another book, the two free books and gifts are mine to keep forever.

105/305 IDN F49N

Name _____ (PLEASE PRINT) _____

Address _____ Apt. # _____

City _____ State/Prov. _____ Zip/Postal Code _____

Signature (if under 18, a parent or guardian must sign)

Mail to the Harlequin® Reader Service:
IN U.S.A.: P.O. Box 1867, Buffalo, NY 14240-1867
IN CANADA: P.O. Box 609, Fort Erie, Ontario L2A 5X3

**Are you a subscriber to Love Inspired books
and want to receive the larger-print edition?
Call 1-800-873-8635 or visit www.ReaderService.com.**

* Terms and prices subject to change without notice. Prices do not include applicable taxes. Sales tax applicable in N.Y. Canadian residents will be charged applicable taxes. Offer not valid in Quebec. This offer is limited to one order per household. Not valid for current subscribers to Love Inspired books. All orders subject to credit approval. Credit or debit balances in a customer's account(s) may be offset by any other outstanding balance owed by or to the customer. Please allow 4 to 6 weeks for delivery. Offer available while quantities last.

Your Privacy—The Harlequin® Reader Service is committed to protecting your privacy. Our Privacy Policy is available online at www.ReaderService.com or upon request from the Harlequin Reader Service.

We make a portion of our mailing list available to reputable third parties that offer products we believe may interest you. If you prefer that we not exchange your name with third parties, or if you wish to clarify or modify your communication preferences, please visit us at www.ReaderService.com/consumerchoice or write to us at Harlequin Reader Service Preference Service, P.O. Box 9062, Buffalo, NY 14269. Include your complete name and address.

LIDIR13R

REQUEST YOUR FREE BOOKS!

2 FREE CHRISTIAN NOVELS
PLUS 2
FREE
MYSTERY GIFTS

$\heartsuit$

HEARTSONG
PRESENTS

HSPDIR13R

REQUEST YOUR FREE BOOKS!

2 FREE INSPIRATIONAL NOVELS
PLUS 2
FREE
MYSTERY GIFTS

Love Inspired.
HISTORICAL
INSPIRATIONAL HISTORICAL ROMANCE

YES! Please send me 2 FREE Love Inspired® Historical novels and my 2 FREE mystery gifts (gifts are worth about $10). After receiving them, if I don't wish to receive any more books, I can return the shipping statement marked "cancel." If I don't cancel, I will receive 4 brand-new novels every month and be billed just $4.74 per book in the U.S. or $5.24 per book in Canada. That's a savings of at least 21% off the cover price. It's quite a bargain! Shipping and handling is just 50¢ per book in the U.S. and 75¢ per book in Canada.* I understand that accepting the 2 free books and gifts places me under no obligation to buy anything. I can always return a shipment and cancel at any time. Even if I never buy another book, the two free books and gifts are mine to keep forever.

102/302 IDN F5CY

Name	(PLEASE PRINT)	
Address		Apt. #
City	State/Prov.	Zip/Postal Code

Signature (if under 18, a parent or guardian must sign)

Mail to the Harlequin® Reader Service:
IN U.S.A.: P.O. Box 1867, Buffalo, NY 14240-1867
IN CANADA: P.O. Box 609, Fort Erie, Ontario L2A 5X3

Want to try two free books from another series?
Call 1-800-873-8635 or visit www.ReaderService.com.

* Terms and prices subject to change without notice. Prices do not include applicable taxes. Sales tax applicable in N.Y. Canadian residents will be charged applicable taxes. Offer not valid in Quebec. This offer is limited to one order per household. Not valid for current subscribers to Love Inspired Historical books. All orders subject to credit approval. Credit or debit balances in a customer's account(s) may be offset by any other outstanding balance owed by or to the customer. Please allow 4 to 6 weeks for delivery. Offer available while quantities last.

Your Privacy—The Harlequin® Reader Service is committed to protecting your privacy. Our Privacy Policy is available online at www.ReaderService.com or upon request from the Harlequin Reader Service.

We make a portion of our mailing list available to reputable third parties that offer products we believe may interest you. If you prefer that we not exchange your name with third parties, or if you wish to clarify or modify your communication preferences, please visit us at www.ReaderService.com/consumerschoice or write to us at Harlequin Reader Service Preference Service, P.O. Box 9062, Buffalo, NY 14269. Include your complete name and address.

Reader Service.com

Manage your account online!

- Review your order history
- Manage your payments
- Update your address

---

*We've designed
the Harlequin® Reader Service
website just for you.*

Enjoy all the features!

- Reader excerpts from any series
- Respond to mailings and special monthly offers
- Discover new series available to you
- Browse the Bonus Bucks catalog
- Share your feedback

Visit us at:

ReaderService.com

RS13